Tomfoolery
(Tommy Fox Book 3)

Graham Ison

© Graham Ison, 1992

Graham Ison has asserted his rights under the Copyright, Design and Patents Act, 1988, to be identified as the author of this work.

First published in 1992 by Macmillan.

This edition published in 2017 by Endeavour Press Ltd.

Table of Contents

Chapter One	5
Chapter Two	15
Chapter Three	26
Chapter Four	36
Chapter Five	43
Chapter Six	53
Chapter Seven	62
Chapter Eight	74
Chapter Nine	84
Chapter Ten	94
Chapter Eleven	104
Chapter Twelve	113
Chapter Thirteen	123
Chapter Fourteen	130
Chapter Fifteen	137
Chapter Sixteen	148
Chapter Seventeen	161
Chapter Eighteen	169

Chapter Nineteen 180

Chapter Twenty 189

Chapter One

It was an American who first discovered what had happened.

And he was extremely displeased.

In fact, he considered that he had been a victim not only of an audacious crime, but also of a distant travel agent who had deceived him into taking a holiday in London on the grounds that the crime rate there was considerably lower than in his native country.

Still wearing a Stetson that he would not have been seen dead in back home in Lynchburg, Virginia, he was now telling the manager exactly what he thought of him and his hotel, and was thumping the fist of his left hand into the palm of his right to emphasise the salient points of his argument.

The manager was no less concerned about it than the American. After all, the reputation of a high-class West End hotel depends much upon the ambient well-being of its guests.

The American was joined by a loud Yorkshire industrialist who protested in language so strong and raucous that it caused the manager to wince and privately take the view that the money was in the wrong hands these days. Then a German woman arrived who made a similar complaint in strident and heavily accented English.

Reluctantly, the manager picked up the telephone and called the police.

Charlie One, the police area car responsible for covering that part of West End Central Division in which the hotel was situated, had been cruising in Piccadilly and arrived within two minutes of receiving the call.

By the time the two officers had locked their Ford Sierra — car theft being ever on the increase in London — and donned their uniform caps, the security officer of the hotel, a retired policeman, had been peremptorily summoned from his office by the now-irate manager, and was hovering at the front entrance in the hope that he might steer the two PCs away from the curious stares of the idlers sitting around in the lobby.

But that was not all. Detective Inspector Jack Gilroy of the Flying Squad had picked up the call on his radio and directed his driver to the hotel.

Detective Chief Superintendent Tommy Fox, operational head of the Flying Squad, had also heard the call on his way back from lunch with a crime reporter. He too told his driver, the mournful Swann, to make his way to the hotel.

Which was to prove unfortunate for quite a number of people. Not least of whom was Detective Inspector Jack Gilroy who needed his governor breathing down his neck like he needed a hole in the head.

But then, substantial jewel thefts are of great interest to the Flying Squad.

The crew of Charlie One had been quite happy to be dismissed from all the activity on condition that they committed nothing to paper beyond a few lines in their incident report books and the entry in the area car log that was required by the regulations. Fox, or Gilroy — and the latter was the more likely — would make the entry in the major crime book at West End Central police station once the full extent of the thefts was known. The crime might yet prove to be less serious than the first garbled outpourings of the hotel manager had appeared to indicate. If that were the case then Fox would be saved the explanations that were required when a major crime was downgraded to a minor one. But then Fox was a supreme optimist.

'Well, Jack, what's it all about?' Fox stood in the centre of the lobby and gazed around as he spoke. He was always impressed by big London hotels, and envious of the well-dressed patrons who appeared to have no visible means of support and little else to do all day but sit around drinking.

Gilroy examined the brief notes he had made. 'Walk-in thief, guv,' he said. 'Ripped off a dozen or so rooms ... maybe more. Jewellery every time. According to the losers, total value about eighty grand.' Glancing up, he added with a grin, 'But that might be what they propose to see the insurance people off for, rather than the true value of what's been nicked.'

'Oh dear,' said Fox. 'What a terrible shame.' He smoothed the lapels of his Gieves and Hawkes suit and checked that his side flaps were not tucked wholly or partly inside his pockets. Fox's sartorial idiosyncrasies were well known at Scotland Yard, but it would be a foolish man who suggested that he was a dandy. And despite retaining his native Cockney accent, Fox took as much care over his spoken English — when the mood took him — as he did over his clothes. He described himself as a man of good taste and his concern for what he wore merely underlined the care he took with his job as a pursuer of the unrighteous. And if anyone was in any doubt about that, Fox was the holder of the Queen's Gallantry Medal which he had been awarded for disarming a villain who had been so ill-advised as to pull a gun on him. 'Do we have any witnesses, dear boy?' he enquired.

'Sort of. The linkman.'

'Any good?'

Gilroy shrugged. 'Might be, guv.'

'Well, have you spoken to him yet?'

'Been too busy taking the details of what these villains had off, sir.'

'Villains? In the plural, Jack?'

'Second-hand so far, guv. The manager reckons that the linkman saw a car he was a bit sussy about. Man and a woman. Plus the driver.'

'Oh!' Fox spoke flatly and shrugged. 'Where is the manager?'

'Over there,' said Gilroy. 'Him in the natty black jacket and pinstripes, surrounded by a crowd of happy holiday-makers.'

'We'll have a chat with him, then. The merry throng comprises the losers, I take it?'

'Yes, sir.' Gilroy crossed the lobby and whispered to the manager, who, with a look of relief at having been rescued, led Gilroy and Fox into his office.

'Well, Mr, er —?'

'Hawkins. Mr Hawkins,' said the manager.

'Well, Mr Hawkins, what seems to be the problem here?' Without waiting for an invitation, Fox sat down in a gilt reproduction armchair.

'The problem!' Hawkins sounded outraged. 'I would venture to suggest that it's a bit more than a problem.' He paused. 'Who are you, anyway?'

Fox smiled disarmingly. 'How remiss of me,' he said. 'Thomas Fox ... of the Flying Squad.' He raised himself an inch or two off his chair and shook hands.

'Well, the problem, as you put it, consists of about twelve of my guests having had their rooms burgled and jewellery to the tune of about eighty thousand pounds stolen. So far.'

'So far?' Fox raised an eyebrow.

Hawkins sat down in the chair behind his ornate desk, suddenly deflated by the monstrous events of the day. 'Not all the guests are in the hotel at the moment,' he said wearily. 'For all I know, others may come in at any time to complain of a loss.'

'You may well be right,' said Fox sympathetically. 'Yes, indeed.'

'What I want to know,' continued the manager, 'and certainly what my directors will want to know ...' He paused briefly to emphasise his erroneous belief that mention of his directors would persuade Fox to give some priority to his enquiries, 'is what the police are doing about it.'

Fox smiled benignly. 'We shall pursue the investigation with vigour,' he said. 'Now, Mr Hawkins, my detective inspector tells me that your linkman has some valuable information to impart to me.'

'Er, yes. Shall I ...?' The manager's hand hovered over the telephone.

'Fetch him in? If you would be so kind.' Fox crossed his legs, half turned in his chair and gazed at a David Gentleman print on the wall. 'Superb picture, that,' he murmured.

Despite the warmth of the mid-July day, the linkman wore a greenish-grey greatcoat and held a top hat of the same colour against his chest. As if in the presence of royalty, he bobbed his head and addressed the manager. 'You sent for me, sir?'

'Yes, Dibbens. This is ...' Hawkins paused. 'I'm sorry,' he said, 'I've forgotten your —'

'Detective Chief Superintendent Thomas Fox ... of the Flying Squad.' Fox carefully appraised the linkman's livery. 'Herbert of Bruton Street, I should think,' he said.

The linkman grinned. 'Yes, sir. All our stuff comes from there.'

'Thought so,' said Fox, nodding amiably. 'Very decent cut, that.'

'Ahem!' The manager coughed discreetly. 'Dibbens was the man who saw the motorcar,' he said.

'What exactly did you see?' Fox became incisive.

'Must have been about half past one, sir,' said Dibbens. 'Always a bit of a rush at lunch time, but I noticed these two coming out. Man and a woman. She was a bit of all right, she was.' He grinned, and the manager coughed again.

'Why did you notice them particularly?' asked Fox.

'Well, I asked them if they wanted a cab, but they said no, they'd got a car. And they walked across the forecourt to this Jag.'

'Go on.'

'A new one, it was. An XJ6, dark green. I've the number here.' Dibbens produced a handful of paper money from his pocket and sorted through it. Then he extracted a five-pound note and peered at it. 'I wrote it down on this,' he said. 'There you are.'

Fox waved a hand towards Gilroy. 'My detective inspector will take the details. Now, what alerted you to these people?'

'It was his suit, sir,' said the linkman.

'His suit?' Fox looked suddenly interested.

'Yes, sir. Very poor cut, it was.'

Fox nodded knowledgeably. 'I see.'

'And I thought to myself, that suit doesn't go with that motor. That's what I thought.' And by way of explanation added, 'You get to know the real class in this job, sir. And you get to know them as who ain't got two ha'pennies to rub together. If you get my drift, sir.'

'Oh, I do, I do,' said Fox warmly.

'And he had dirty shoes, an' all,' said Dibbens with a sniff. In his view that was the final condemnation.

Fox tutted. 'Descriptions?'

*

The investigation dragged on for most of the afternoon. Victim after victim was interviewed by Jack Gilroy's team and all told much the same story. They had left jewellery — without which their womenfolk had refused to travel — in their hotel rooms. Yes, they admitted, the management had advised placing it in the hotel safe, but, well, you know how it is. On their return from seeing the Changing of the Guard, or visiting the shops, or lunching at some expensive restaurant, they had discovered that various items of jewellery were missing from their rooms. For the most part these items consisted of necklaces, earrings, brooches and rings, but in one case an attractive French woman reluctantly admitted to the loss of a pair of diamond nipple clips.

The scenes-of-crime team arrived and spread fingerprint powder about, more as a sop to the losers than in any belief that the thieves might have left any traces of their crime. Then they started to take elimination prints from guests and staff. But their hearts weren't in it. Like Tommy Fox, they knew a professional heist when they saw one.

Detective Inspector Gilroy set his team to taking statements from the guests, the linkman, the manager and anyone else who might subsequently be called to give evidence. Then he went back to Scotland Yard. By which time the canteen was closed.

*

Late that evening Gilroy held a briefing in his office at New Scotland Yard. 'To sum up,' he said, gazing round at his team, 'the bill has now risen to about a hundred grand's worth of tomfoolery. The likely runners are a bloke and a bird … and the driver.' He glanced down at the sheet of paper on his desk. 'According to the linkman, the man was aged anything between thirty and fifty, medium build, medium height, darkish hair. Poor-quality suit and dirty shoes.'

'And the bird, guv?' asked a DC with more than professional interest.

Gilroy scoffed. 'Legs all the way up to her arse and boobs that'd stop her ever falling flat on her face. Apart from that, zilch! And no description of the driver, except that he can't drive. Took off so fast he left half a hundredweight of rubber on the forecourt of the hotel.' He screwed up the piece of paper and tossed it into the waste-paper basket. 'As for the car,' he continued, 'it was nicked. Taken from Hyde Park Gate this morning. It's been circulated, of course, but not a sign of it so far. But that does seem to point to the three persons aforementioned having been involved.' Gilroy scowled. 'Perhaps,' he added cautiously. Jack Gilroy had been a detective for too long to jump to rash conclusions.

'So where do we go from here, guv?' asked DS Crozier.

Gilroy shrugged. 'The scenes-of-crime lads dusted for dabs,' he said. 'All the usual places, but they're not hopeful. They've got a stack of elimination prints to wade through, but you know as well as I do that at the end of the day there won't be anything. I've got SO11 doing a run through their criminal-intelligence files just to see if there are any likely runners on the outside —' Gilroy paused as the door to his office opened.

Tommy Fox stood on the threshold. 'Jack, an interesting snippet has just come through from Hawkins, the hotel manager.' He waved down the assortment of detectives who were struggling to their feet out of deference to Fox's rank.

'What's that, guv?'

'They've lost a receptionist, Jack.'

'Lost one?' Gilroy looked puzzled.

'Yes. A bloke, apparently. He'd worked there for about five or six weeks. Today, would you believe, he took it into his head to do a runner. Gone. No trace.'

'When was this, guv?'

'Strange to relate, Jack. When the tumult and the shouting had sort of petered out, the manager went to look for this finger and he'd gone to lunch. Looks like a long lunch a long way away. Didn't come back. Look into it, Jack. Might mean something.'

'If he's in on it, guv'nor, it might explain how the villains knew which rooms to make for. And how it was they had keys to get in with.'

'Now you're beginning to think along the right lines, Jack.' Fox turned and then paused. 'Ron.'

'Yes, sir,' said DS Crozier.

'I've got your Long Service and Good Conduct Medal in my drawer, seeing that you refused to have it presented by the Commissioner. Been there for about two weeks now. Pick the bloody thing up, will you.'

'Yes, sir.'

*

The next morning Gilroy pursued the matter of the missing receptionist.

'I understand that a member of your staff has disappeared, Mr Hawkins.' Gilroy smiled as he eased himself into one of the manager's chairs.

'Yes.' Hawkins had a sour expression on his face. 'It was shortly after the robbery yesterday that the duty assistant manager came to see me to say that this man Wilkins had gone.'

'Not gone sick or anything like that, I suppose?'

'Well, if he has I wasn't advised,' said Hawkins angrily. Such an omission would, in his book, be unthinkable.

'Wilkins, you say?' said Gilroy. Hawkins nodded. 'D'you have an address for him?'

'Yes. I've written it down for you. At least that was the address he gave when we took him on. Of course, he lives in.'

'What, here?'

'Certainly not.' Hawkins looked suitably shocked that such a menial might actually be accommodated in the same building as paying guests. 'In the hostel.'

'I see. And have you checked his room there?'

'Good God, no. It's in Earl's Court.' Hawkins spoke as if it were in the middle of the Gobi Desert.

'Right, then,' said Gilroy. 'That'd better be the first thing we do. Now then, when did he start here?'

Hawkins dropped his gaze. He was not at all pleased at being interrogated about his errant receptionist and had the feeling that this policeman was silently smirking at what he probably thought was gross incompetence. 'I have a note of it here,' he said, absently pushing at the sole piece of paper on his desk. 'The fourth of June.' He switched his gaze to a calendar. 'Just over five weeks ago.'

'References? Did you take up references?'

For a moment or two, Hawkins stared at Gilroy. 'I shall have to enquire of my personnel manager,' he said finally.

'Would you do so, please. Now.' Gilroy grinned. It did little for the manager's self-esteem.

Hawkins grabbed at the handset of his telephone and pressed a button. 'This Wilkins person,' he said to whoever had answered. 'What about references?' For some seconds he listened, a frown slowly settling on his brow. 'I'll speak to you later,' he barked before replacing the handset. 'It would seem not,' he said with obvious embarrassment. 'The man had been employed in the South of France, Cannes, apparently, and produced written references. The personnel manager saw fit not to check them. Stupid man muttered something about the cost of international telephone calls.' He puffed out his chest. 'I shall advise him as to his future conduct, you may rest assured.'

'Bit late now,' said Gilroy with another grin. 'This Wilkins. Reliable, was he?'

'There were always reservations about him.'

'Seems reasonable for a receptionist,' murmured Gilroy, but the humour was lost on Hawkins. 'You had occasion to be dissatisfied with him, did you?' he asked.

'No ...' Hawkins drew the word out. 'But there was just something about him that made me feel uneasy.'

Gilroy dismissed that as Hawkins being wise after the event. 'We'll look into it, Mr Hawkins, just in case there's any connection.'

Hawkins shook his head wearily. Recent occurrences had all been a bit too much for him. Added to which, the chairman of the company that owned the hotel had made it plain, in a short and acrimonious interview, that he was not unduly impressed by Hawkins's management skills. 'I really don't understand it. Any of it.' He shook his head again. 'The hotel business never used to be like this,' he added miserably.

Gilroy could see that he was unlikely to make much progress here. 'Perhaps if I have a word with your personnel manager, he can give me full details,' he said.

'Yes, of course.' Hawkins's hand moved towards the telephone.

Gilroy stood up. 'Don't bother,' he said. 'I'll pop into his office on the way out.'

*

'I spoke to some of the staff —' began Gilroy.

'Naturally,' murmured Fox.

'But there wasn't much they could add. Wilkins, they said, kept himself very much to himself. He liked a flutter on the gee-gees and he was always willing to give out a few tips about what to back, but he never talked about himself or his family, if indeed he had one.'

'Got to be something in it, Jack. This Wilkins doing a runner straight after the blagging. It's too good to be kosher.' Fox shook his head slowly. 'Right, then, the plan is this ...' Gilroy looked nervously expectant. 'First of all, have a look at Wilkins' room in Earl's Court, and his home address. Then have a word with the National Insurance people in ...' He paused, flicking his fingers.

'Newcastle, sir.'

'Very likely.' Fox smiled. 'They might have a record of our Mr Wilkins.' He sucked through his teeth. 'We should be so lucky,' he added. 'See to it, Jack.'

*

The room in Earl's Court was clean. Not clean domestically, but clean evidentially. The scenes-of-crime team went over it methodically, but there was nothing. No fingerprints, no tell-tale pieces of correspondence, nothing of a personal nature. In fact, nothing that would indicate that Wilkins had ever been there. Or, for that matter, had ever existed. That view was confirmed by another resident at the hostel who said that he had never seen Wilkins there.

The address in Pimlico where the mysterious Wilkins claimed to have been living when he applied for his job at the hotel did not exist.

'He's obviously a bloody villain, guv'nor,' said Gilroy.

Fox looked pensive. 'I think you're probably right, Jack. Find him, there's a good chap.'

Chapter Two

On the Sunday afternoon following the jewellery theft that was now occupying much of Detective Inspector Gilroy's time, the police launch that covered that stretch of the River Thames between Teddington Lock and Shepperton was making its way slowly up river. The crew, a sergeant and two constables, gave a friendly wave to a foot-duty PC standing on the embankment and then carried on admiring the numerous young ladies who were stretched out, in the briefest of swimsuits, on the decks and roofs of the cabin cruisers that crowded the river during the holiday season.

But the PC on the bank cupped his hands and shouted. 'Ahoy, Thames Division,' he cried.

'Blimey,' said one of the river policemen, 'he must be a Captain Hornblower fan,' and grabbed a loud-hailer. 'What's the problem, mate?'

'Something in the river,' shouted the PC.

'I hope it's not a body,' said the sergeant. He was not averse to dealing with dead bodies, in fact they were almost a commonplace, but he was only too aware of how difficult it was to get hold of a coroner's officer on a Sunday afternoon. He eased the throttle down, put the launch about and edged it into the bank. Then he throttled up again slightly, sufficient to hold the vessel against the current. 'What's up, mate?'

'A bloke in a launch, Sarge,' said the foot-duty constable, leaning forward and supporting himself against the cabin roof of the police launch, 'reckons he saw something pretty solid down there.' He pointed to a spot about four or five yards out from a slipway.

The sergeant yawned. 'We'll take a look,' he said, opening the throttle. The foot-duty PC relinquished his hold of the cabin roof just in time to prevent himself from falling in the water.

'You'll have to be a bit sharper than that, skipper,' said one of the crew with a grin. 'He got away.'

*

'It seems,' said Fox, appearing in the doorway of Gilroy's office, 'that our water-borne colleagues have found the car.' He let go of the message flimsy so that it floated down on to Gilroy's desk. 'These villains had the bloody audacity to dump it in the river practically within spitting distance of Kingston nick, in whose station yard it now drips, surrounded no doubt by signs bearing the legend "Preserve for Fingerprint Examination".' He lit a cigarette. 'Well, it'd better be,' he added darkly.

Gilroy glanced at the message. 'I suppose we might get something out of that,' he said. 'Can only have been in the water for three days at most. Could get the local lads to do house-to-house, I suppose.'

Fox shook his head slowly. 'My dear Jack, the bloody thing was found in a stretch of the river miles from any dwelling. You don't seriously think that the sort of villainry we're dealing with would have dumped it in broad daylight with a gaggle of witnesses looking on, do you? Waste of time, that'd be.'

Gilroy shrugged. 'We'll get the lab boys to give it a going over then, sir.'

'Indeed, Jack,' said Fox. 'Bring all our scientific resources to bear, eh?'

They came up with a single fingerprint.

'And whose is it?' asked Fox.

'Bloke called Murchison, guv,' said Gilroy. 'James Murchison. He's thirty-five now. Got a bit of form for breaking, but he's been clean for a while, it seems.'

'Splendid. Find him, Jack.'

'Yes, sir,' said Gilroy and sighed. But not until the door had slammed behind Fox.

*

At Gilroy's behest, Detective Sergeant Percy Fletcher put himself about. Making use of his string of informants, he let it be known that he was seeking the whereabouts of one Jim Murchison who, it was thought, could assist the police with their enquiries. Nothing happened. No one seemed to have heard of Murchison, or if they had they didn't know where he was, or if they did they weren't saying.

*

Detective Chief Inspector Maurice Barker had joined the Metropolitan Police after the momentous decision of a former Commissioner to place the Criminal Investigation Department under the command of the

Uniform Branch. Nevertheless, on the basis of received prejudice, it was something that Barker resented.

'Maurice.' The chief superintendent in charge of the Kingston Division was a young man, graduate of the Special Course at Bramshill, but, in the view of most of the CID officers at the station, suffered the grave disability of lacking experience. It was a view based upon the fact that he had never been a detective.

'Yes, sir?' Barker stopped at the foot of the stairs.

'That missing person report …' The chief superintendent paused. 'Harley, Thomas Harley. Somewhere up Kingston Hill, Coombe Lane, perhaps.'

'Not seen it, sir.'

'Oh?' The chief superintendent raised an eyebrow. It looked like a criticism. 'Well, perhaps you'd look into it. Seems a strange business.'

'Right, sir.'

'Good.' The chief superintendent turned on his heel.

Barker stood on the threshold of the CID office and glared. 'Missing person. Harley. Who knows anything about it?'

'That'd be a Uniform job, wouldn't it, guv?' said a detective sergeant, a youngster called Purvis.

'Not any more it isn't. Get me the report. Now.' Barker was not happy.

Moments later DS Purvis appeared in Barker's office with the Missing Persons file that he had collected from the front office of the police station. He placed it on the desk and turned to go.

'Hold on,' said Barker. He scanned the report, made a few notes and then stood up. 'Take that back to the front office and get the car out. We're going to see this Mrs Harley.'

'But, guv —'

'But guv nothing. Get a move on.'

*

The house lay between Kingston Hill and Coombe Lane. The entrance was guarded by wrought-iron gates, but the drive, which could have taken three cars, was empty. To one side there was a double garage, and on the other, but lying well back, a swimming pool.

'I should think this drum's worth a bob or two,' said Purvis.

Barker grunted before ringing the bell.

Susan Harley was about thirty years of age. She was wearing a shapeless grey tweed skirt and a cream blouse, and her brown hair was straight and short with a fringe. The overall appearance was one of dowdiness, not helped by the unfashionable horn-rimmed glassed she wore.

Introductions over, Barker followed her into the spacious sitting room that looked out on to the landscaped gardens. 'I've come about your husband, Mrs Harley,' he began.

'You mean you've found him?' Susan Harley contrived to look anxious and hopeful at one and the same time.

'No.' Barker shook his head.

'Then —'

'My chief superintendent has directed that the CID make some enquiries.'

'I see. Well, about time. It was three days ago that I telephoned the police station. Since then I've heard nothing.'

'Mrs Harley,' said Barker patiently, 'hundreds of people are reported missing every year. It doesn't necessarily mean that there is anything suspicious about such disappearances —'

'But you think there is about this one?'

'Not necessarily.'

'Then why are you —?'

'Until I have the facts, I shan't know. Now perhaps you'd tell me about it.'

Mrs Harley leaned back in her chair and crossed her legs. 'I was expecting him home last Thursday, nearly a week ago. He didn't arrive and I haven't seen or heard from him since. That's all there is to it.'

'Yes,' said Barker. 'That much we have on record at the station.' He glanced across at Purvis to make sure that he'd started taking notes. 'You expected him home, obviously?'

'Yes, of course.'

'And you've had no phone call? Nothing like that?'

Susan Harley shook her head. 'Nothing.'

'And when did you last see him? Incidentally, his first name's Thomas, isn't it?'

'Yes.' She paused for a few moments. 'That morning. When he went to work.'

'What time would that have been?'

Mrs Harley considered the question and then, 'About half past seven, I suppose.'

'And that was the last time you saw him or heard from him, was it?'

'Yes.'

'Where does your husband work, Mrs Harley?'

'A firm of insurance brokers in the City.'

'What's the name of this firm?'

'Good heavens, I don't know.' Susan Harley tidied her fringe with her fingers. It was a nervous gesture and she started to look a little distraught.

'You don't know where he works?' Barker raised his eyebrows.

'For God's sake, Inspector, or whatever you are, there are some married couples who don't know all each other's business. Why are you treating me like a criminal? All I did was to telephone the police station and tell them that my husband was missing.' Mrs Harley opened her handbag and rummaged around until she found a tissue. Then she dabbed at her eyes.

Barker waited until she had calmed herself. 'I'm sorry, Mrs Harley, but we do need to know as much as possible about your husband's life-style. Are you sure that you don't know where he works?'

Mrs Harley sniffed and put the tissue back in her bag. 'No,' she said, 'except that I think it's …' She paused. 'No, it's no good. I really can't be sure.'

Barker tried another tack. 'Has this sort of thing ever happened before? Your husband going off without telling you, I mean.'

'No.' The woman looked up at him, her eyes slightly red. 'Well, yes, once or twice, but he's always turned up again. It was usually some sort of urgent business, so he said, but it's never been as long as this before. And he usually telephoned.'

'I see. Has he ever been away from home before? When you've known where he's gone, I mean.'

'Quite frequently.'

'On business?'

'Yes. Sometimes.'

'And sometimes not?' Barker was puzzled by this woman. She had reported her husband missing but seemed very reluctant to assist in discovering his whereabouts.

'He was a very keen golfer. He'd sometimes go away for golf weekends.'

'And where does he play golf?'

'Over Richmond way somewhere, I believe. I don't really know.'

'Richmond?' Barker sounded surprised. He was not a golfer, but he knew that the famous Coombe Hill Club was on the division and wondered why Thomas Harley wasn't a member of a club that was practically on his doorstep. Judging by the house, he could certainly have afforded it. But then Barker didn't know about waiting lists.

'I'm afraid I'm not much interested in golf.' Susan Harley sounded resigned to being a golf widow.

'What about friends?'

'What about them?'

'Did he have any?'

'Well, of course he did. Everyone has friends, but if you mean did I ever meet any, then the answer's no.'

'You mean he never brought any of them home, here? Business acquaintances ... that sort of thing?'

'No. We were never great ones for dinner parties, if that's what you mean.'

'Did he ever mention any of them ... by name?'

Susan Harley gave that some thought. 'I think there was someone called Frazer ...'

'Was that a surname, or a Christian name?'

'I really don't know. I think it was someone he played golf with.'

It was rapidly becoming apparent to Barker that he was not going to get very far with Harley's wife.

'D'you know whether he had any enemies? People he may have upset in the course of business. Anything of that sort.'

Mrs Harley looked suddenly alarmed. 'Why d'you ask that? Are you suggesting that he may have been murdered?' There was a probing intensity about her question.

Barker wondered about that, but showed no signs that it interested him. Instead, he shook his head and smiled. 'No, but we have to explore every possibility. D'you have a photograph of Mr Harley, by any chance?'

Susan Harley pursed her lips. 'Not that I can immediately put my hands on. There might be some old holiday snaps, but I think they're in a box room somewhere.'

'It would be helpful if you could look them out, Mrs Harley. Perhaps you could give me a ring at the station.'

'Yes, all right.' She sounded hesitant. 'My husband wasn't a great one for having his photograph taken, as a matter of fact.'

'One other thing, Mrs Harley. Did your husband travel to work by car?'

'Yes. Always.'

'Can you tell me what sort of car he owns?'

'A red one.'

Barker smiled patiently. 'Yes, Mrs Harley, but what make?'

'Oh, a Ford, I think.' Susan Harley looked vacantly at the chief inspector. She obviously took little interest in cars.

Barker nodded. 'And the number?' he asked hopefully.

'No idea, I'm afraid.'

*

Barker slammed the door of the car and put on his seat belt. 'There's something bloody odd about that woman,' he said, 'and I don't think she's telling us all she knows. Either she's frightened out of her wits, or she's covering something up.' He glanced at his detective sergeant. 'Did you get the impression that she doesn't want to find her husband?' he asked.

'Funny things, women,' said Purvis with a wisdom beyond his years.

*

Detective Sergeant Purvis turned out to be much luckier than most CID officers are, or, indeed, ever expect to be. The very first golf club he telephoned in the West London area had one Tom Harley among its members. But the secretary, a Major Carfax, having claimed that at one time during his military service he had been in 'intelligence', would not say any more on the telephone. He expressed the view that just because his caller said he was a police officer did not necessarily prove that he was one. It was an argument which Purvis could not refute.

Having attempted to lay the enquiry off on his DCI, only to find that Barker bounced it straight back, Purvis took a car and drove to the club.

'Major Carfax?'

'Yes.'

'DS Purvis, Kingston CID, I telephoned —'

'Yes, of course. D'you have a —?'

'Yes,' said Purvis, and produced his warrant card.

'Well,' said Carfax, indicating a chair with a sweep of his hand, 'what can I do for you?' He was a bristly sort of man with a clipped moustache, and wore a hacking jacket of a cut that would have drawn Tommy Fox's unstinting approval.

'You told me on the phone that Thomas Harley was a member of this club …'

'Was? He still is.' Carfax looked enquiringly at the detective.

'Yes, well that's just the point,' said Purvis. 'He's missing.'

'What d'you mean, missing?'

'Just that. He went to work last Thursday morning and hasn't been seen since. His wife's had no phone calls, no letters, nothing.'

'How very strange.' Carfax thought about that for a moment or two and fingered his moustache. 'What d'you suppose has happened to him, then?'

'That's what I'm attempting to find out,' said Purvis patiently.

'Well, I don't quite see how I —'

'Perhaps if you were able to tell me when he was last seen at the club …'

Carfax looked pensive. 'I can probably tell from the Greens Register when he last played,' he said, 'but he may have popped in just for a drink after that. A lot of members do, you know.' Then, as an afterthought, he asked, 'D'you play, at all?'

'No,' said Purvis.

'Mmm!' said Carfax. 'Well, I'll have a look.'

'Thank you,' said Purvis. 'That would be a start.'

'Shan't keep you a moment, then,' said Carfax and strode from the office. A few minutes later he was back, holding a piece of paper. 'Looks like Saturday the seventh of July.'

'That's nearly a fortnight ago.'

'Very likely,' said Carfax mysteriously. There was a vacant expression on his face. 'But, as I said, he may have been in for a drink …' He spoke the last few words in a distracted way as he rose slowly from his chair and peered out of the window. 'Ah,' he said, 'the club captain's just arrived.'

Purvis turned as a large cream BMW crunched to a standstill on the gravel outside the secretary's office window.

'Might be a good idea if you were to have a word with him,' said Carfax. 'Keeps his finger on the social pulse of the club, don't you know.'

Purvis followed the club secretary through into the bar just as the captain was raising a large gin and tonic to his lips.

'Oh, Captain, this is Detective Sergeant Purvis,' said Carfax.

The gin and tonic never quite made it. The Captain placed his glass firmly on the bar and turned. 'First today, old boy,' he said with a guilty grin, and shook hands vigorously. 'Charles Fowler, club captain. What can I get you to drink?'

'Nothing, thanks. I'm driving.'

Fowler laughed. 'Yes, but you're a copper. You don't have to worry, surely?'

'If I get caught, I get the sack,' said Purvis. He did not like the Charles Fowlers of this world.

'Ah! Yes, I see. Sauce for the gander and all that, I suppose.' Fowler laughed, but not very convincingly. 'Well, what can I do for you, old boy?'

'Thomas Harley.'

'Old Tom. What's he been up to?'

'We don't know. That's why I'm here. I was just explaining to Major Carfax that he's missing from home … according to his wife.'

Fowler screwed his face into a frown. 'Damned funny business. Never knew he had a wife. Got a girlfriend. As a matter of fact, she's a member here too.' He paused. 'Are you sure about that drink, old boy? Just the one won't hurt, surely?'

'No, thanks.' Purvis could have used a Scotch, but decided, out of sheer bloody-mindedness, that he would refrain. He knew that all the while he wasn't drinking, Fowler wouldn't touch his own drink either, not with a car outside, anyway. 'There's no possibility that they're married, is there? Could this girlfriend be his wife?'

'Good God, no,' said Fowler. 'She's called Jane Meadows. Stunning-looking girl.'

'Really?' Purvis wasn't surprised to hear that. He had come to the conclusion that Susan Harley was completely devoid of sex-appeal.

'You know Jane Meadows, don't you, Geoffrey?' Fowler glanced at Carfax.

'Oh yes,' said Carfax. 'Often in here.' He paused. 'But usually with Tom.'

'When was she last here, do you know?' asked Purvis.

Fowler stared at the detective. 'I thought it was Tom you'd lost.'

'So it is, but this might be relevant.'

'About ten days ago. With Tom, I think. A Saturday it was.'

'Could you describe her?'

'A rather gorgeous blonde, actually. Quite a figure, believe me —'

'Age?'

'Oh, let me see. Thirty at most, I'd say,' Fowler paused and then signalled to the barman. 'Dennis, have you still got those photographs behind the bar? The ones we had taken after that Pro-Am thing in the spring.'

'They're in the office, sir. Won't keep you a moment.'

'We've not done it before,' said Fowler while they were waiting for the barman.

'Not done what before?'

'Hired a professional photographer to take candid camera shots.' Fowler paused. 'That's just reminded me,' he said. 'The only chap who objected was Tom Harley. I'd forgotten all about that.'

'Why should he object?'

'No idea. But now you tell me he's got a wife, he might not have wanted ...' Fowler grinned. 'Well, you know what I mean.'

'I can only find the one, sir,' said the barman, returning with a bulky photograph album.

'I think that's all there was, Dennis. Now, should be here somewhere.' Fowler started to flip through the pages. 'Had these up in the bar for weeks, then we bunged them in a book. You know what people are like. Love to buy photographs of themselves getting sloshed. Ah! Here we are.' He prodded a photograph. 'That's the boy.' He half turned the album. 'There he is. That's Tom. And that ...' He reached across and pointed. 'And that is Jane Meadows.'

Purvis looked closely at the photograph. 'Good-looking girl.'

'Plays off ten,' said Fowler. He was obviously more impressed by the girl's handicap than her sexual attraction. 'Damned odd, though,' he continued. 'Tom having a wife. Never mentioned it.' He shook his head. It could have been wonderment, but it might just have been envy that Harley had managed to have a wife and a mistress. He glanced at the club secretary. 'I say, Geoffrey, that's not on, is it? Using the club for womanising.'

Purvis grinned at that. 'I wonder if I might keep this photograph, sir?'

'Have the lot, old boy. We were going to sling them out anyway.'

'D'you happen to have an address for this Jane Meadows, Mr Fowler?'

'Oh, I'm sure we do. Geoffrey, you'll have that in that complex filing system of yours, won't you?'

'On the computer,' said Carfax. 'I'll get it.'

'Now, are you sure you won't change your mind and have a drink?' said Fowler.

'Well,' said Purvis slowly, 'perhaps I will.'

'Splendid.' Fowler took a gulp of gin and tonic. 'What can I get you, then?'

'Tomato juice, please,' said Purvis.

Chapter Three

When it became apparent that DS Percy Fletcher's informants were not coming up with the goods on James Murchison, Fox took a hand. 'Spider,' he barked into the phone, 'I want to see you.'

'Who's that?' enquired a suspicious voice.

'Don't ponce about, Spider, you know bloody well who it is. Meet me in the Albert at half past two.'

'That's a bit close to you-know-where.'

'If you mean the Yard, Spider, it's bloody near on top of it, but I'm feeling idle today. Be there.' Fox slammed down the receiver.

*

Dressed as usual with a total disregard for the weather, the raincoated figure of Spider Walsh, clutching a roughly furled umbrella, edged slowly through the door of the pub and peered round. Fox, seated in a corner, looked at the ceiling in exasperation.

Walsh bought himself a pint of Guiness and after an unconvincing display of indecision sat down near Fox. But not too near.

'Come here,' said Fox.

Walsh moved reluctantly. 'I don't like it, Mr Fox,' he said.

'D'you have to bugger about like that every time I meet you?' said Fox. 'You waste one hell of a lot of time.'

'I don't like it, Mr Fox, straight I don't.'

'You've already said that,' said Fox. 'But I haven't arranged this meeting for your pleasure. Nor for mine,' he added as an afterthought. 'Now, to business.' He took a sip of Scotch and lit a cigarette. After a moment's hesitation, he dropped one in front of Walsh. 'I'm looking for Jim Murchison.'

'Who?' Walsh looked genuinely puzzled.

'Something wrong with your hearing?' asked Fox. 'Murchison. Got a bit of form for burglary. But it seems he's moved up in the world. To wit, he has come to the notice of the Flying Squad. And he's wasting my time and that of my officers.'

'I've never heard of him, Mr Fox.'

'Then you'd better start listening around, Spider. I want to know, like yesterday.' Fox took out a pound coin and laid it on the table in front of Walsh. 'Buy yourself another pint,' he said.

Walsh looked at the coin. 'Here, Mr Fox,' he said, 'a pint costs more than —'

But Fox had gone.

*

'What's happening?' asked Detective Chief Inspector Barker impatiently.

'I got an address from the club for this Jane Meadows, sir,' said Purvis. 'It's Mrs Meadows apparently.' He stressed the marital status.

'Well, you'd better shove off and see what you can find out,' said Barker. 'Although why the hell we're wasting time on a missing person I don't know,' he added. 'It's pretty obvious that Harley's decided to trade in the dowdy Susan for a decent-looking bird.'

*

Detective Sergeant Purvis had been a policeman for ten years. He had passed the inspectors' examination and was sweating on a promotion board, which is why he had to take all this trouble with a tuppenny-ha'penny enquiry that was a waste of everyone's time. At least that was what Barker had said, but if it went wrong it would be Purvis's career that would suffer, not Barker's.

He rang the bell twice before a woman came to the door. Two children, a boy and a girl, clung to her skirt. The boy had a dirty face and gazed up at the detective with a screwed-up expression.

'Yes?'

'I was looking for Mrs Meadows.'

'She doesn't live here any more. Moved out a year ago.'

The woman had given Purvis the name of the estate agent through whom she and her husband had purchased the flat. Next morning Purvis rang them. They had no address for Jane Meadows. But they gave him the telephone number of the solicitor. The solicitor either didn't know or wouldn't say.

'That's that, then,' said Barker. 'But there is one more avenue you can try.'

'Like what, sir?'

'The DSS. They might have a record of Harley's employment. Not that there's much chance that he's still there. If you draw a blank, give it a few days and then circulate the details in *Police Gazette*.'

As far as Barker was concerned the enquiry was over. He — and Purvis — had done all they could.

*

'Just had a report of another one, sir.' Gilroy held out the message form.

'Another what?' asked Fox.

'Another jewellery heist, same method as the one we're looking at. But the take was nothing like as big.'

'Where?'

'Hotel just outside Windsor, sir.'

'Windsor!' Fox snorted the word. 'That's Thames Valley police area.'

'Yes, sir.'

'Damn it all,' said Fox. 'These villains seem to know nothing about police boundaries. Don't they know that that makes it unnecessarily complicated, blast 'em.'

Gilroy nodded sympathetically. 'Yes, sir,' he murmured.

'Get on to it, Jack, there's a good fellow. Find out what it's all about.'

Gilroy retrieved the message flimsy. 'Yes, sir,' he said.

*

DCI Barker put down his pen and looked up at DS Purvis.

'Nothing from the DSS, sir. They gave me the name of a firm of insurance brokers in the City, but he hasn't worked there for about two years. That's the last record of UK employment they have. File's marked "Gone abroad".'

'Bloody terrific.'

'But something might come of this.' Purvis held out a tabloid newspaper.

'What's that?'

'There's a bit about Harley's disappearance, guv.' Purvis laid the paper on Barker's desk.

'What does it say?'

'Not a lot. Just that he's been reported missing by his wife and that police are making enquiries.'

'Where did they get that from? His wife?'

Purvis shook his head. 'No, sir. I rang her and asked.'

'What did she say?'

'Did her nut, guv.'

'Strange,' said Barker. 'I said at the time that she didn't want him found.'

'She put it firmly down to us, sir.'

'And was it down to us?' Barker looked accusingly at his sergeant.

'No way, guv. Leastways, not me. Probably down to that gin-swilling pillock Fowler that I spoke to at the golf club.' Barker shrugged. 'Well, I don't suppose it'll do any harm,' he said. 'Except that we'll now have the Press on our backs, and sightings from Land's End to John o'Groats that'll have to be looked into.' He sighed. 'Why can't the Uniform Branch do their own bloody jobs once in a while?'

*

'It's a blow-out, guv.'

'What's a blow-out, Jack?' asked Fox.

'The Windsor job. They've nicked a bloke for it. Trying to flog the gear at a jeweller's in Maidenhead.'

Fox moved his perpetual calendar a fraction of an inch. 'Why is it, Jack, that these outside forces always get the easy jobs?' he asked.

'It's because these second-rate villains know better than to come up to the Smoke and tangle with you, guv'nor,' said Gilroy with a grin.

Fox nodded gravely. 'You're right, of course, Jack. Absolutely right. Incidentally, has this villain got anything to do with our job?'

'Not a chance, guv. He's only just come out. He was in Reading jail when our heist took place.'

Fox smirked. 'Didn't write ballads by any chance, did he?'

'Pardon?' said Gilroy.

Detective Sergeant Purvis laid a newspaper on his DCI's desk. 'They've gone one better this morning, guv'nor,' he said. 'There's a picture of Tom Harley in today's paper.'

'Where the hell did they get that from? I'll bet it wasn't his wife. Didn't ring back to say she'd found one, did she?' Barker frowned. He had enough serious crime to investigate without looking for a missing businessman whom he was convinced had run away with Jane Meadows, the gorgeous-looking blonde.

'No, sir,' said Purvis. 'I'm pretty sure that this is another one from the club's spring Pro-Am thrash. It's only a blow-up of his head and shoulders, but you can see he was wearing a dinner jacket.'

'I thought you said that you'd got all those photographs.' Barker studied his sergeant suspiciously.

'Fowler said that's all there was, but now I come to think of it the barman mentioned something about only being able to find one book. If they did find another one Fowler might have flogged it to the Press. Or Carfax ... or even Dennis the barman, I suppose.'

'Cynical mind you've got,' said Barker thoughtfully.

*

'It's Mr Hawkins,' said the voice of the hotel manager on the phone. 'Is that Mr Fox?'

'Yes, Mr Hawkins. What can I do for you?'

'There was a photograph in the paper this morning of someone called Harley, Thomas Harley. It said that he was missing from home.'

'Really, Mr Hawkins? I can't say that I've seen it.' Fox sighed. 'What about it?'

'Well, I've shown it to several members of my staff, Mr Fox, and we're all agreed that it's Wilkins.'

'Wilkins?'

'Yes, you know, the receptionist who disappeared from the hotel on the day of the robbery.'

'Really?' said Fox, his interest aroused. 'How fascinating. And which newspaper was this in?'

Fox slammed down the phone and marched into the main office of the Flying Squad, an appearance that was immediately greeted with an expectant hush. For a moment he looked round, then started sorting through the various newspapers that littered the desks.

'Help you, guv?' asked a detective sergeant.

'I'm looking for a newspaper,' said Fox darkly. 'One of you low-life layabouts must read the rag I want.'

*

Detective Chief Inspector Maurice Barker was having lunch, in the senior officers' dining room at the top of Kingston police station, when the telephone rang. A uniformed inspector answered it, then held the receiver out. 'It's for you, sir,' he said to Barker.

Barker paused and then put a potato in his mouth. 'It's my bloody lunch-time,' he said. 'Tell them I'll ring them back.'

'It's Detective Chief Superintendent Fox of the Flying Squad, sir.'

Barker stood up abruptly. 'I'll speak to him,' he said.

*

'Ah, Tommy, good afternoon.' Commander Alec Myers, who had charge of several branches of the Criminal Investigation Department at the Yard including the Flying Squad, was Fox's boss.

'Good afternoon, sir.'

'This walk-in theft of jewellery, Tommy ...'

'Yes, sir.'

'How's it going?'

'We're still looking for Murchison, who was probably the wheelman, guv. The lads are out and about talking to faces. He'll come ... in the fullness.'

Myers nodded knowingly. 'And Wilkins, the missing receptionist from the hotel?'

'Not found him yet either, sir, but enquiries are continuing.'

'But surely there's been an interesting development there, Tommy? Might he not be identical with a missing businessman called Harley? On Kingston's ground?'

Fox looked at Myers with a crafty expression on his face. 'Oh, you've heard about that, sir?'

Myers smiled. 'I've just been talking to the Commander CID Five Area about it, as a matter of fact.'

'I'm not wholly convinced that there's a connection, sir.'

'You mean you don't think that they're identical?' Myers leaned back with a half smile on his face. He had known Tommy Fox for twenty years and enjoyed playing him along as he might a recalcitrant fish that had been well and truly hooked.

'Ah, but —'

'But that's what you led me to believe, Tommy, isn't it? That the missing Wilkins was definitely implicated?' Myers consulted a sheet of paper on his desk. 'Or have I got it all wrong?'

'Well not exactly, sir, but —'

'That's good, because Commander Five Area and I have agreed that the Harley enquiry should be taken over by you, Tommy. Would make more sense, don't you agree?'

'Oh!' said Fox. 'That's very kind of the Commander Five Area, sir.'

'I thought you'd appreciate the gesture,' said Myers, and studied Fox with a pensive expression.

*

'Jack, remind me to send the Commander Five Area a bloody Christmas card,' said Fox.

*

'Oh, Captain, this is Detective Chief Superintendent er —' Major Carfax paused. 'I, er …'

'Thomas Fox … of the Flying Squad,' said Fox, smiling amiably. He shook hands with Charles Fowler.

'Oh, splendid,' said Fowler, massaging his hand. 'Will you have a drink?' he asked tentatively.

'Most kind,' murmured Fox. 'A large Scotch, if you please.'

'Good, good.' Fowler turned to the barman and ordered a double whisky and a large gin and tonic. 'Well,' he said, after downing a substantial quantity of his gin, 'always a pleasure to see the boys in blue.' He put his glass down. 'Had one of your young fellows here the other day, as a matter of fact.'

'So I believe,' said Fox, taking a sip of his Scotch. 'Good health.'

'A sergeant, he was,' said Fowler. 'Bit touchy about drinking and driving.'

'Very wise,' said Fox. 'Very wise indeed.'

'I s'pose it doesn't worry you more senior chaps?'

'Good heavens no.'

'No, I thought it wouldn't. Experience breeds worldliness, as they say.'

'Oh, it's not that,' said Fox. 'I've got a driver.' He waved a hand towards the window. 'Sitting out there waiting for me now.'

'Ah, yes, of course,' said Fowler, relinquishing his hold on his gin and tonic. 'Well, what can I do for you, Chief Superintendent?'

'Harley. How well do you know him?'

'Ah, that's what your young chap came about the other day.'

'Yes, I know.'

'Mmm! Gone missing, they tell me.'

'And you told the Press.'

'Well, I, er, thought it might help, you know.' Fowler looked guilty.

'Yes,' said Fox slowly. 'Could have been construed as interfering with a police enquiry, of course.' He put his empty glass on the bar. 'I'd buy you one,' he said, 'but we don't want to fall foul of the licensing laws, do we?'

'Oh, er, no, of course not.'

'Allow me, Captain,' said the unctuous Carfax.

'How long has Tom Harley been a member of this club?' asked Fox, carefully positioning his whisky glass in the centre of the mat on the bar.

'Not sure, as a matter of fact.' Fowler paused. 'I daresay that you can tell us from that magic computer of yours, Geoffrey, eh?'

'Of course,' said Carfax. 'I'll pop in and have a look now.'

'Splendid,' said Fowler. 'Don't bother coming back, Geoffrey. You can ring it through.'

'Yes, of course, Captain.' Carfax strode irritably towards his office.

'Mustn't take up too much of his time,' said Fowler. 'Busy man, our secretary.' He took a very small sip of his gin. 'Funny business, this Harley affair,' he continued. 'Did your young chap tell you that we didn't even know he had a wife?'

'Yes.'

'Mmm! Very friendly with our Jane Meadows, y'know. Crafty bugger.' Fowler shot a sideways glance at Fox. 'Now there is a woman,' he said.

'So I gather.'

Fowler was rapidly learning what many others had learned before him, that Fox wasn't going to give much away. He tried another tack. 'Bit unusual, a big noise like you from the Yard taking an interest in all this, isn't it?'

'All depends.' Fox took a sip of whisky.

'Yes, I suppose so.' Fowler leaned closer and dropped his voice. 'You don't think he's been murdered, do you?'

'Whatever makes you think that?' asked Fox, an expression of mock amazement on his face.

'I don't know, really, but one hears such terrible things these days, doesn't one?'

'One does indeed,' said Fox.

'Secretary for you, sir,' said the barman, holding up the handset of the telephone.

'Thank you, Dennis.' After a brief conversation Fowler returned to his place next to Fox. 'About four years, it would seem,' he said.

'What is?'

'That Tom Harley's been a member here.'

Fox nodded, as though this information was of great significance. 'I see,' he said thoughtfully. 'Tell me, Mr Fowler, what did he do for a living?'

Fowler's brow creased with what, in his case, passed for concentration. 'D'you know, I'm not awfully sure. Something in the City, I believe.'

'Yes, but what?'

'I honestly don't know, old boy. Some sort of brokerage, I believe.' Fowler shrugged. 'Futures market, perhaps.'

'Strange,' said Fox.

'What is?'

'I always thought that golf clubs were the places where a lot of business got done.'

Fowler laughed. 'Well, sometimes.'

'This Jane Meadows. About thirty, blonde and good looking, I think you told the sergeant.'

'Oh, absolutely. A dashed attractive girl.'

'And she always came with Harley, did she? Didn't come on her own, at all? In her own car, for instance?'

'Used to come on her own quite often at first.'

'At first?'

'Yes, she's been a member here probably for about five or six years. Some time before Tom joined us, in fact.'

'But recently they've spent quite a lot of time in each other's company, is that right?'

'Yes ...' Fowler looked unhappy. 'Thought they might get married, to be honest. Bit of a bad show, that. Didn't know that Tom'd already got a wife.'

'Or that Jane Meadows had got a husband?'

Fowler's jaw dropped. 'Really? I never knew that. Well I'll be damned.' He shook his head. 'She never mentioned him. Perhaps they're divorced.'

'Perhaps,' said Fox.

Fowler laughed, nervously. 'Of course, if we'd known there was going to be some funny business we'd have paid more attention.'

'Funny business?'

'Yes, you chaps getting involved, I mean. That sort of thing. Look, I'm awfully sorry about that photograph in the paper. I really thought it might help.'

'Oh, it did,' said Fox. 'Immeasurably.'

*

'Well, guv'nor?' asked Gilroy.

'Blow-out,' said Fox. 'That man Fowler's a complete prat.'

'Didn't have much to say, then?'

'Didn't know much,' said Fox. 'You don't learn a lot looking at the world through the bottom of a gin glass.'

Chapter Four

'I really don't know why the police have to keep bothering me,' said Susan Harley. 'I should have thought that you'd be better employed looking for my husband rather than badgering me.' She was beginning to realise that there was more to reporting a missing husband than just ringing the police station. She had imagined that they would make a few notes and leave it at that. After all, the first policeman who had called had said that hundreds of people went missing every year. But now this man from Scotland Yard had turned up and she knew enough about the ways of the police to know that senior detectives didn't investigate missing persons, not unless they believed them to be an integral part of a motorway bridge somewhere. She shuddered inwardly.

'Yes,' said Fox sympathetically. 'It's quite understandable for you to think that, but we can't just send officers out willy-nilly, looking for people.' He smiled benignly. 'Firstly, we have to satisfy ourselves that they really are missing.'

'Well of course he's missing. He's not here, is he?' Susan Harley tossed her head impatiently.

'The fact that he's not here doesn't necessarily mean that he's missing,' said Fox. 'He might just have decided to leave the marital home.' And I wouldn't blame him, he thought.

'What d'you mean?'

'Had you considered the possibility that he might have gone off with another woman.'

'How dare you!' Susan Harley tried to inject outrage into her voice, but it was unconvincing. 'Why on earth should he do a thing like that?'

'I don't think it, necessarily,' said Fox. 'But such questions need to be asked before we start looking for someone whose absence may have a perfectly logical explanation.' He had decided that there was something insincere about Mrs Harley, and he didn't mind applying a little pressure. She was certainly hostile, a strange attitude for a woman whose husband had gone missing, and it appeared that she was not being entirely open.

'Did your husband ever have any extra-marital relationships?' Fox beamed at her.

'If he had, he wouldn't have remained here. I can assure you of that.' Susan Harley sounded so adamant that for a moment Fox believed her.

But Fox had spent a lifetime interviewing witnesses, and knew that many of them told lies. And he could tell when they were telling lies. He also knew that any suggestion of a husband's infidelity might be seen by the deserted wife as a criticism of her own qualities. On the other hand, he wondered if she knew about the jewellery heist, or had even taken part in it. After all, a blonde wig would fit very neatly over Susan Harley's short brown hair. But the linkman's description of the female thief tallied with Jane Meadows. And Harley was almost certainly Wilkins. And Harley and Meadows were known to be close friends ... at the very least. 'Just a thought,' he said.

'Ours was a perfect marriage,' said Susan Harley, but just a little too quickly and a little too emphatically to be credible. 'I really don't understand it.'

Fox made a pretence of referring to his pocket book. 'Have you ever visited your husband's golf club?' he asked suddenly.

Susan Harley's reply was immediate. 'No. I have no interest in golf. Why d'you ask?'

'No particular reason.' Fox determined to apply a little more pressure. 'Mrs Harley,' he said, leaning forward earnestly. 'I have no wish to upset you, but for all I know your husband may have been murdered. And if that is the case, I would not wish to have my investigation obstructed. By anyone.' Fox didn't think for one moment that it was a murder enquiry, and judging by Susan Harley's lack of reaction neither did she. Like DCI Barker at Kingston police station, Fox was pretty certain that right now, somewhere, Tom Harley was enjoying the delights of a nubile blonde called Jane Meadows. Looking at Mrs Harley, he wouldn't be at all surprised. And he didn't think that Mrs Harley would be too surprised either.

*

Police Constable Walter Crabtree of the Devon and Cornwall Constabulary had been the officer responsible for the three villages of Cray Magna, Dibley and West Ponding for about three years. During that time he had got to know all their local residents very well. And their handful of minor local villains. But the caller at his house-cum-police station this morning was not a villain. He was the vicar of Cray Magna and its surrounding hamlets. A youngish-looking forty years of age, the vicar was broad-shouldered and athletic.

'Good morning, Wally.'

'Good morning, Vicar. What can I do for you? If it's a squash match, I'm tied up for the rest of the week.' Crabtree and the vicar were long-standing squash partners.

The vicar laughed. 'Not sure you're still in my league, Wally, not after the thrashing I gave you last time. No, it's this.' He spread out a newspaper on the counter.

Crabtree raised his eyebrows. 'Now I wouldn't have thought that you read that sort of paper, Vicar.'

'I don't normally, Wally, but my verger showed it to me this morning. It's yesterday's paper, as a matter of fact.' The vicar pointed to a photograph on one of the inside pages. 'It's this,' he said. 'This man Thomas Harley, who's missing from home.'

'What about him?'

'I buried a man of that name about a month ago.'

*

'Mr Fox?' The voice on the telephone was bronchial.

'Yes, Spider.'

'I think I've tracked him down, Mr Fox.'

'Who? Murchison?'

'Yes, Mr Fox.'

Fox sighed. 'Have you just rung me to tell me that, or are you actually going to tell me where he is?'

'Well, I was just wondering if you could see your way clear to, well, like …'

'If I thought you were trying to negotiate with me, Spider, I'd reach down this telephone and squeeze your scrawny neck until you squealed … in more ways than one.'

'No, nothing like that, Mr Fox. Honest.'

'Don't use words you don't know the meaning of, Spider,' cautioned Fox. 'Now where is Murchison?'

Walsh whispered the address.

'Right, then,' said Fox and jotted it down on a pad on his desk.

'That's got to be worth something, Mr Fox,' said Walsh hopefully.
'Yeah, don't worry, Spider. I'll remember you. Come Christmas.'
'Blimey, Mr Fox, that's months away.'
'Something to look forward to, then. But don't hold your breath.'

*

Jack Gilroy knew villains, and he knew that the sort of villain who specialised in walk-in thefts from classy West End hotels was unlikely to carry a firearm. But in recent years the specialist categories of the villainry have tended to overlap and policemen have been shot at by villains they didn't think would carry firearms. Consequently, the commander's authority was obtained for Gilroy to arm his team.

According to Spider Walsh, and confirmed by what the police call quiet enquiry, Murchison was staying with a lady of ill repute at her small terraced house in one of the numerous back streets in the Honor Oak Park area of London, not far from Brockley Rise. The paintwork of the house was peeling, the windows dirty, and the garden overgrown. But for the fact that the police had satisfied themselves to the contrary, they could have been forgiven for thinking that the house was unoccupied, or at best used as a squat.

At five o'clock in the morning, armed with Smith and Wesson police specials, a search warrant and a seven-pound sledgehammer, Gilroy's team of Flying Squad officers drove in from opposite ends of the silent street and stopped a few yards either side of the target house. They approached the front door stealthily, having waited for a radio call from other officers in a third car now in the next street, just in case Murchison decided to do a runner over the back gardens.

'Try 'loiding it, Ron,' said Gilroy to DS Crozier. 'Makes less noise.'

Crozier produced a credit card and slid it between the edge of the front door and the frame, gently teasing it up and down until he succeeded in pushing back the tongue of the rim-latch. Then he pushed the door open. 'There you go, guv,' he said, looking gloomily at his mutilated credit card.

'Well done, Ron.'

'Well, it is an Access card, guv,' said Crozier, 'but they're getting a bit fed up with me always trading it in. Probably think I'm a burglar or something.'

Gilroy grinned and led the way into the house, leaving a disappointed DC on the doorstep leaning on his sledgehammer.

Quickly and quietly the detectives moved through the ground floor, but found no one. Then they climbed the stairs and gently pushed open the door of the front bedroom. A man and a woman were engaging in the oldest pleasurable pastime in the world to the discordant accompaniment of protesting bed springs.

Gilroy surveyed this activity for a moment or two. 'James Murchison?' he enquired loudly.

The woman screamed as her partner rolled off her, although whether it was from terror or delight was not immediately apparent, and hurriedly grabbed at the bedclothes in an attempt to cover her nakedness.

'What the bloody hell —?' said the man.

'Are you James Murchison?' asked Gilroy again.

'Who the bloody hell are you?'

'Flying Squad.'

'Jesus Christ,' said Murchison.

'Bastards,' said the woman.

'Get up and get dressed,' said Gilroy. 'Both of you. You're nicked.'

'You needn't think I'm putting on a free show for an audience of coppers,' said the woman, a brassy redhead.

'Well, we're not paying,' said Gilroy with a grin. 'You can come as you are if you like.'

The woman threw back the bedclothes defiantly and stood up. Placing her hands on her hips and pushing one knee forward in what she thought was a classic pose, she glared at the policemen. 'Satisfied, are you?' she shouted.

Crozier gazed at her pale body and at the red hair tumbling around her shoulders. 'Don't know what all the fuss is about,' he said. 'You're no oil painting. But,' he added, 'at least you're a genuine redhead.'

*

'How many times have I got to say it? I don't know nothing about no jewellery, and that's straight.' Murchison sat on a hard wooden chair in the interview room at Lewisham police station, a truculent expression on his face.

Tommy Fox appeared not to have heard, and continued to walk around the room, smoking a cigarette. It was an unsatisfactory form of interview from Murchison's standpoint because it meant that he had to keep turning his head. His criminal instincts told him that it was unwise to let this rather nasty detective out of his sight.

'So you can get stuffed,' continued Murchison. 'You've got nothing on me, copper, and anyhow I want a brief. I know my rights.'

Fox paused momentarily in front of the table and smiled at Murchison but still said nothing.

'And another thing. Your bloody hoods broke in my drum this morning and woke me up —'

'Oh?' Fox stopped in front of the prisoner again and looked puzzled. 'From what my officers told me, you were already aroused,' he said. 'In fact, I am reliably informed you were well at it.'

'I never —'

'Incidentally, I don't go much on your choice. Where did you pick up that scrubber?'

'She's my girlfriend,' said Murchison defensively. 'And it's got sod-all to do with you.'

'Yeah,' said Fox. 'And everybody else's girlfriend as well. You do know who she is, I suppose.'

'Course I do. Sandra Nelson.'

Fox scoffed. 'Is that what she told you?'

'What d'you mean?'

'Your Sandra Nelson's real name is Jeanie Thom, from Glasgow.' Fox laughed. 'Not that I blame her for changing it. Any bird with a name like Thom'd change it if she was on the game, I suppose.'

'What d'you mean, on the game?'

'Jeanie Thom, alias Sandra Nelson, has got a string of previous for soliciting and outrage on public decency. Mind you, she'd be an outrage on public decency just by standing there.'

'I don't have to take that. Not from you nor no one else.' Murchison started to rise to his feet.

'Sit down and shut up,' said Fox. 'I'm doing you a favour. Take a word from the wise, my son, and get yourself tested. You're probably HIV positive. Furthermore,' he continued, deliberately switching back to his original theme with a suddenness that thoroughly alarmed Murchison, 'I am reliably informed that you've been up to your old tricks, my son.'

'I dunno what you're talking about. Look, I want to see whoever's in charge.'

'I am,' said Fox mildly.

'Well I ain't saying nothing ... not without a solicitor.'

'No need, dear boy. I'm going to do the talking. Just for a bit, anyway.' Fox sat down in the chair opposite Murchison and stubbed out his cigarette. 'You see, Jim —' He paused. 'Don't mind if I call you Jim, do you ... Jim? You see, your problem is that we found some litter ... in the river.' Murchison went to say something but Fox held up a staying hand. 'Very unwise of you to dump it in a busy river like the Thames. All those people chugging up and down in their expensive boats. Bound to find it. And another thing, the Thames Water Authority is very upset with you. It's an offence, you know, putting litter in the river like that.'

Murchison sneered. 'Are you telling me that your hoods pulled me in because of some bleeding litter in the river?'

'Well, yes ... in a manner of speaking, Jim. But it was the quality of the litter that interested them, you see. It's not every day that our lads find a new Jaguar XJ6 dumped in the river.' Fox lit another cigarette and pointedly ignored Murchison's hungry look. 'And it got us thinking. I know the ashtrays were full, but that doesn't warrant throwing away a brand new Jaguar, does it now?'

Murchison was starting to get worried. Never in his chequered criminal career, which spanned some two-thirds of his life, had he come across a detective like the one who now faced him. 'I don't know nothing about no car,' he said desperately.

'Funny, that,' said Fox, glancing round the room as though appraising the décor, 'because your dabs were all over it.' That was something of an exaggeration; there had been only the one mark, and the fingerprint officer was not too optimistic about finding sixteen points of similarity that would prove, to the satisfaction of the court, that it was Murchison's. But it was good enough for Fox. As a start, anyway.

Chapter Five

'I'm not saying anything.' Sandra Nelson, known to the police as Jeanie Thom, sat sideways on to the table in the interview room and drew deeply on her cigarette.

Detective Constable Rosie Webster, one of the Flying Squad's few women officers, stood for a moment and surveyed the red-haired prostitute. 'Really?' she said with a smile. Rosie Webster was six feet tall and weighed fourteen stones, but all her curves were in the right places; as usual, she was expensively dressed and wore a perfume that must have nigh-on bankrupted the male admirer who had bought it for her. 'Well, we'll see.' Rosie sat down, lit a cigarette and studied the woman opposite through a haze of smoke.

'It's no an offence to have it off with my feller in my own bed, is it?' Sandra Nelson spoke sarcastically and with a deliberate coarseness. Both were wasted on Rosie Webster.

'No offence at all, within certain limitations, of course.'

'Meaning?' Sandra snarled the word.

'Unless he paid you for it, after having been solicited by you in a public place.'

'You don't think I'm on the game, do you?' asked Sandra nastily.

Rosie smiled again and opened a file. 'Twenty-seven previous convictions for soliciting for an immoral purpose. Three for outrage on public decency.' She glanced up. 'Want me to go on ... Jeanie.'

'Oh!' Sandra lit another cigarette from the butt of her first. 'So, I'm on the game. So what? Anyway those OPDs were a swing. There's dozens of people doing it in Hyde Park ... every night. Why's it only girls like me who get done for outrage on public decency? What about all the rich layabouts having it off with their bimbos, eh? They don't get nicked, do they?' Her Scots accent had become more pronounced since Rosie's revelation that the police knew all about her, and she puffed angrily at her cigarette so that the tip glowed fiercely. 'Anyway,' she continued, 'since when have the Sweeney done dawn raids just to nick a girl for tomming?'

'On the twelfth of July,' said Rosie slowly, 'two men and a woman were concerned with stealing jewellery to the value of about one hundred thousand pounds from a hotel in the West End of London. Jim Murchison was one of them. We know that for sure. We found his fingerprints in the vehicle that was used.' She paused to add emphasis to what she was to say next. 'And the description of the woman involved fits you like a glove.' In fact, Sandra Nelson was nothing like the woman the linkman had described, but Rosie Webster knew from experience that descriptions were often far from accurate and it was possible that if Sandra had been wearing the blonde wig that police had found in her house at Honor Oak Park her appearance would have been altered quite dramatically. There again, the description could have fitted a thousand other blondes.

'Hold on,' said Sandra. 'That was nothing to do with me.' She had gone white in the face and was gripping the sides of the table. 'I don't know anything about it.' She had done one stretch in Holloway Prison for persistent importuning, and she had no desire to return to that gaunt North London pile.

'Don't you?' Rosie raised a quizzical eyebrow.

'No, I don't, and that's straight. And you can't prove it.'

'Well in that case you won't mind if we put you up on an ID parade, will you?'

Sandra Nelson placed her hands flat on the table and for a moment or two glared at her chipped nail varnish. The criminal fraternity with whom she mixed had always told her that if you got picked out on an identification parade there was a good chance of finishing up in prison, guilty or not. Slowly she raised her head. 'Look,' she said, 'I'll square with you. Yes, I'm on the game, but I had nothing to do with any robbery.'

'So?'

'I never even knew Jim then. It's only the last week or so we've been shacked up together,' said Sandra. Rosie looked doubtful. 'Well, ask him if you don't believe me.'

'We did.'

'And what did he say?'

'He said the same thing.'

'Well there you are, then.' Sandra smiled and leaned back in her chair.

'Well, he would, wouldn't he? But let's hear your version.'

'I was working Shepherd Market, you know?' Rosie nodded. 'And Jim gave me a pull. Well it was pouring with rain, and I said I'd go the night for a ton.'

'And that's what he paid you? A hundred pounds?'

Sandra shrugged. 'If he wants to bankrupt himself for a screw, that's his business. Any road, he told me that he was on the run, and asked if he could shack up with me. Only temporary, like. And he'd pay.'

'He'd still got plenty of money, then? Even after what you'd charged him?'

Again Sandra shrugged. 'He didn't seem short.'

'And how long ago was this?'

'Like I said, about a week ago.'

Rosie Webster looked dubious. 'And how do I know that you hadn't fixed up that alibi beforehand, so that you could trot it out when the pair of you got nicked?'

'Oh, Christ!' Sandra ran a hand through her hair. 'Don't you bloody coppers ever believe anything?'

'Not without proof.' Rosie smiled cynically.

'Look, you've got all my gear, haven't you?'

'Yes. Why?'

'Can you let me have a look at my diary?'

A few minutes later, Rosie returned with a large plastic bag containing the property that had been taken from Sandra Nelson at the time of her arrest. She broke the seal and emptied the contents on to the table. Picking a dog-eared diary out of the handbag, she passed it across. 'Is that it?'

'Yeah, that's it.' Sandra thumbed quickly through the diary. 'There,' she said triumphantly. 'Thursday the twelfth of July. I was in bed with an Arab all day ... and all night.'

Rosie examined the scrawled entry. 'Since when have girls on the game kept records? Or are you paying VAT now?' she asked. 'Anyway, that doesn't mean a thing. You could have put that in there as insurance in case you were arrested.'

'Oh, Jesus!' said Sandra. 'How else can I prove it, for Christ's sake?'

'All you've got written down there is the name of the hotel and a room number. There's no time. And there's no name.'

'Oh, leave it out. You don't honestly expect me to put names in my diary, do you? You trying to get me striped?'

Rosie dropped the diary into Sandra's handbag. 'Looks like we're back to square one, then, doesn't it?'

'All right, I'll level with you.' Sandra was now looking very scared. It seemed to her that she was faced with the stark choice of either being convicted of a crime she hadn't committed or naming her client. The first was a terrifying prospect; the second breached the unwritten code of the prostitute and could have very dire consequences. 'I'm no good with these Arab names, but he was called Aziz-something. And if you speak to the hall porter at the hotel, Charlie, his name is, he'll tell you. I had to give him a ton, or he wouldn't have let me in.'

'You gave the hall porter a hundred pounds?' asked Rosie. Sandra nodded. 'How much did you get from the Arab, then?' Sandra paused briefly. 'A grand,' she said reluctantly.

'A grand? That sounds like easy money.'

'Easy money! I earned every penny of the thousand I got from that cruel bastard,' exclaimed Sandra with feeling. 'You wouldn't believe the disgusting things I had to do for that.'

'Try me,' said Rosie and pushed her cigarette packet across the table. Not for the first time she felt some sympathy for a prostitute.

*

Rosie Webster did not believe in wasting time on enquiries. Not when there was a short cut, anyway. After racing back to the Yard and changing into what she called her Vice Squad gear, she and Detective Sergeant Crozier made for the hotel where Sandra Nelson claimed to have spent a distressing twenty-fours with an Arab.

'This shouldn't take long, skip,' she said to Crozier as she got out of the car. 'But you know what to do if I'm not out in ten minutes with a statement, don't you?'

Crozier looked slightly alarmed. 'What?' he asked.

'Volunteer me for the Juvenile Bureau,' said Rosie. She smiled her usual devastating smile and walked towards the hotel entrance.

The doorman's brief glance took in Rosie's tall well-built figure as she swept past him. Her appearance convinced him that he knew what she was there for. Which was not altogether surprising. Her shiny black raincoat was open to reveal a knitted black dress that was well above the knee and low enough at the neckline to reveal her deep cleavage, and she wore black nylons and patent leather shoes, the spindly heels of which clacked across the marble flooring of the lobby.

The hall porter looked up and smiled knowingly. 'Can I help you, Madam?' he asked in a tone just short of sarcastic. He too thought that he had assessed Rosie.

'Are you Charlie?' asked Rosie.

'I am indeed, madam.' The hall porter paused. 'How can I help you?' he asked tentatively. It was a deliberately ambiguous question. He thought he knew what she did for a living, but he was being cautious. He knew from long experience that it was not always easy to distinguish between prostitutes and some of the very rich women who patronised his hotel.

Rosie leaned confidentially towards the hall porter. 'I've come to see an American gentleman,' she said as she made a pretence of searching in her handbag. She looked up. 'He said that if I were to give you a little something, you'd be able to tell me the number of his room … discreetly.' She smiled sweetly.

'What would his name be, madam?'

'He said it was Clint Farman.' Rosie repeated the name that DS Crozier, using a fake American accent, had given to the hall porter on the telephone not thirty minutes previously when he had arranged for the use of a room … for a fee, of course. She pursed her lips. 'I don't think he's registered under that name, of course, but then I got the impression that he's a very tactful sort of gentleman.'

'Of course, madam,' said the hall porter and looked expectant as Rosie opened her handbag once again.

'Oh dear,' said Rosie. 'I don't seem to have any money, but I do have this.' She laid her warrant card on the counter.

The hall porter looked as if he had been pole-axed. 'Christ!' he said, his cut-glass accent disappearing along with his confidence. 'Is this "Candid Camera" or something?' His feeble joke was more to hide his fear than any attempt to amuse Rosie.

'The only camera you're likely to be staring into is the one we keep at West End Central for photographing prisoners,' said Rosie with no trace of a smile. 'Now, on the twelfth of July last, a tom called Sandra Nelson gave you a hundred pounds to let her in to see an Arab called Aziz-something.'

'I don't know anything about that,' said the hall porter automatically.

'That's a pity,' said Rosie. 'It looks as though we're going to have to continue our conversation down at the station. But I'd better have a word with the manager first. He'll have to arrange a relief for you, won't he?'

'What the hell's this all about?' The hall porter's anguished glance took in a couple of guests who were waiting patiently to speak to him.

'Perhaps you'd better deal with your customers first, Charlie.' Rosie dropped her warrant card casually into her handbag and walked to the other end of the lobby.

'What's coming off here, then?' asked the hall porter, rushing back to Rosie after having dealt somewhat cursorily with the two guests.

'Same question,' said Rosie, 'and I'm running out of time.'

The hall porter's shoulders drooped. 'All right,' he said. 'Yeah, I know Sandy Nelson. She's often in here, but I've never took anything from her, God's honest truth.'

'Really?' Rosie looked sceptical. 'Well, for the moment I'm not interested in whether you did or not, Charlie, unless …' She left the threat hanging in the air. After hearing Sandra Nelson's account of precisely what her Arab punter had put her through, Rosie would have had great pleasure in swifting the hall porter straight into the charge room of the nearest police station, but she knew that it would be impossible to get him convicted of living on the Scots girl's immoral earnings. There just wasn't the evidence. 'Tell me what time she came in and what time she left.'

Charlie gave up. 'OK,' he said. 'I s'pose she came in about ten in the morning and went up to this Arab's suite. Room four-oh-four, it was. She stayed all day and all night, as far as I know. Left next morning about ten.' He sniffed. 'Poor little cow looked as though he'd given her a right hard time. I tell you straight, I wouldn't have had anything to do with it if I'd known what he was up to.'

'And how d'you remember that so clearly, might I ask?' Rosie looked at the hall porter with a penetrating stare.

'Are you going to do me for this?'

'Possibly, but all I'm interested in right now is eliminating certain persons from a serious crime. I'll think about your little scam later.'

For a moment or two the hall porter considered his position, then, 'I set it up for this Arab,' he said at last. 'But I didn't think it was ... well, you-know-what. He asked me if I could find a nice young lady to keep him company for dinner —'

'What, at ten o'clock in the morning?'

'Oh, yeah, I see what you mean. I didn't think about that.'

'That's understandable, Charlie. I wouldn't imagine that thinking's your strong point.'

'Well, I thought he wanted an escort, like. He didn't say anything about sex. He said he was lonely, and away from home, and —'

Rosie leaned closer to the hall porter. 'Don't take me for a fool, Charlie, it makes me angry,' she said menacingly.

The hall porter moved back sharply. 'No, honest, miss, I —'

'If you've forgotten that it's a police officer you're talking to, you can see my warrant card again,' said Rosie with heavy sarcasm.

'But they all expect it,' said Charlie. His voice had now assumed a wheedling tone, and despite his elaborate livery Rosie knew that she was dealing with just another small-time villain. 'It's very difficult not to oblige.'

'I'm sure it is,' said Rosie. 'Just as you're going to find it difficult not to oblige me now.' She opened her handbag again and took out some statement forms. 'Now we'll just go somewhere quiet and you can give me a written statement to that effect.'

'You must be joking,' said the hall porter in alarm.

Rosie looked pointedly out of the window. 'Ah, good,' she said. 'My car and driver are still there.' She turned back to the hall porter. 'D'you want to slip a mac on over your uniform before we go, Charlie?' she asked.

'All right, all right.' Charlie held up his hands in an attitude of surrender.

'I knew you'd see it my way,' said Rosie.

*

Rosie Webster dialled the number of the Operations Chief Inspector at West End Central police station. 'Hallo, guv,' she said when the chief inspector answered, 'I've got a snippet of information for you about a naughty hall porter at a certain hotel not a million miles from where you're sitting.'

'It's a terrible waste of my time, going over all this again, Jim,' said Fox, 'but I am known to be an exceedingly fair man.'

James Murchison looked at the detective doubtfully. 'Oh, yeah?'

'Indeed, Jim.' Fox smiled at the prisoner.

'What about Sandra?'

'What about her?'

'What's happened to her?'

'Oh, we threw her out. Not connected.'

'Well, I told you that,' said Murchison.

'Indeed you did, Jim, but unfortunately we can't just take the word of a small-time villain like you. We have to check these things, you see. But as it happened, you were quite right.' Fox leaned closer, like a Harley Street consultant about to discuss a rather unsavoury complaint with a rich patient. 'In fact, Jim, she was getting her arse screwed off by some rich Arab in a West End hotel not very far from another West End hotel where you were doing some screwing of an entirely different nature.'

'You're putting me on.' Murchison's hands had started to open and close, but whether from fear or anger was not entirely clear.

'Alas, Jim, it's true,' said Fox, who never saw any point in giving aid and comfort to the villainry. 'And she got a grand for her pains.' He smiled owlishly. 'And I do mean pains. Twenty-four hours she was at it.' He paused for a moment, calculating. 'By my reckoning that works out to roughly forty-two quid an hour. Not a bad rate of pay, that.'

'I'll bloody kill her,' said Murchison.

Fox tutted. 'Now, now, Jim. I have to point out that a threat to murder constitutes a criminal offence, but as I said earlier I'm an eminently fair man, so I'll overlook it on this occasion. But be warned.' He lit a cigarette. 'Now then,' he continued, 'about this heist in which you played a not insignificant part …'

'Don't know nothing about it.'

'A hundred grand is a pretty big one, Jim,' said Fox as if the other had not spoken.

'How much?' Murchison's eyes opened wide.

Fox whistled softly. 'That was very good, Jim, the way you did that. Almost as if you didn't know. And how much did you get out of it, eh?'

'Don't know what you're talking about. All right, so I nicked a car. So what? What's that, a carpet at worst?'

'Three months is a very conservative estimate of the amount of porridge you're lined up for, Jim,' said Fox. 'But the thing that astounds me' — he glanced reflectively at the walls of the interview room — 'is the number of poor little buggers like you who get sod-all out of a job and are then prepared to stand it all on their tod.' He turned to Gilroy. 'Often said that, haven't I, Jack?'

'Indeed you have, guv'nor.'

'Tell me,' said Fox, looking at Murchison once more. 'What did you get for that little bit of wheel-artistry? Not that it was up to much, from what I hear. The management of the hotel were apparently quite aggrieved at the amount of rubber you left on their nice clean forecourt.'

'I'm telling you, copper —'

'The interesting thing, Jim, is that there were at least three other people involved.'

'Two,' said Murchison without thinking.

'Well, well.' Fox beamed at Murchison and leaned forward. 'So tell me.'

'I keep telling you, I don't know nothing about no jewellery heist.'

'Then how did you know how many people were involved, dear boy?'

'It's what you said,' said Murchison lamely.

'I said three.'

'No, before that. You said two.'

Fox shook his head. 'Now listen, my friend. The Jaguar XJ6 that you dumped in the river had your fingerprints on it, in parts of the said vehicle that prove categorically that you were the driver. I've already told you that. And you are going on the sheet for stealing that elegant vehicle. And you're going on the sheet for stealing a hundred thousand pounds' worth of jewellery. Although we have recovered the car, we haven't recovered the jewellery. Now that's not very helpful. But if you insist that no one else was involved you can have it all by yourself.' Fox folded his arms and gazed at the prisoner. 'And, for your information, judges' wives always seem to own a lot of jewellery, and they seem to stay in hotels quite a lot. Get my drift, Jim?'

'Sorry to interrupt, sir,' said DS Crozier, as he opened the door of the interview room.

'What is it?'

'Thought you might want to see this message.' Crozier held out a computer printout. 'Came in a couple of minutes ago.'

Fox read the message twice, slowly shaking his head as he did so. 'Interesting,' he said, handing it back to Crozier.

'Want me to do anything, sir?'

'Not for the moment, Ron.' Fox faced Murchison again. 'Things are definitely worsening, Jim,' he said, a sympathetic expression on his face. By Fox's standards there was great profit to be derived from receiving arcane and significant information in the middle of an interrogation and he was a great one for leaving his suspects with something to worry about. As he often said, it tended to concentrate their minds wonderfully.

'What the bloody hell are you talking about?' The naked fear was quite apparent on Murchison's face. He knew all about the Flying Squad and their methods, and had a terrible premonition that he was about to get stitched up.

'Oh dear,' said Fox. 'I do believe you're going to be awkward.'

'You're trying to con me into making a statement,' said Murchison.

'If you make a statement,' said Fox airily, 'it'll be entirely of your own free will.'

'You're trying to lean on me,' said Murchison. 'And that's what my mouthpiece'll say.'

Fox scoffed. 'Lean on you,' he said. 'Believe me, my dear James, if I was leaning on you, you'd be under no illusions about it.'

Chapter Six

'The Department of Social Security have turned up a bit more on Harley, sir. They'd already been approached by Kingston CID and gave them the information about the insurance brokers where he worked, but now they've found a trace of him at another West End hotel where he was working until about a year back. Left suddenly.'

'What have you done about it, Jack?'

Gilroy grinned. 'Ordered a car, sir. I'm going up there now.'

'Good. And when you've done that, go and see these insurance brokers and see what you can dig up there.'

'I would have thought you'd know all about Tom Harley,' said the impeccably dressed hotel manager.

'You would?' Gilroy frowned.

'Surely you remember the robbery we had here about a year ago, Inspector.'

'Not offhand, no.' Gilroy was always amazed that people in London expected detectives to be familiar with every crime that had been committed in the capital over the last twenty years.

'We had about ten thousand pounds taken from the safe one night. Obviously an inside job.'

'Was that proved?'

'No one was ever arrested, if that's what you mean,' said the manager. 'But it was proved to my satisfaction. Harley was employed here as an assistant manager and he had access to the safe. He was on night duty that night and in the morning ten thousand pounds had gone. And so had Harley. That's good enough for me.' The manager gazed cynically at Gilroy as though he were not awfully bright.

'You don't know who investigated it, I suppose?' asked Gilroy, hoping to save himself a search of records.

The manager pursed his lips, thinking. 'Some fellow from Savile Row,' he said slowly. 'Can't remember his name …' He paused again. 'Brace? Could it have been Brace?'

'Gavin Brace. Detective Chief Inspector at West End Central?' said Gilroy.

'That's the chap. He'll put you in the picture.'

'Thanks,' said Gilroy. 'And you've never seen or heard of this Harley again?'

'No, I haven't. Believe me, you chaps would have been the first to know if I had.'

'Have a look at this photograph, will you?' Gilroy produced the golf club print.

'Yes, that's him,' said the manager without a moment's hesitation. 'You've found him, then?'

'Not yet,' said Gilroy, 'but we're working on it.'

*

Detective Chief Inspector Gavin Brace ran a hand through his thick grey thatch of hair and made a big show of looking behind him. 'I always get nervous when the Squad come wandering into my nice, quiet little nick,' he said.

'Quiet? West End Central. Do me a favour, guv,' said Jack Gilroy. 'I wanted to talk to you about a finger called Thomas Harley.'

'Do you indeed?' said Brace. 'Better shut the door and pull up a chair, then.' He produced a bottle of Scotch and two glasses from the bottom drawer of his desk and poured a liberal measure into each. 'Are you going to tell me you've found him, Jack?'

'I should be so lucky. No, but we've got him in the frame for another job.'

'The jewellery heist?'

'That's the one.'

Brace grinned. 'I'm glad you copped that and not me,' he said. 'I've quite enough on my plate without grieving foreigners wanting their tomfoolery recovered before they go home.'

Gilroy took a sip of Scotch. 'Fat chance of that,' he said, 'but an early arrest is anticipated.'

'That's nice.' Brace grinned. 'What can I tell you about Harley, then?'

Gilroy outlined what the Flying Squad had learned about Thomas Harley so far. 'I'd just like a bit of background on this safe job, guv. Might help to fill in the gaps.'

'Straightforward, really,' said Brace. 'Except that we can't find the bastard. He'd been employed as an assistant manager at this place for nearly a year. Eleven months, perhaps. No complaints about him up to the time the safe got screwed. Anyhow, friend Harley was night duty manager. The assistant managers take it in turn. Usual thing for big hotels ...'

'And had the key of the safe, I suppose?'

'Yes,' said Brace. 'Quite simply, when the day assistant manager turned up to take over, Harley had gone ... and so had ten grand from the safe.'

'What about the keys?'

'Cunning bastard had taken those with him,' said Brace. 'So that he'd delay discovery. The manager had the only other set and he didn't arrive until about nine. It would have been later, but they tried ringing Harley first — no answer — so then they rang the manager. Not best pleased, he wasn't.'

Gilroy laughed. 'Sounds a bit like that business last year. That nick north of the river. D'you remember? Sixty quid of prisoners' property went adrift from the station safe.'

Brace laughed. 'Yeah, I heard about it. Panic for twenty-four hours and then they found it in the chief superintendent's safe. Some stupid skipper had forgotten to enter it in the book.'

'Anyway,' continued Gilroy. 'You got nowhere, I presume?' Brace shook his head. 'No. We knew who we were looking for, but he just vanished. Put it in *Police Gazette* and Informations, but nothing. Tried the DSS at Newcastle and the DVLA at Swansea, and everywhere else we could think of.'

'If only the Uniform Branch at Kingston had thought to do a computer search when Harley first went missing, we'd've been ahead of the field ... slightly,' said Gilroy. 'The DSS said he used to be an insurance broker.'

'That's right, but he wasn't there any more, obviously. They didn't know where he'd gone, but they seemed to think he was out of the insurance business.'

'Sounds as though he's insuring himself now,' said Gilroy. 'Yeah, does a bit. But that still didn't help. So when you find him, Jack ...'

Gilroy waited until he had reached the door. 'Perhaps I shouldn't tell you this, guv,' he said. 'But for the past four years Harley has belonged to a golf club in the Richmond area. Under his own name.' He shut the door quickly enough to drown Brace's cry of anguish.

*

'How far's that hotel from the one where the heist was, Jack?'

'About twenty minutes' walk, sir,' said Gilroy.

'Is it indeed?' said Fox. 'Now that's what I call taking the piss.'

'Shall I get the Devon and Cornwall police to make a few enquiries about this moody funeral, sir?'

'No thank you, Jack,' said Fox, adjusting his tie, a beautiful silk creation he'd picked up at Liberty of Regent Street. 'You see, what will happen is that they will go round there, trampling all over the place, metaphorically, of course, and they will doubtless obtain a statement. But because they are not conversant with the intricacies of the enquiry' — he paused, savouring the phrase — '... they will not ask all the relevant questions. The result is that we will have to go down there and do the business ourselves. So we might as well do it from scratch ... So get on the blower to this vicar of Bray —'

'Cray, sir.'

'What?'

'He's the vicar of Cray. Cray Magna, sir.'

Fox stared briefly at Gilroy. 'If you say so, Jack, if you say so. Anyway, get on to him and tell him that he's been specially selected for a visitation.'

*

The chief security officer at the insurance broker's office was a retired detective sergeant called Stan Druce. He had forgotten how busy working policemen were and all he wanted to do was talk about old times and old friends.

But Gilroy had a lot on his plate. 'This Harley, Tom Harley, who used to work here, Stan. What can you tell me? I spoke to some clown in personnel, but he either didn't know or didn't want to say.'

Druce scoffed. 'Funny lot up there,' he said, shutting the door of his minute office. 'Want a cup of tea, Jack?'

'No thanks, I'm a bit pushed.'

'Yeah, I s'pose so,' said Druce. 'Job's changed, hasn't it? To be perfectly honest, I'm glad I'm out of it.' His wistful expression told Gilroy that that was a lie. 'Harley.' He leaned back in his chair, fingertips together, gazing at the ceiling. 'Went out under a cloud.'

'What sort of cloud? Thieving?'

'No, nothing like that.' Druce grinned. 'The gee-gees,' he said.

'I've heard he likes a flutter,' said Gilroy.

'You can say that again. Word is that he was into the bookies for about fifteen grand. This was about two years ago.' Druce rocked forward and placed his elbows on his desk. 'Well, you know how it is, Jack. Once you've been in the job you pick up the vibes. One or two phone calls. A snippet here, a snippet there. Know what I mean? Anyhow the upshot was that the partners got to hear about it, and that was that.'

'Gave him the chop, then?'

'Not half. Brokers are terrified of taking risks anyway, but one of their own who's into the bookies for that much, well …' Druce inclined his head. 'Know what I mean, Jack?' he said again, and tapped the side of his nose.

*

'I do hope there's nothing wrong,' said the vicar of Cray Magna.

'Remains to be seen,' said Fox without enthusiasm. 'Tell me about the burial of the late Mr Thomas Harley. If he is the late …'

The vicar nervously explored the muddle on his desk until he found a large book and several accompanying pieces of paper. 'This is the burials ledger,' he said. 'Interesting, you know, that a ledger is also a flat gravestone.'

'Is that so?' said Fox. 'That's very interesting indeed. I didn't know that. Did you know that, Jack?' he asked Gilroy.

'No, sir. Can't say that I did.'

The vicar resumed his seat and opened the burials ledger on his knees. 'Ah, here we are,' he said. 'The nineteenth of July.'

'What was?'

'The day of Mr Harley's interment.'

'His what?'

'Interment, Chief Superintendent.'

'Of course,' said Fox with a grin. 'For a moment I thought you said internment.'

The vicar smiled bleakly. 'It was a perfectly ordinary funeral ... except —'

'Except what?' Fox sat forward, an interested gleam in his eyes.

'Well, it wasn't handled locally. It was a London firm of funeral directors.'

'Was it really? Well, well. Which one, may I ask?'

'Er, yes.' The vicar examined his records again. 'Firm called Marloes ... of Edgware Road, I think. I must say that I'd never heard of them.'

'Nor me,' said Fox, who regarded himself as something of an authority on undertakers in London. 'Do go on.'

'I got a telephone call about four days beforehand asking if I could arrange the burial of a Mr Thomas Harley.'

'And you were able to fit him in, to coin a phrase.' Fox grinned.

The vicar swallowed. 'Oh, yes. We don't have that many funerals down here. The residents of Cray Magna have quite a reputation for longevity.'

'Didn't you think that it was a little strange?'

'Unusual, but not strange.'

'How so?'

'They explained that Mr Harley had died from a heart attack ... in London, and that it was his widow's wish that he be buried in the churchyard of the village where he was born.' The vicar paused. 'I have known it happen before. Not here, but in my last living.'

'And you didn't question it? Didn't, for instance, examine your parish registers to see if, in fact, Harley had been born in the parish?'

The vicar smiled benignly. 'Gone are the days when the parish priest keeps a register of births, Mr Fox. We would only have a record if the individual had been christened here.'

'And was he?'

'I've no idea. It would certainly have been before my time, that's for sure.'

'But did you check?'

The vicar shook his head. 'No,' he said. 'There would have been no point. Apart from anything else, people often turn to the workings of Christ late in life. In any event, not having been christened wouldn't constitute grounds for refusing anyone a Christian burial.'

'Did you view the body, by any chance?'

'Of course not. I was furnished with the death certificate and the authority to bury so I went ahead.'

'So a coffin turned up, you did the business and bunged him down below?' Fox grinned. 'Is that a fair assessment of the proceedings?'

The vicar gulped. Never before had he heard a funeral summarised in such a way. 'I suppose so,' he said, unhappy that he could not fault Fox's rough-and-ready description.

'And how did the, er, cadaver, arrive, may I ask?'

'In a plain black hearse.' The vicar spoke as though he could conceive of no other way for a coffin to arrive.

'Didn't happen to take a note of the registration number, I suppose.'

'Why on earth should I have done that?' The vicar was incredulous.

'How many people turned up for the funeral, Vicar?'

'Just his widow ... and a friend.'

'What sort of friend?'

'A man.'

'Could you describe him?'

The vicar gave that some thought. 'Ordinary, I suppose.'

'Very helpful,' murmured Fox. 'And you didn't think that unusual, either?'

'No. Mrs Harley explained that they didn't live in this country any more. Apparently they were over here on holiday from ...' The vicar paused. 'Tasmania, I think she said.'

'Tasmania, eh?' Fox nodded. 'Yes,' he said thoughtfully, 'it would have to have been somewhere like that. And all the relatives were miles away. On the other side of the world probably.'

'Well, yes, as a matter of fact that is exactly what she said. Mrs Harley, that is.' The vicar was beginning to look disconcerted. 'Is there some suggestion of irregularity? I mean, the bishop would have to hold an enquiry, and —'

'Not before I do,' said Fox with a measure of finality that further anguished the vicar.

'Well, I don't see —'

'This wife of the deceased, Mrs Harley. Any idea what her first name was?'

Again the vicar sought solace in his books and papers. 'Yes,' he said eventually. 'Susan. Mrs Susan Harley.'

'And what did she look like? D'you remember?'

The vicar thought about that for a bit. 'Yes,' he said eventually. 'About thirty, I suppose. Long blonde hair.' He glanced guiltily at Fox. 'A very good-looking woman as I recall,' he said.

'What an extraordinary thing.' Fox grinned, stood up and fastened the centre button of his grey chalk-striped suit. The vicar stared at him. 'One of the best that Hackett had,' Fox volunteered.

'I beg your pardon?'

'The suit,' said Fox, smoothing the lapels. 'It came from Hackett of Covent Garden.'

'Oh, I see,' said the vicar, who had been unable to afford a new suit in three years. 'What happens now?'

'What happens now, Vicar, is that I make further enquiries. In the meantime, perhaps you would be so good as to give my detective inspector here the full details of this funeral parlour that purports to trade from the Edgware Road.'

'There are no undertakers called Marloes in the Edgware Road ... or anywhere else in London as far as I can see, sir,' said Gilroy.

'What a strange business,' said Fox. 'And what about the phone number?'

Gilroy grinned. 'The subscriber to that number is a Mr Jeremy Benson, who lives in a flat near Marble Arch. As a matter of interest, guv, he's got a wife called —'

'Don't tell me. It's Susan!' said Fox. He fiddled with his paper knife for a while.

'No, sir. It's Jane.'

'Now there's a coincidence,' said Fox. 'Something evil is going on here, Jack,' he added.

'Yes, sir.'

'Marble Arch, you say?'

'Yes, sir.'

'Good,' said Fox. 'We'll pop across and have a chat with this Benson finger.'

Chapter Seven

'It's empty.' A grey-haired woman who must have been close on seventy had emerged from the door of the flat opposite.

'Is that so, madam?'

'They moved out a few weeks ago.'

'I see.' Fox stepped across to within a few feet of the helpful neighbour.

'Are you from the agents?'

'No, madam, the police.' Fox produced his warrant card. 'Detective Chief Superintendent Thomas Fox … of the Flying Squad,' he murmured.

The woman nodded knowingly. 'I can't say that I'm surprised,' she said.

'That's very interesting,' said Fox. 'And why d'you say that?' He was at his suave best when dealing with cultured old ladies.

The woman briefly examined Fox's well-dressed figure and concluded, despite his Cockney accent, that he was a gentleman. 'Perhaps you'd better come in,' she said. 'It doesn't do to discuss matters of this sort in public, does it?'

'Indeed, madam, it does not.' Fox beamed and he and Gilroy followed the woman into her apartment.

The sitting room was richly furnished with what Fox's practised eye told him were genuine antiques. The expensive carpet was overlaid with a valuable Persian rug and the loose covers on the chairs matched the curtains. Fox rapidly assessed that he was in the presence of substantial wealth.

'Do sit down.' The woman paused. 'Perhaps I may offer you a glass of sherry?'

'Thank you.'

She filled elegant crystal glasses and handed them round. 'A strange couple, the Bensons,' she began.

Fox sipped his sherry. 'This is quite splendid,' he said.

'It's an Oloroso Extra Solera. One of the best sherries there is, so I'm told.'

'I can quite believe it.'

'It is rather fine, isn't it?'

'Forgive me, ma'am,' said Fox, 'but you have the advantage of me. I don't know your name.'

'Oh, how remiss of me,' said the woman. 'It's Morton, Alice Morton.'

'Well, Mrs Morton …' Fox paused. 'Or is it Lady Morton?' he asked, with a flash of intuition.

'How very clever of you, Mr Fox. Yes, it is Lady Morton.' She fluttered her ageing eyelashes. 'Not that it matters. Before he became chairman of the bank, my late husband was a general.' She took a sip of sherry. 'It came with the rank … or "up with the rations" as he used to say.' She gave a nervous little giggle.

Gilroy took a tentative sip of his sherry, a drink he didn't much care for, and thought once again what a smarmy bastard his governor was.

'You were saying … about the Bensons,' said Fox, carefully placing his glass on a lace mat on the Chippendale side table.

'Well,' said Lady Morton, 'to use modern parlance, she was a flighty piece.' She smiled at her own boldness.

Fox smiled too, but at Alice Morton's belief that a phrase some forty years out of date could still be considered risqué. 'Is that so?' he said.

'Of course, she was much younger than her husband.' Lady Morton gave a knowing smile.

'How interesting.'

'I think she married him for his money.'

'He was wealthy, then?'

'Oh yes.' Alice Morton lifted her chin slightly. 'These flats are quite expensive, you know.'

'Indeed, Lady Morton, I can see that.'

'But they never seemed to do things together. Rather strange, I thought. I didn't know them very well, mind you. Tended to keep themselves very much to themselves, but one can't help noticing.'

Not for the first time in his experience Fox concluded that the Lady Mortons of this world were probably worth ten full-time surveillance officers. He also knew there was little point in prompting her. It would all come out, given time.

'They used to go on holiday separately,' continued Lady Morton with enough inflexion in her voice to indicate that it was an arrangement that did not meet with her approval.

'Really?' Fox contrived to sound quite amazed.

'I happened to be coming out one morning as she was leaving. The chauffeur was taking her luggage out.' Lady Morton fluttered a lace handkerchief towards her nose and sniffed genteelly. 'I suppose she felt that she had to say something.'

'And did she?'

'Said that she was taking a holiday in Morocco.'

'I see.'

'I was able to give her a bit of advice, as a matter of fact.' Lady Morton placed her empty glass on a table and glanced at Fox's half-full one. 'More sherry?' she asked.

'Thank you very much.'

Lady Morton topped up Fox's glass and poured herself another full measure. She noticed that Gilroy had hardly touched his and silently dismissed him as a social inferior. 'Oh, yes,' she continued, sitting down again opposite Fox. 'I was able to tell her some of the more useful things, like not drinking the local water and what to do about gippy-tummy, and how much to tip the natives. That sort of thing.'

'You know Morocco well, then.'

'I should say so,' said Lady Morton enthusiastically. 'The general and I knew it like the backs of our hands.' She paused to sip her sherry again, prompting Fox to believe that she got through quite a few bottles in the course of a week. 'I said I hoped that she and her husband would enjoy their holiday, and she said that she was going alone. Well, I suppose that I must have raised an eyebrow ...' Fox could visualise the effect that would have had, and envied it. 'And she said that her husband was very busy with his work and couldn't possibly get away.'

'What was Mr Benson's work?' asked Fox. 'Not an undertaker by any chance, was he?'

'An undertaker?' Lady Morton threw back her head and laughed, a tinkling, girlish laugh. 'My dear man,' she said, 'what a quite absurd thing to say.'

'Only a passing thought,' said Fox, joining in Lady Morton's infectious laughter. Behind him, Gilroy smirked.

'No, I believe he was a company director of some sort, but, as I said, they kept themselves very much to themselves. Of course' — Lady Morton lowered her voice to a conspiratorial whisper —'she had other men here when her husband was away, you know.'

'Did she really?' Fox leaned forward.

'Oh, yes.'

'Might you recognise any of them again?'

'I very much doubt it. I'm not one to pry, you know.'

'Of course not.' Fox paused. 'I wonder, ma'am, if you can recall whether the Bensons were here during the last week in July.'

'The last week in July …' Lady Morton spoke slowly as if trying to recall the events of that week. 'No,' she said eventually. 'I'm afraid that I really can't remember.' She looked quite disappointed at being unable to provide this vital piece of information. By way of compensation, she nodded at Fox's glass. 'Another sherry?' she asked.

'No thank you,' said Fox, 'but there is one other thing …'

'Yes?'

'D'you happen to know where the Bensons went when they moved out?'

Lady Morton looked crestfallen. 'I'm afraid I can't help you there,' she said. 'One minute they were here, the next they were gone, so to speak.'

'Never mind,' said Fox, rising to his feet. 'You've been most helpful.'

'Not at all. I feel that one should always assist the police whenever possible.'

'How refreshing,' said Fox as he moved towards the door.

'Er … is there some sort of trouble?' Lady Morton held the front door of her apartment ajar.

Fox smiled disarmingly. 'Good heavens, no,' he said. 'I was just hoping that the Bensons might be able to assist us with our enquiries.'

*

'The flat's not on the market, guv'nor,' said Gilroy. 'According to the managing agents, the Bensons are away on an extended holiday.'

'But you got an address for them … obviously,' said Fox.

'Of course, sir.'

'Where is it?'

'In the South of France, sir. Nice.'

Fox smiled. 'Is that a fact?' he said. 'Well, well. They tell me that it's very pleasant there at this time of the year.'

'D'you want me to book a flight, guv?' asked Gilroy hopefully.

'Not yet, Jack. There are still things to be done here.' Fox stood up. 'Yes, indeed, things to be done.' As an afterthought, he added, 'I'm sure you'll be able to fit them in, Jack.'

*

'The doctor whose name appeared on the death certificate does actually exist, sir.'

'I would have been surprised if he didn't, Jack.'

'So I went to see him.'

'Good, good.' Fox inclined his head in expectation.

'Thomas Harley was not one of his patients. In fact, he'd never heard of Thomas Harley and most certainly did not sign a death certificate in respect of the said Thomas Harley.'

'There are days, Jack, when you absolutely astound me,' said Fox. 'However,' he added, 'today is not one of those days.' He stood up, ran a finger along a ledge on his bookcase and then examined it despairingly. 'I think it would be a useful course of action, at this stage of the enquiry, Jack, for us to obtain an exhumation order.'

'Yes, sir.' Gilroy waited patiently.

'Well, put it in hand, Jack, there's a good fellow,' said Fox. 'It's a very straightforward administrative process.'

'It is, sir?'

'Nothing to it, Jack.' Fox assumed a crafty look. 'Application to the coroner under Section 25 of the Burials Act 1857, I should think. Perhaps the Coroners Act. Is it 1887? Or is there a later one? Needs the Home Secretary's authority, of course. Look it up in Archbold, just to be sure.' He waved a dismissive hand in the air.

'Yes, sir,' said Gilroy, turning towards the door.

'And when you've done that, come back and we'll pay another visit to Jim Murchison ... the man least likely to become the next world champion driver.' Fox lifted his jacket carefully from his shoulders and settled it back into place.

*

'It's no bloody good you bleeding coppers coming in here harassing me,' said Murchison as he was escorted through the door.

The prison officer gave one of Brixton's latest remand prisoners a malevolent glare, and left him to the mercies of Fox and Gilroy.

'Why did you agree to see me, then?' asked Fox.

'Makes a break, don't it? Someone to talk to.' Murchison sat down sideways-on to the table, crossed his legs and folded his arms.

'Splendid,' said Fox. 'Exactly what I had in mind.'

'Well, I ain't saying nothing to you, and that's flat. Not without my brief, anyhow. And probably not then.' Murchison gazed at the far wall with a truculent sneer.

'It's a funny thing, Jack,' said Fox, turning to Gilroy, 'but we travel all the way down here to do this fellow some favours and that's all we get by way of gratitude.' He shook his head wearily.

Murchison swung round and stared at the two Flying Squad officers. 'What d'you mean, favours?'

'As a matter of fact, Jim,' said Fox, exhaling cigarette smoke towards the ceiling, 'I wasn't being quite honest with you there.'

'Huh, tell me something new.'

'I am the bearer of bad tidings, Jim.'

To a prisoner on remand the suggestion of bad tidings usually means one thing: another count or two on the indictment. 'I got sod-all to say without my brief, and that's it. I shan't say it again. In fact …' Murchison stood up. 'I don't think I'm staying here any longer.'

Fox sat still, an amused expression on his face, and waited until Murchison had reached the far side of the room. 'It's about your mate Wilkins, or Harley, or whatever you like to call him.'

Murchison stopped, just as he was about to hammer on the door that led back to the cells, and turned. 'Never heard of him,' he said. It sounded unconvincing.

'Oh!' said Fox. 'So you wouldn't have gone to his funeral anyway.'

'Funeral? What funeral? What the hell are you talking about?' Murchison slowly retraced his steps, an apprehensive expression on his face.

'Sit down,' said Fox.

Murchison slumped into the chair. 'Well? What are you on about? If this is another con, it won't bleeding work. I'll tell you that for nothing.'

'Your esteemed friend and erstwhile colleague, Mr Thomas Harley, died of a heart attack in London on or about the fourteenth of July, dear boy. And on the nineteenth of July was laid to rest in a churchyard in Devon —'

'I don't know what you're going on about,' said Murchison desperately. 'I tell you I don't know no one called Harley or Wilkinson.'

'Nice try, Jim,' said Fox, 'but it's Wilkins not Wilkinson. And he's dead.'

'This is a bloody con. I know what you're —'

'And may the Lord have mercy on his soul,' said Fox.

'It's a bloody wind-up. You're trying to stitch me up.' Murchison picked nervously at the edge of the table. 'What are you up to?'

'But it's true, Jim.'

'Nah! I'm not buying it,' Murchison scoffed. 'My father always said never to trust a copper.'

'That's amazing,' said Fox.

'What is?'

'That you had a father. You're full of little surprises, Jim.' Fox turned to Gilroy and held out his hand. 'This, Jim, my lad, is a photostat copy of the death certificate of the said Thomas Harley, signed, as you can see, by a qualified medical practitioner.' He laid the sheet of paper in front of Murchison, carefully smoothing it with both hands.

Murchison examined the copy of Harley's death certificate, reading it several times. Finally, he pushed it in Fox's direction and leaned back in his chair. 'So what?' he said.

'I take it that Mr Harley's demise does not upset you greatly,' said Fox, folding the copy of the certificate and handing it back to Gilroy. 'At least, not in the way that one is normally afflicted by news of the death of a close and dear friend.'

'I keep telling you, I've never heard of him.'

'I see. Just a working partner, was he?'

Murchison weighed up the pros and cons of his predicament. After what seemed an eternity of soul-searching and introspection he looked at Fox and said, 'I ain't saying nothing and that's final.'

'Is that a fact?' Fox appeared to be quite unmoved by Murchison's rehearsal of his rights.

There was a long, silent pause during which Murchison continued to pick at the table's edge.

'I hope you're not intent on destroying the whole of Her Majesty's table,' said Fox, nodding towards Murchison's nervously active fingers.

'All right, so I nicked a set of wheels. I'll have that —'

'You don't have a great deal of choice there, Jim,' said Fox mildly.

'But I'm not having no bleeding robbery. I never heard nothing about it till after.'

'Till after what?'

'Till after the job.'

'Perhaps you'd better begin at the beginning, Jim.'

Murchison paused yet again. 'Will this help me out, Mr Fox?' he asked finally.

Fox smiled and leaned forward across the table. 'Give it your best shot, Jim, and we'll see what we can work out, eh?'

That was not an entirely satisfactory reply for Murchison, but he knew that it was about the best he could hope for at this stage. 'I never knew no Harley nor no Wilkins. It was another geezer what set me up.'

'Name?'

Murchison looked thoughtful. 'Harry something.'

'Harry what?'

'Never knew his last name,' said Murchison.

'That reckons,' said Fox. 'Go on with your fairy tale, then.'

'Well, he said as how he'd got a little tickle lined up —'

'What sort of little tickle?'

'It was a scam, like.'

Fox sighed. 'This is like pulling teeth,' he said. 'For Christ's sake, get on with it.'

'Yeah, well like I said, it was a scam. This Harry and his bird was con merchants, see. They were going to this hotel to meet this geezer and take him for a few grand. Something to do with stocks and shares, he said.'

'Oh, God!' said Fox.

'That's what they told me.' Murchison sounded defensive. 'And they wanted a set of wheels so's they could look the real thing, like. That's why I was wearing chauffeur's rig. But when they come out, this Harry said as how it had all gone bent and I'd better take off like the clappers because the Old Bill'd be there in no time.'

Fox smiled disconcertingly. 'What a fascinating yarn, Jim. But there are one or two flaws in this little fantasy of yours …'

'Do what?'

'For instance, why steal a car? Why not hire one?'

'Hire one!' Murchison sounded horrified at the prospect. He could not see the logic in hiring a car when the streets of London were littered with them, just waiting to be stolen. 'Bloody hell,' he said.

'And secondly,' continued Fox, 'none of my reliable witnesses happened to mention that you were wearing chauffeur's livery.' That was true. Not that it meant anything. Although the linkman at the hotel was the only person to have seen the getaway car, he had said nothing about the driver being in uniform. There again, of course, Dibbens had not had a great deal of time to absorb such minor details. 'Furthermore, we didn't find any such uniform at your address when we searched it.'

'Yeah, well I dumped it, didn't I?'

'Where?'

'Can't remember,' said Murchison sullenly.

'And the woman you mentioned. Who was she?'

Murchison shrugged. 'Search me. A blonde piece, she was. Quite tasty. I only ever saw her the once.'

'Know her again, would you?'

Murchison shrugged again. 'Might do,' he said. 'Who's to tell? One bird looks much the same as another.'

'Describe her, then.'

'Medium height, I s'pose. Like I said, blonde.'

'Age?'

'Twenty-eight. Thirty, maybe. Dunno, really.'

'Did she have a name, this woman?'

Murchison grinned. 'I expect so. Most people do, don't they?'

Fox struck the table top with the flat of his hand, and Murchison moved back sharply. 'Don't ponce about with me, sunshine. You're not holding a very good hand at the moment. A hundred grand's worth of tomfoolery's gone adrift from this hotel, and right now it's all down to you.' Fox paused. 'And that, Jim, is because you're the one we've got banged up.'

Murchison looked decidedly nervous. 'Yeah, well what I meant,' he said, licking his lips, 'was that I never heard her name. This Harry bloke never used it, see.'

'As a matter of interest, Jim, where did you drop the said Harry and his female accomplice?'

'Er ...' Murchison's brow wrinkled in thought. 'Park Lane. Well, Marble Arch, really.'

'Did you indeed? Well, well, well.' Fox stood up and walked across the room. For a moment or two he stood and read a few paragraphs of the Prison Regulations which were pinned to the wall. Then he turned and sauntered back. He sat down again and smiled disconcertingly at the prisoner. 'And where did you meet this Harry finger?'

'In a pub.'

'Oh dear.' Fox shot a glance at Gilroy. 'I fear that we're about to chart familiar territory here, Jack,' he said. He turned back to Murchison. 'Where was this pub, pray?'

'Dulwich.'

'Would be,' said Fox phlegmatically. 'And does it have a name, by any chance?'

Murchison scratched his head. 'The Oak and Apple,' he said eventually. 'I think.'

'Would that be the Oak and Apple or the Oaken Apple?' Fox enquired.

'Yeah!' said Murchison, somewhat mystified by the question.

'Never mind,' said Fox. 'No doubt the resources of Scotland Yard will find it, should that be necessary. And what happened?'

'Well, I was in there, having a quiet drink, see, and this Harry come up to me and says how did I fancy a bit of an earner. No risks, and that.'

'Beautiful,' said Fox. 'And you fell for it.'

Murchison looked contrite. 'Yeah, well I never thought I was getting into nothing heavy.'

'That's your trouble, Jim, you don't think, period.' Fox lit a cigarette and thought. 'So who's idea was it to nick a motor?'

'Oh, his, Harry's,' said Murchison a little too quickly.

'Yes,' said Fox. 'I somehow thought it would be. And how much did you get for this little venture?'

'Nothing, the bastard.'

'Which particular bastard are you talking about now, Jim?'

'Harry. He promised me a cut. A monkey, it was. But he welshed on me.'

Fox laughed, a grating laugh that quite upset Murchison. 'Five hundred quid? Deary me, Jim, you have been seen off, haven't you?' He laughed again. 'That little team calmly walks into a hotel, removes jewellery to the value of a hundred grand, and you're the only one who gets ID'd. And all for five hundred notes that you didn't get anyway. What frightfully bad luck. And here you are, all tucked up in Brixton, waiting to take the rap.'

'It ain't funny, Mr Fox.'

'Depends where you're standing, Jim. This Harry, incidentally. Ever see him before?'

'Nah!'

'Right. Let me see if I've got this straight. A bloke you've never seen before comes up to you in a boozer and props a job that involves nicking a set of wheels and dressing yourself up as a chauffeur. He offers you a monkey for the inconvenience, and you just take it on. And you don't even get paid. Is that about the strength of it?'

'Yeah.'

'Now, about Wilkins, alias Harley.'

'I told you, I never heard of him.'

'When you took it into your head to terminate this interview earlier, Jim, and started walking towards the door, I mentioned the names Wilkins and Harley, and you stopped dead, like you'd walked into a brick wall. How come that the mention of someone you claim not to know had such an effect on you?'

'Well, it was Harry, see.'

'You mean that Harry was also Wilkins otherwise known as Harley?'

'Nah, course not.'

'I thought not. Well?'

'It was what Harry said, before I dropped him and the bird off. He told me what the job was, and how this Wilkins was the boss. He said he was the inside man, and had been grafting there on the desk, see, so's he'd know what rooms to screw. He said that Wilkins was the one what was going to knock out the gear, and that once he'd done that I'd get my cut.'

'Oh, I see. And where was this pay-out going to take place?'

'He said he'd get in touch. In the boozer.'

'And you agreed to that?'

'Yeah, but I said I never knew it was no jewellery heist. So I told him straight he'd better come across with more'an a monkey, or I might just get a bit nasty.'

'That must have terrified the life out of him,' said Fox mildly. 'What did he say to that.'

'He got a bit shirty at first, but then he said he thought it was reasonable and that he'd have a word with Mr Wilkins and see what he could do for me.'

'Very generous,' said Fox. 'But he didn't turn up, I suppose?'

'No, he bloody didn't, the shyster.'

'What d'you reckon, then, Jim?' Fox smiled.

'I reckon that Harry done a runner, probably on his tod ... or with the bird.'

'And the shock of being thus defrauded gave Mr Wilkins, alias Harley, a heart attack, eh?'

'Yeah, you could be bloody right there, Mr Fox.'

'Mmm! D'you know, Jim, you're thicker than I thought,' said Fox. For a moment or two, he seemed to ponder Murchison's IQ. Then he stood up. 'I think it's only fair to issue you with a government health warning, Jim,' he said. 'Don't try and have me over. It could do your future career no end of harm.'

Chapter Eight

'Well, Jack, there's a pretty kettle of fish,' said Fox.

'What d'you reckon, guv'nor? Is he kosher, this Murchison?'

'Quite definitely not, Jack. He's bobbing and weaving like mad. He's well into this little lot, but he's been left holding it. He knows he's in bother and he's wriggling. Unfortunately for him, he's not too smart. He's yet another of your front-line expendables who's been caught in the cross-fire. Just a soldier, you see, Jack. Just a soldier.'

Gilroy looked faintly bemused. 'Right, guv,' he said. 'But what do we do now?'

'We find this Harry. And we find Harley. And we find Jane Meadows. I suggest that you sit down in front of our expensive computer and play a brief concerto, Jack. See what sort of music you can make.'

'Tried it, sir,' said Gilroy. 'A villain called Harry is not enough to put into the computer, let alone get anything out. And I've tried Wilkins alias Harley and a blonde who could be either Susan Harley in a wig, or Jane Meadows.'

'And?' asked Fox thoughtfully.

'Nothing, sir. No previous in any of those names.' Gilroy grinned. 'Apart from a marker from Gavin Brace at West End Central who wants to talk to Harley about a missing ten grand from a certain hotel safe.'

'Oh dear,' said Fox. 'I never did think that the purchase of all those expensive computers was a wise investment, Jack.'

'Well, you know what they say, guv ...'

'No, Jack.' Fox looked enquiringly at Gilroy. 'What do they say?'

'Rubbish in, rubbish out, sir.' Gilroy grinned.

'Exactly my point, Jack, but Harry — when we find him — may well be persuaded to give us some information about this distressing matter. Looks as though we shall have to rely on old-fashioned methods after all.' For a few moments Fox lay back in his chair, an expression of tranquil contemplation on his face. Then he sat up, sharply. 'Jack, pop round and see Lady Morton, well known friend of the police, and show her the picture of Jane Meadows that was obtained from that clown down at the golf club, and ask her if she recognises same as Mrs Benson.' Fox stood up and buttoned his jacket. 'I do believe we're starting to motor, Jack,' he said.

*

'I've got an associate of Jim Murchison's here, sir,' said DS Crozier, pushing a computer printout in Fox's direction.

'Well, where is he?' asked Fox, glaring round the office as if expecting him suddenly to appear.

'Mr Gilroy said you wanted any we'd got, sir.'

'What I want, Ron, is a body. The body of whoever that is.' Fox waved menacingly at Crozier's hand. 'Not a bloody paper villain.'

'Yes, sir,' said Crozier. 'I mean, no, sir.'

'Who is he, by the way?'

'Oswald Bryce, guv.'

'Is that a joke?' Fox gave Crozier a penetrating stare.

Crozier looked hurt. 'No, sir. He used to run with Jim Murchison. Known as Ozzie Bryce.'

'Yes,' said Fox, 'he would be. What else do we know about him?'

'Nothing, sir.'

'Nothing?' growled Fox. 'Well get something, for Christ's sake. Get out and beat on the ground, Ron. And find him.'

'Yes, sir,' said Crozier. 'Why me?' he added. But not until he was back in his own office.

*

'I wonder if you would be so good as to look at this photograph, Lady Morton,' said Gilroy.

Lady Morton peered over Gilroy's shoulder. 'Is Mr Fox not with you?' she asked.

'No, ma'am. He's very busy.'

'I suppose so. Well, you'd better come inside.'

Gilroy stepped into the hallway but it was evident that that was as far as he was going to get.

'Now,' said Lady Morton, 'what is this photograph that you want me to look at?' She put on a pair of spectacles that were permanently attached to her by a gold neck chain.

'Can you tell me, ma'am, if you have ever seen either of these people before?' Gilroy handed her the photograph of Harley and his partner that had been taken at the golf club.

Lady Morton stared at it for some seconds before handing it back. 'No,' she said decisively. 'I've not seen either of those people before.'

'Oh,' said Gilroy, somewhat taken aback. 'You're quite sure?'

'Young man,' said Lady Morton severely, 'I may be getting on in years, but I haven't lost any of my faculties.'

'Er, no, ma'am, of course not.'

'Why did you think I should know who these persons are?'

'Mr Fox,' said Gilroy, hoping that mention of his governor's name might defrost Lady Morton, 'wondered if they could be Mr and Mrs Benson.'

'Good gracious!' Lady Morton now thrust the photograph back into Gilroy's hand. 'Just wait one moment, young man,' she said, and walked down the hallway and into a room at the far end. Gilroy heard the sound of several drawers being opened and closed, and then Lady Morton returned clutching a large magnifying glass. 'Let me see that again,' she said. For some time she stared at the photograph through the glass. 'I suppose it's just possible that that is Mrs Benson,' she said.

*

'I should like you to know that I strongly disapprove of this,' said the vicar of Cray Magna, thrusting his hands deeply into the pockets of his waxed jacket.

'I must admit I'm not greatly struck on it myself,' said Fox. He too was wearing a Barbour. And a tweed hat that would undoubtedly have drawn some witty and sarcastic comments from his subordinates. If they had been there. And if they hadn't been his subordinates.

'It's un-Christian, and it's … it's a desecration. That's what it is.' The vicar spluttered on. 'And why does it have to take place at the unearthly hour of five in the morning?' He turned so that his back was against the penetrating drizzle that was gusting up the exposed hill from the tiny church.

'So that it will not be apparent to too many people what we're up to,' said Fox, gazing gloomily at the canvas screens. Behind the canvas a group of Devon and Cornwall police officers, under the supervision of

DI Gilroy, were taking it in turns to dig up the coffin of the recently buried Thomas Harley.

'But why? I don't understand what this is all about.'

Fox sighed. 'Vicar,' he said, 'I have satisfied the Home Secretary that there is a good and valid reason for the disinterment of the late Mr Harley. And we're doing it at five o'clock in the morning so that if it turns out to be a monumental cock-up, there won't be too many people who find out what complete prats we've been.' Fox unscrewed the cap of his vacuum flask and poured himself some black coffee. Then he added a goodly measure of Scotch from a small silver hip-flask. 'Care for some?'

'No, thank you.'

'You've got to admit, Vicar, that it's a bit odd. A bloke arrives in London, allegedly from Tasmania, and drops dead. And his widow wants him buried in some out of the way place that nobody's ever heard of … if you'll excuse the expression.'

'Well, I don't see that —'

'Furthermore, I would remind you, Vicar, that it was you who drew the attention of the police to the fact that Thomas Harley was the name of a man who had been reported missing from his home in Kingston upon Thames and whose photograph appeared in the newspaper.'

'Yes, but —'

'Further enquiries,' continued Fox relentlessly, 'indicated that the death certificate was not signed by the doctor whose name appeared thereon and that the firm of funeral directors that you say delivered the coffin did not exist.'

'Good grief.'

'Exactly. Sure you won't have a snifter?'

'Perhaps I will,' said the vicar.

'Of course,' said Fox, 'it is possible that it's a different Thomas Harley, I suppose. Be a bit of a coincidence, though, wouldn't it?'

'They've got down as far as the coffin, sir.' Gilroy appeared from behind the screens.

'Well done,' said Fox. 'Get them to fetch it out, then.'

One of the local officers also appeared round the screen. 'We'll have to go a bit deeper, sir, so's we can get the straps round her,' he said in a ringing Devonshire accent.

'Him,' said Fox absently. 'Here, have a drop of Scotch. Keep your spirits up, so to speak.' He held out his flask.

The constable looked shocked. 'No thank you, sir. Not on duty,' he said, and disappeared behind the screen again.

'Jack,' said Fox, shaking his head, 'I do believe the police force is changing.'

'Not that much,' said Gilroy, holding out his hand. Reluctantly Fox handed over his flask.

It took another twenty minutes of digging before a number of grunts and groans indicated that the coffin was being raised. 'Cor,' said a voice, 'here be an 'eavy bugger.' Another voice told the first to watch his language.

Fox stepped into the canvas enclosure and gazed down at the mud-encrusted coffin that the perspiring policemen were struggling to get on to the ground beside the grave.

'There's a brass plate on it, sir,' said one of the constables. 'It says "Thomas Harley, 45 years".'

'Well, that's a bit of luck,' said Fox. 'Probably means you've got the right coffin.' He looked round at the assembled policemen. 'Anyone got a screwdriver?'

'Oh aye, sir, we've got all the necessary,' said one of the officers.

'Open it up, then.' Fox turned to the incumbent of Cray Magna. 'Here we go, Vicar,' he said, but the vicar appeared to be praying.

As the last screw was withdrawn, Fox stepped closer and waited expectantly as the heavy lid was removed.

'Well, I be buggered,' said one of the policemen. 'That's a bit unusual, sir. There b'ain't no shroud nor nothin'.' He looked more closely at the body and then stood up. 'I think you'd better take a look at him, sir.' He turned one of the arc-lights by which they had been working so that the interior of the coffin was fully illuminated.

Fox stepped a pace nearer and gazed down at its naked occupant. Even without the benefit of a pathologist's expert opinion, it was quite evident that the man had been shot several times in the chest. 'Oh, Christ!' said Fox. It was not an expression of abhorrence — he had seen many victims of violent death in his service — but the realisation that he had just been lumbered with a murder enquiry. 'What d'you reckon, Jack?' he said, turning to Gilroy.

Gilroy grinned. 'Certainly doesn't look like a heart attack, guv,' he said.

'Oh, I don't know,' said Fox, pursing his lips. 'A few rounds in the chest is enough to give anyone a heart attack. But more to the point, does he look anything like the photograph we've got of Thomas Harley, Esquire?'

Gilroy peered closely at the face of the body and shook his head. 'This bloke can't be more than about thirty. He's fatter in the face than Harley — in fact, he's fatter altogether — and he's got a moustache. In short, guv'nor, he doesn't look anything like Harley.'

Fox shook his head. 'What have I done to deserve this?' he asked and glanced at the vicar.

'I could hazard a guess,' said the vicar drily.

'There's something between his legs,' said one of the PCs who had helped to remove the lid.

'There would be,' said Fox laconically. 'It was his chest that got hit.'

'No, sir, I meant that sack down there, see.'

'Well, well,' said Fox, rubbing his hands together, more from expectation than from cold. 'Fetch it out.'

The policeman lifted out the small canvas sack and up-ended it on to a groundsheet. For several seconds Fox and the others gazed down at a quantity of jewellery glinting in the glare of the floodlights.

'There are evil doings here,' said the vicar in a melancholy voice.

'You're dead right there, Vicar,' said Fox. 'For a start it's the wrong body, and it's a racing certainty that that's bent gear. Furthermore, I'll wager seven-to-four-on where it came from.' He looked down at the occupant of the coffin. 'The first thing, Jack, is to discover the identity of the resident of this six-foot bungalow.' He paused. 'Well, not quite,' he added. 'Get on the blower to Pamela Hatcher and ask her how she fancies a dirty weekend.'

*

'So you've caught another murder, Tommy?' said Pamela Hatcher, peeling off her rubber gloves. 'Seem to be making a habit of it.'

'Yeah,' said Fox disconsolately. 'I go out looking for them. Well, what's the verdict?'

Pamela Hatcher was an experienced Home Office pathologist in her late forties and had worked on several previous cases with Fox. She undid her single pigtail and shook her long grey hair around her shoulders. 'Been dead about five weeks,' she said.

'You cheated,' said Fox. 'You asked the vicar.'

'Can't do better than that, Tommy. Not in the circumstances. Death was caused by gunshot wounds to the chest. I gave Jack Gilroy the three rounds I took out.'

'Thanks,' said Fox, 'but it won't be much help until we find the weapon. If we find it. Probably at the bottom of the Thames ... along with all the others. There must be more weapons in that damned river than in the whole of the British Army.'

'I think you'll be able to get fingerprints all right.' Pamela Hatcher sat down and started to take off her rubber boots. 'If not, I'll amputate the fingers and you can take them with you.' She grinned. 'Well, good luck, Tommy.'

*

'No go on the fingerprints, guv'nor,' said Gilroy.

'What?' Fox did not sound pleased.

'Fingerprint Branch have done a run through on both main collection and scenes-of-crime. Nothing.'

'Terrific,' said Fox. He leaned back in his chair and scowled at the map of the Metropolitan Police District opposite him. 'Why do I always have to get the difficult ones? What about Photographic Branch?'

'They managed to get a few decent portraits, guv. We've circulated them, and it might be worth showing them to Murchison ...'

Fox nodded. 'Anything's worth a try, Jack. We've got little else at the moment.'

*

The little else they had got amounted to the information that Lady Morton had given the police about Jeremy and Jane Benson, her former neighbours at Marble Arch. That, of course, would come to nothing if the vicar of Cray Magna had made a mistake about the telephone number he said he had been given by Thomas Harley's 'widow'. According to Lady Morton, Jane Meadows might be Mrs Benson, but there again, she might not, given that women have the ability to change their appearance quite easily. Nevertheless, Fox had not ruled out the possibility that the two women were one and the same. 'Get a warrant, Jack,' he said, 'and take a team of fingerprint blokes up to the Bensons' flat and get them to give it the once over.'

*

'We got a result, sir,' said Gilroy.

'Meaning?' asked Fox.

'The bloke whose body we found down a hole in Cray Magna had been in the Bensons' flat at Marble Arch, guv,' said Gilroy. 'And it wasn't portable evidence, either.'

Fox nodded his understanding. What Gilroy meant was that the mystery man had actually been at the flat; his prints had not been found on something which could have been taken there by someone else. For a few seconds he stared out of the window. Then he swung round. 'How old did Lady Morton say Jeremy Benson was?'

'She didn't, sir, not in as many words.' Gilroy consulted his pocket book. 'She just said that his wife was much younger than he was.'

'And our information is that Jane Meadows was about thirty at most. That came from Fowler, the captain of the golf club, and from the weasel we've got banged up in Brixton. Right?'

'She's exactly thirty, sir. We got that from the DSS at Newcastle.'

'And how old did Pamela Hatcher reckon our cadaver was?'

'Between thirty and forty, sir.'

'It said forty-five on the brass plate.'

Gilroy chuckled. 'It also said "Thomas Harley" on the brass plate, guv.'

'Wish I'd got enough service to retire,' said Fox gloomily.

*

'We've released it to the Press, sir, as you said.' Gilroy spread a copy of the *Daily Express* on Fox's desk.

'Yes, I saw it,' said Fox. He gazed down at the picture that the Yard's Photographic Branch had prepared. 'Almost looks alive, doesn't he? Anything come of it yet?'

Gilroy grinned. 'Only one call from some nut in Inverness who swears he had a drink with him last night guv'nor.'

Fox scoffed. 'That's always the trouble with this sort of caper, Jack. Brings out all the loonies.'

'What now, sir?'

'I think we'll have to pop down to Kingston and have another word with the not-so-bereaved Mrs Harley. The blonde wig we found at Sandra Nelson's drum and a few smart clothes and there's no telling what she might have got up to, is there? But that can wait for a while. First, I think, we'd better pay the Bensons a visit. See if Jeremy and Jane are still in the land of the living. And, more to the point, see if they can explain what our unidentified dead body's fingerprints were doing in their elegant flat.' Fox stood up. 'And find out when they stopped trading as undertakers. South of France, I think you said, Jack?'

'Yes, sir. Nice.'

'Right, Jack, we shall go.'

'Go where, sir?' Gilroy fidgeted nervously with the corner of the file he was holding.

'Nice, of course.'

'What, now, sir?' Gilroy could see his social life being disrupted yet again ... and at a moment's notice.

Fox gave the question a little thought. 'Well, not immediately.' He glanced at his watch. 'But as soon as you can book a flight and talk to the French police.'

*

Fox marched on to the concourse of the airport, stared at a sign bearing the legend '*Bienvenue à Nice Côte d'Azur*', and turned to the young Special Branch officer next to him. 'What's that mean, Les?'

Detective Constable Leslie Reed was a fluent French speaker and had been assigned to assist Fox in any dealings he might have with the French police. 'It means, Welcome to Nice Côte d'Azur, sir.'

'Right,' said Fox. 'Just testing.'

'You are Detective Chief Superintendent Thomas Fox of the Flying Squad?' The clean-cut young man spoke in flawless English.

'Yes.'

'Good. I am Inspecteur Principal Pierre Ronsard of the Police Urbaine of Nice. I have been deputed to assist you in your enquiries.'

'Oh,' said Fox. 'How kind. This is Detective Inspector Jack Gilroy and Detective Constable Les Reed.' He put a hand on Reed's shoulder. 'Les is my interpreter,' he added.

Ronsard smiled. 'Ah,' he said. 'You thought that we did not speak English, perhaps?'

'That was the rumour,' said Fox, who had had dealings with the French before.

Ronsard shook hands with the three of them. To Reed he said, 'Perhaps your chief will give you a holiday in the circumstances, eh?'

'Not bloody likely,' said Fox. He was suspicious of any police force outside London, let alone abroad, and he was going to make sure that Reed was with him all the time. Just so that nothing would get lost in the translation.

Chapter Nine

The address Gilroy had obtained from the agents who managed the Bensons' London flat was nearly two kilometres inland from the Promenade des Anglais, not far from the Place de la Liberation. It was a pleasing villa, not large but undoubtedly expensive.

The man who answered the door was about sixty, wore an orange shirt and white trousers, and was clutching a book. 'Yes?'

'You are M'sieur Benson?' asked Ronsard in French.

'Yes, I am,' said the man in the same language. 'What d'you want?' He looked at the four policemen on his doorstep as though suspecting them of being either salesmen or missionaries.

'We are from the police, m'sieur. These gentlemen are from Scotland Yard.' Ronsard indicated the three Englishmen.

The expression of doubt remained on Benson's face until Fox produced his warrant card. Then he said, in English, 'Well, I don't know what this is ail about but you'd better come in. There seem to be a lot of you,' he added as he led the way into a long, cool room that ran the width of the villa and looked out on to a swimming pool. He indicated chairs with a sweep of his hand and the four officers sat down. 'Well,' he continued, 'what can I do for you?'

'We had occasion to search the flat at Marble Arch in which you lived until recently,' said Fox.

'Whatever for?' Benson looked genuinely puzzled.

'I am investigating a murder,' said Fox. 'And the fingerprints of the dead man were found in that flat.'

Benson's mouth dropped open. 'But how on earth did they …? I mean, who was this man?'

'We don't know, Mr Benson. We haven't been able to identify him. We hoped that you might know.'

'But —' Benson stopped and shook his head. 'I'm sorry,' he said, 'but I don't understand any of this.'

'Nor do I,' said Fox drily.

'But why look in my flat in the first place?' Benson frowned. 'You're not saying that you found this man there, are you?'

'No,' said Fox. 'Strange to relate, we found him in a coffin in a churchyard at a place called Cray Magna. Do you know the place at all? It's in Devon.'

'No.' Benson surveyed the four detectives before centring his gaze on Fox once more. 'Is this some sort of a joke?' he asked.

'I only wish it were,' said Fox, and decided that, suspect or not, Benson would have to be told more. Briefly he outlined the story of the missing Harley — a name which evinced no reaction from Benson — and an account of how the vicar of Cray Magna had alerted police to the fact that Harley, the missing man, had been buried in his churchyard. Except that he wasn't Harley. But Fox decided that he would not, at this stage, mention the jewellery theft at the hotel.

Benson listened patiently. 'But,' he said, 'I still don't understand what caused you to examine my flat at Marble Arch.'

Fox explained that the telephone number that the vicar had been given for the non-existent undertaker had been the telephone number of Benson's flat.

'This is really the most bizarre thing I've ever heard,' said Benson. 'Undertakers? I really don't understand any of it. I mean, is it possible that your vicar got the number wrong?'

'I'll explain it again, Mr Benson,' said Fox patiently. 'A woman telephoned the vicar to arrange the funeral. She gave him the phone number of the firm of undertakers who were supposedly handling the arrangements. But those undertakers don't exist. We traced the phone number to your flat, and when we searched it we found fingerprints that matched those of the body the bogus undertakers delivered. Be one hell of a coincidence if it was a mistake, don't you think?'

'Yes, I see.' Benson sat forward, his elbows resting on his knees.

'A woman turned up at the funeral claiming to be Mrs Harley, widow of the dead man. Presumably the woman who made the initial phone call. But the Mrs Harley I saw denies all knowledge of the matter, and in any case her description is nothing like that of the woman at the funeral. That Mrs Harley was aged about thirty, blonde and good-looking.' He watched Benson closely to see what sort of reaction that statement would produce.

'Good God,' said Benson, 'that sounds like my wife.'

'Yes, I know,' said Fox. He turned to Gilroy. 'Got the photograph, Jack?'

'Yes, sir.' Gilroy handed Benson an enlargement of the photograph taken at the golf club.

There was no hesitation. 'That's her,' said Benson. 'That's Jane.' He looked up sharply. 'Where did you get this from? And who's this man she's with?'

'As far as we know, Mr Benson, that's the Thomas Harley I mentioned earlier, and we want to talk to him about a rather large jewellery theft. We would also like to have a chat with him about a certain dead body we found. Does the name mean anything to you?'

'No, it doesn't. I've never heard it before.'

'Show Mr Benson the photograph of the body, Jack,' said Fox.

Gilroy handed over one of the prints that Photographic Branch had prepared.

Benson studied it for a moment or two before handing it back. 'That's Donald Dixon,' he said.

'And who is Donald Dixon?' asked Fox as though the answer was not of much interest to him.

'A business partner of my wife. I met him a couple of times. Once at the flat — he was there when I got home one day — and again when Jane and I were lunching at the Savoy. He was with someone else on that occasion.'

'Don't know who, I suppose?'

Benson shook his head. 'Sorry, no idea.'

'What is your wife's business, Mr Benson?'

Benson looked up, a tired expression on his face. 'I'm not absolutely sure,' he said. 'I know that sounds silly, but she's always had her own life … I think it's something to do with hotels.'

Fox refrained from saying that that came as no surprise. 'Perhaps we might have a word with her, Mr Benson.'

'That's not possible, I'm afraid.'

'Oh?'

'My wife's left me. She ran off with another man. Last month, it was. That's why I gave up the flat in London and came out here.'

'I see,' said Fox. 'It wasn't Donald Dixon by any chance?'

Benson shrugged. 'I don't know,' he said.

'Well, perhaps you'd be so good as to give us her present address.'

'I'm afraid that I've no idea where she is,' said Benson. 'And quite frankly,' he added bitterly, 'I don't care.'

But Fox had one more question to ask. 'What was your wife's maiden name, Mr Benson?'

'I don't know,' said Benson. There was a blank expression on his face and he spoke listlessly. 'But her married name was Meadows.'

And that appeared to be that. Fox knew from years of experience that he would have to be satisfied with the limited replies he had got so far. But it was something. A few inches further on. Benson had obviously been badly shaken by Fox's revelations, and would take some time to digest them. In time, he might remember something else, but that would have to wait. Fox was acutely aware that he was in a foreign country, and in the presence of a local police officer. In London he would probably have removed Benson to the nearest police station. Right now, he would just have to leave it. But Fox was a wise and patient detective. The information he required would come in time. Of that he was sure.

But he had far from dismissed the possibility that Benson was implicated.

*

'Some more of the jewellery's turned up, sir.' DS Crozier appeared in Fox's office the day after the latter's return from France.

'Tell me about it,' said Fox.

'It was flogged to an unsuspecting jeweller but when he tried to lay if off, someone told him it was bent, sir. Enquiries were made through Interpol, and it turns out that some of it came from our hotel heist.'

'Through Interpol?' Fox frowned. 'Where does this innocent jeweller have his premises, then?'

Crozier looked hesitant and moved towards the door. 'Nice, sir.' He paused. 'It's in the South of France.'

'I know where Nice is,' said Fox darkly. 'I've just come back from the bloody place. Incidentally, how are we getting on with identifying the jewellery found in the coffin?'

'Slowly, sir. Most of the losers have gone back from whence they came … like America, France and Saudi Arabia.' Crozier grinned. 'It's a mammoth task, you know.'

Fox looked gloomy. 'Why do I always have the difficult jobs?' he asked.

'That's life, sir.' Crozier refrained from pointing out that all the hard work was being done by Fox's subordinates. And most of it by Detective Sergeant Crozier.

*

Fox's Ford Granada stopped in front of the Harleys' Kingston Hill house and he and Gilroy alighted. Fox had decided to have another talk with Susan Harley, mainly to check her story. It was an old theory. If her second account was inconsistent with her first, then there was a strong possibility that she was not as innocent as she had first claimed.

'Looks sort of deserted, Jack.'

'Does a bit,' said Gilroy, pressing the bell-push.

There was no answer, and Fox walked along the front of the house and peered into one of the windows. 'The furniture's gone, Jack. That bitch has done a runner.' He sounded outraged. 'I reckon she knows more than she's told us,' he added ominously.

'Racing certainty, guv,' said Gilroy helpfully. 'Perhaps we should have charged her.'

'Regrettably, Jack, we had nothing with which to charge her. The fact that she might know that her old man's a villain does not at present constitute an offence known to English law … unfortunately.'

'Could have a chat with the neighbours,' said Gilroy.

'Oh, do leave off, Jack. You can't even see any other houses from here. What are they going to tell us?'

'Just a thought, sir.'

Fox stood with his hands in his pockets, staring morosely at the perfect gardens. 'Tell you what,' he said. 'Get Crozier to do the rounds of the local estate agents. See if any of them have got it on the market. I know that Harley's thieved a few quid in his time, but surely to God he wouldn't walk away and leave a drum that must be worth damn' near half a million.'

Gilroy shrugged. 'Be a London agent, I should think, for a gaff this size,' he said. 'Or an advert in one of those glossies … like *Country Life*.'

Fox nodded. 'Could well be right, Jack,' he said. 'But tell Crozier to give it his best shot. In the meantime, get a warrant and do the place. Fingerprints are what we're after.'

*

'I've spent several hundred pounds of the Commissioner's money on telephone calls, sir,' said Crozier, appearing round the door of Fox's office.

'Congratulations, Ron. I'll tell him. But what's the result?'

'Zilch, guv.'

'What?'

'Nothing, sir. I've tried every estate agent in the Kingston area and practically every agent in London who might handle that sort of property. Nothing.'

'Sod it,' said Fox and stood up. 'Tell you what, Ron, try the removal companies. See if you get any joy there.'

'I did, sir.'

'Oh, wonderful!' said Fox sarcastically. 'You going to tell me about it, then?'

'A firm in Wimbledon's got their furniture in store. Moved it out of the house a few weeks ago.'

'Go on, then.'

'Mrs Susan Harley paid for six months' storage in advance, sir. Said that she would contact them again before the period was up.'

'Leave an address, did she, Ron?'

'Yes, sir. Her bank.'

*

It took four days to get a result from Fingerprint Branch. A day to examine the house thoroughly, and three days to do an intensive search of fingerprint records. On the fifth day, Sam Marland, a senior fingerprint officer, sauntered into Fox's office.

'Well, Sam? Got good news, have you?'

Marland grinned and laid some files on the edge of Fox's desk. 'Depends what you mean by good news, Tommy,' he said. 'We found dozens of marks, but only two sets that meant anything.'

'Go on then, ruin my day.'

Marland pushed a couple of files towards Fox. 'These were found in various places in the Harley house, and we've ID'd them.'

'Really?' Fox showed a spark of interest. 'Whose are they?'

'Would you believe Jim Murchison's and the bloke down the hole at Cray Magna,' said Marland. 'The bloke you say is Donald Dixon.'

*

'It seems that the jewellery was sold in Nice about four weeks ago, sir,' said Gilroy. 'But not all of it came from our job. There's some yet to be identified.'

Fox looked at his desk calendar. 'So ...' he said slowly. 'That means that it was knocked out about a week after Harley's funeral ... or rather the funeral of one Donald Dixon. Whoever he might be. And it could mean that there's been another heist we know nothing about.'

'Yes, sir.'

'Is it Ronsard at Nice who's handling this job, Jack?'

Gilroy shrugged. 'Don't know, sir. It doesn't say on the message. But probably not or he'd have mentioned it when we were there, surely?'

'Never mind, give him a bell — Pierre Ronsard, I mean — and get him to have a chat with this French jeweller. See if he can get any further details. Like who flogged him this gear. Description. Anything like that. You know the form, Jack.' Fox glanced at his watch. 'And then I think we'll pop down to Brixton and have another little chat with friend Murchison. I've got a feeling that he knows more than he's saying. Time we rattled his bars a bit.' He paused. 'We'll get him to look at the photo of our Donald Dixon. That should get him going.'

*

'Never seen him before,' said Murchison after a brief glance at the photograph.

'Really?' said Fox. 'I wondered if it was the hood who chatted you up in a pub in Dulwich and invited you to participate in a jewellery heist for an inadequate fee.'

'I said before, I never knew it was a jewellery job,' said Murchison. 'Anyway, who is he? Got him banged up in here, have you?'

Fox grinned. 'Oh, do leave off, Jim. I've got him banged up all right ... in the deep-freeze. When we found him he had three very painful holes in his chest.'

'You what?'

'Don't play the innocent with me,' said Fox. 'Right now you're well in the frame for topping him.'

Murchison leapt to his feet with such violence that his chair almost fell over. His face had gone white and his fists were clenching and unclenching with an agitated rhythm. 'You're not laying no bloody topping on me,' he said, his voice choking with fury.

'Sit down, you prat,' said Fox, 'and stop play-acting.' Murchison sat down abruptly. 'Look at it from my point of view,' continued Fox conversationally. 'You, a male anon and a blonde woman blag a hotel for about a hundred K. They do a runner but we nick you. And then, lo and behold, we find a body in a coffin in a churchyard two hundred miles away. And, would you believe, it was the body of the said male anon who took part in the heist aforementioned and whom you spirited away from the scene in a motorcar which you subsequently scuttled in the River Thames.'

'That's a load of balls,' said Murchison. 'I don't know sod-all about it. I told you, I dropped the pair of them off at Marble Arch, and I never saw neither of them again. As for him,' he said gesturing at the photograph of the unknown of Cray Magna, 'I tell you I've never seen him before.'

Fox's face took on a pitying expression. 'If I was in your shoes, James,' he said, 'I should consider my position very carefully.' 'Sod off,' said Murchison.

Fox stood up and grinned. 'See you again soon,' he said. 'In the meantime you take good care of yourself.'

*

'What d'you reckon, guv?'

'Murchison knew that was Dixon all right, Jack,' said Fox, 'but until we get some decent evidence to screw him down with, he's just going to sit in Brixton laughing like a drain. We haven't even got an ident that'll put him at the scene of the heist, and although I'm happy with the fingerprint that tied him to the car, Marland says he can't get sixteen points off it that'll even put him down for nicking it. All right, he's put his hands up to it, but Murchison's right when he says that it's only worth a carpet.' He shook his head gloomily. 'Frankly, I'll be surprised if he even gets that. It's a sad business, Jack.'

'Why didn't you put Dixon's name to him, guv?'

Fox looked at his DI sharply. 'Never show your hand, Jack,' he said. 'We'll let the bastard sweat. And we'll let him think we're floundering.'

'Well, aren't we, sir?' said Gilroy.

*

'Ronsard says that the jeweller doesn't remember much about the woman who sold him the stuff, guv'nor, except that she was English, a blonde, youngish and good-looking.'

'Aha!' said Fox, pleased that his detective instincts were still on course. 'What a coincidence. And do we have a precise date for this business transaction, Jack?'

'Yes, sir,' said Gilroy. 'The second of August. It was a Thursday,' he added helpfully.

Fox stared at his DI for some seconds. 'Really?' he said eventually. 'That's particularly useful. A Thursday, eh?'

'Yes, sir.' Gilroy looked puzzled. 'Does that have some significance, then?'

'None whatsoever, Jack.'

*

'How far is Nice from Cannes, Jack?'

'About twenty miles, sir,' said Gilroy promptly.

Fox looked suspiciously at his DI. 'You've just looked that up, haven't you?'

*

'Runs a second-hand car business in south-east London, guv. Lewisham way,' said DS Crozier.

'Who does?' Fox looked malevolently at the sergeant. 'I do wish people wouldn't come into my office talking in riddles and expecting me to understand what they're going on about,' he added.

'Ozzie Bryce, sir. The bloke I said used to run with Jim Murchison.'

'Ah! Lewisham, eh?' Fox smiled. Nastily. 'I think we'd better pay Mr Bryce a visit. Nip up to Horseferry Road and get a "W". And tell Mr Gilroy to assemble a team.' Fox rubbed his hands together. There was nothing that he enjoyed more than executing a search warrant on the premises of a dodgy car dealer.

'Yes, sir.' Crozier went. There was nothing he liked less than going to a magistrates' court to get a search warrant. Or a 'W', as Fox insisted on calling it.

Chapter Ten

The one thing that Tommy Fox could never do was disguise the fact that he was a policeman. Despite the elegance of his dress, it was the confidence of his step, the expression on his face — a mixture of arrogance and pity — and the direct, granite-like gaze that tended to alert the wicked to the disconcerting fact that the Old Bill had come among them. And so it was now.

'Which one of you is Oswald Bryce?' Fox stood in the doorway of the office and examined the two seedy men who were seated behind the desks. Each wore a shabby suit, and one of them had a smudge on his top lip that could have been mistaken for a moustache. Their furtive expressions implied that they were more than familiar with dubious business transactions and had never in their lives paid full price for anything.

'I am. Who wants to know?' The question was rhetorical. Bryce knew perfectly well who wanted to know.

But Fox knew anyway. He had studied the photograph on Bryce's file before he had left the office. 'Thomas Fox ... of the Flying Squad.'

'Oh!' said Bryce.

'Thought you might say something like that,' said Fox. He looked round the dilapidated office and cast a loving eye in the direction of the filing cabinet where he knew, by instinct, he would find documents relating to the forlorn group of cars that stood on the forecourt.

'You won't find anything dodgy here, guv'nor,' said Bryce nervously.

Fox sat down. 'You own this little set-up, do you?' he asked, well knowing that to be the case.

'Yeah.'

'When did you last see Jim Murchison?'

'Who?'

Fox remained silent and leaned back in his chair. Slowly he took a cigarette from his case and lit it. Then he watched the spiral of smoke drifting towards the ceiling before levelling his gaze, once more, at the car dealer.

'Er — well, not lately,' said Bryce.

'How much not lately?'

Bryce appeared to give the matter some thought, then he glanced at his business partner. 'Must be about a year, I should think, wouldn't you, Sid?'

Fox pointed his cigarette at Sid. 'And who is that?' he enquired.

'That? Oh, that's Sid Meek —'

'Meek, eh?' Fox smiled. It was disconcerting. 'How interesting. And where do you fit into this establishment?' he asked the other man.

'I'm — well — like, I'm an associate.'

'Fascinating,' said Fox as though much impressed by this particular crumb of information. 'And how long have you been an, er … associate, may I ask?'

'Couple of months, I s'pose,' said Meek.

'Then how would you know that it was a year since your partner — your co-associate, as one might say — had seen Jim Murchison?'

'Well, I —'

'You too are a friend of the said Murchison, then, is that it?'

'Well, I sort of know him.'

'Sort of know him. I see.' Fox savoured that. 'And how would you sort of know him, may I ask?'

'Sort of seen him around, you know.' Meek struggled on.

'When, for instance?'

'Can't rightly remember.' Meek scratched his temple with a grubby forefinger and assumed a frown that suggested he was giving the matter his complete and undivided attention.

'What's this about?' asked Bryce, boldly taking the conversation back, but trying to sound helpful rather than hostile.

'This, Oswald, dear boy, is about murder.'

'Oh, Christ!' Bryce paled slightly. 'Not Jim. You don't mean he's been topped, surely.'

Fox grinned owlishly. 'Not yet,' he said. 'But given the company he keeps I daresay it's only a matter of time.'

'Well who, then?'

'A gentleman by the name of Donald Dixon,' said Fox. 'I give him the courtesy of calling him a gentleman only because he had no previous convictions … unlike you.' He turned to Meek. 'Or you,' he added.

'I —' began Meek.

'And before you say anything else, Sidney, I got my sergeant to look you up.' It was true. Before he had ventured into the hinterland of Southeast London, Fox had made a point of reading up Meek's criminal biography. And he had known that Meek was in partnership with Bryce even before he had got Meek to admit it.

'Look,' said Bryce. 'I'd like to help, but —'

'Where did you get the hearse that Jim Murchison used?' Fox dropped the question quietly into the conversation. It landed like a boulder hitting a smooth duck pond.

'Hearse? I don't know anything about a hearse.' Bryce mashed his cigarette violently into the ashtray and swallowed. Hard.

Fox shrugged and stood up. 'Oh well,' he said. 'We'll just have to look for it.'

'Hold on, I —' Bryce stood up too and waved his hands aimlessly in front of his body.

Fox stepped out of the office and signalled to Gilroy and the rest of the team who were waiting on the road in two of the Flying Squad's cars. With a panache that only the Squad's drivers seem able to display, they swept on to Bryce's forecourt and stopped, effectively blocking both its entrance and exit.

'Now,' said Fox, turning to face Bryce once more. 'The Horseferry Road magistrate has this day granted me a warrant to search these premises.' He wafted a piece of paper under Bryce's nose. 'Unless you feel like talking about this hearse ...' It was what Gilroy called a leap in the dark. Fox had no evidence to indicate that Bryce — or Meek, for that matter — knew the first thing about the so-called funeral of Thomas Harley, but Fox knew villains. For more than twenty years he had pursued and harried them relentlessly, and he knew their nefarious ways as a formicologist will unerringly chart the habits of ants.

Bryce looked unhappily at the six Squad officers standing on his forecourt. He knew from past and bitter experience that they would find something with which they could charge him. And right now he knew what that was. In any event, his business was such that he could never put his hand on his heart and swear that it was all above board. The second-hand car business didn't work like that. Not Bryce's second-hand car business, anyway.

There was but a moment's pause. 'Right, lads,' said Fox. 'Go!'

'Look, can we talk about this, guv?' said Bryce apprehensively as he watched the group of detectives split up and start to maraud over his premises and his cars.

'By all means,' said Fox in a kindly way. 'That's what I've been hoping for all along.'

'Well what about them?' Bryce waved a hand towards the disappearing Flying Squad officers.

'That's all right,' said Fox. 'They can manage without me for a few minutes.'

'Guv.' Crozier strode out of Bryce's office propelling Meek in front of him.

'What?'

'This finger was on the dog-and-bone, guv.'

'Oh dear!' Fox cast a censorious glance at Meek. 'And to whom were you on the phone?' he enquired loftily.

'Our solicitor, that's who.' Meek spoke truculently.

'Oh dear,' said Fox. 'How tiresome.'

'What the bloody hell did you do that for, you berk?' asked Bryce angrily.

'Well they can't just come in here and turn the place over —'

'Yes they can. They've got a bloody warrant, you stupid bastard.'

'Now, now, girls,' said Fox and grinned. 'Still the same mouthpiece is it, Ozzie?'

'Yeah.' Bryce spoke sullenly. 'Sid goes off at half cock, guv. I've got nothing to hide here.'

'I'm sure you haven't, Ozzie. But we'll just make sure.'

'Excuse me, sir.' DC Bellenger appeared from the rear of the premises. Fox turned. 'Yes, Joe?'

'Found something out the back you might be interested in, sir.'

'Really?' said Fox. 'Not a hearse, is it?'

'No, sir. But I think he might be needing one.' Bellenger cocked a thumb in Bryce's direction and grinned.

Fox followed the detective through the office and out into the storeroom.

'I thought you might like to have a look at this little lot, sir.' Bellenger pointed at about a dozen cardboard boxes stacked neatly in the corner. Next to them was a tarpaulin that Bellenger had just removed.

'What have we got here?' said Fox, a note of contrived incredulity in his voice. 'Video recorders? Oh dear, Ozzie.' He glanced at Bryce who had trailed along behind and now stood miserably in the doorway of the store-room.

'I can explain, guv,' said Bryce.

'It had better be good.' Fox spoke absently as he opened a cupboard. 'And video cameras as well.' He turned to Bryce. 'You taking a coach party abroad or something, Ozzie?' he asked.

'Oh, Gawd,' said Bryce. 'Look, guv, can we have a talk about this hearse business. I mean, can we do a deal, like?'

Fox shook his head slowly and tutted. 'Well, we can give it a try by all means, Ozzie. Never know your luck, do you?' He turned to Bellenger. 'Better start listing that stuff, Joe,' he said. 'And anything else you can find.'

Bryce led the way back to his office and slumped into his chair. He reached out and took a cigarette from the open packet on his desk and lit it, drawing hungrily. 'Look, guv,' he said wearily. 'I did lend Jim Murchison a hearse. I owed him a favour, see. But I don't know anything about a topping as God's my witness, so help me.'

'He's not and he won't,' said Fox drily, 'but do go on.'

'Well I didn't ask any questions. You don't in this business. He said it was all a bit of a giggle. Something about a party he was going to, up west. He wanted a hearse so's him and some of his mates — and their birds — could turn up in this thing for a bit of a laugh, see.' Bryce looked imploringly at Fox, willing him to believe his story.

'Is that what he told you? Or is that what you're expecting me to believe?'

'You can ask him if you like.' Bryce sounded desperate.

'Oh, I shall,' said Fox. 'I've got him banged up in Brixton.'

'Christ! I never knew that,' said Bryce.

'No, I don't suppose you did. And I don't believe that load of crap you've just trotted out, either.'

'Stand on me, guv, I —'

'Listen carefully, Ozzie,' said Fox. 'I'm about to read your fortune for you. On the nineteenth of July last, as it will say on the indictment, a coffin was conveyed, in your hearse, I suppose, to the churchyard of All Saints, Cray Magna, and bunged in a hole in the ground according to the rites and ceremonies of the Church of England. When we dug it up we found therein the body of the aforesaid Donald Dixon. But that's not all we found. We also found a quantity of jewellery, the proceeds of an audacious theft with which James Murchison stands indicted. Oh, and I nearly forgot. We also found three bullets in Mr Dixon's chest. A distinguished Home Office pathologist attributes Mr Dixon's demise to the presence of those same three bullets. There, Ozzie, how's that grab you?'

'Christ!' said Bryce, not for the first time. 'That sounds serious.'

Fox grinned. 'You've got it in one, Ozzie,' he said and then looked up as the door of the office opened. A short, rotund man dressed in a dark suit and carrying a bulging briefcase stood surveying the scene. 'And who might you be?' asked Fox. But he knew.

'I'm Mr Bryce's solicitor.' The man stepped forward and presented his card. 'And you?' he asked.

'Thomas Fox ... of the Flying Squad. As you well know.'

'Of course.' The solicitor smiled. 'And what, might I enquire, is going on here?'

'I am executing a search warrant ... and having a little chat with Mr Bryce.'

'Really?' The solicitor stood his briefcase on the edge of the desk. 'Well, perhaps you'd fill me in on what's happened so far.'

Fox stared at the solicitor's briefcase. 'Now that you are within the ambit of the search warrant, perhaps you will show me the contents of that,' he said, pointing at the briefcase.

'What?' The solicitor sounded horrified at Fox's suggestion. 'That would be most unethical,' he spluttered.

'And you certainly know all about unethical behaviour,' said Fox, smiling. 'But it's not unlawful. On the other hand, you could go away and come back later.'

'If I'm to leave, it will be at my client's request and no one else's,' said the solicitor haughtily. He turned to Bryce. 'What d'you have to say about this, Ozzie?'

'Piss off,' said Bryce.

The solicitor snatched up his briefcase and made towards the door. 'You haven't heard the last of this,' he said to Fox.

Fox nodded amiably and turned to Bryce. 'I think he means he'll be sending you a bill,' he said. 'Now, Ozzie, you were telling me all about this hearse.'

'I told you, guv,' said Bryce miserably. 'That's all there is. He brought it back a couple of days later and I knocked it out to a street-trader a week after that.'

'Name?'

'Bloody hell. I can't remember.'

'You are required by law to keep records of the acquisition and disposal of all vehicles coming into your possession, Ozzie. You know that, of course. I just hope that you're not confessing to failing to keep such records.' Fox waved a hand airily in the direction of Bryce's filing cabinet. 'Or shall I get one of my officers to give you a hand to go through your paperwork?'

'I remember now,' said Bryce hurriedly. 'It was a geezer called Sykes —'

'Oh no.' Fox covered his face with his hands.

'Straight up, guv.' Bryce was starting to sweat. 'But I don't know where you'll find him. He was a pikey, see.'

'I think, Ozzie,' said Fox thoughtfully, 'that you're trying to tell me that your customer was a person of no fixed abode, and that I shall, therefore, have some difficulty in locating him.'

'Well, it might be a problem.'

'But not my problem, Ozzie. You see I've got you. And I shall hold on to you until I find Mr Sykes. If, in fact, he exists.'

'Oh, he does, guv, he does.'

'His first name's not Bill by any chance, is it?'

'Dunno,' said Bryce, a vacant and distressed look on his face.

'Well,' said Fox, standing up, 'it was a good try, Ozzie, but not good enough. You're nicked.'

'What for?' Bryce put his cigarettes and lighter in his pocket. He knew the form.

'For the unlawful possession of a quantity of video recorders and video cameras for a start. Plus anything else my officers have found in the meantime. We'll take it from there.'

'They're down to Sid,' said Bryce hurriedly.

'Oh, good,' said Fox. 'Then we'll nick him too. You'd better lock up, Ozzie. It'll be a while before you're trading again. Still,' he added, 'I've no doubt that you'll get a rebate on your VAT.' He smiled encouragingly. 'Possibly even on your business rate.'

*

The interview room at Lewisham police station was a depressing place, but Bryce would have been depressed anyway. He looked round and sighed. He was more than familiar with such places.

'Well, Ozzie, shall we start again, now that you've had time to think things over?'

'All right,' said Bryce. 'But is there any chance that you can row me out of the video job? They're definitely down to Sid, God's honest truth.'

'Maybe,' said Fox doubtfully, 'but with the shtook you're in, they'd probably only be taken into consideration anyway.'

Bryce looked unhappy and gratefully accepted one of Fox's cigarettes. 'I'll lay it on the line for you, guv,' he began. 'Jim Murchison came to see me and asked if I could get hold of a hearse —'

'Did he say what for?'

'Not straight off, and you don't ask questions in this game. But it seemed kosher, once we got going.'

'Explain.'

'He said he'd got a funeral job to do. And could I get a hearse and give him a hand.'

'Good Lord,' said Fox mildly. 'You don't expect me to believe that, do you?'

Bryce looked hurt. 'It happens a lot these days, doing funerals cheap for friends. You've no idea how much it costs. It's a bloody rip-off. I can remember when I buried my dear old mum —'

'Just stick to the point, Ozzie.'

'Yeah, well, we took this coffin — it was a proper job, nothing cheapjack. Jim's got this mate in the trade and —'

'Ozzie!'

'Yeah, well, we took this coffin down to …' Bryce paused in thought.

'Cray Magna.'

'Yeah, that's it. So, like I said, we took it down to this place and gave him a hand lifting it out and doing the carrying bit. Jim told us to wear dark suits and that, so's we'd look the part —'

'Who's we?'

'Me and Sid Meek.'

'There was just the three of you, then? You, Meek and Murchison?'

Bryce hesitated. 'No, there was another bloke. Never seen him before.'

'Name?' barked Fox.

'Barber, I think.'

'You don't mean Ali Barber ... across in Catford, do you?'

Bryce looked vaguely puzzled. 'Don't know who he was,' he said. 'But even the four of us wasn't enough. Bloody heavy this bloke was. The verger had to give us a hand. Anyway, it all seemed above board. I mean there was a vicar there and everything. And the geezer's widow. I never thought nothing more about it. I drove the hearse back here and, like I said, knocked it out to this Sykes bloke about a week later. End of story.'

'Not quite,' said Fox. He turned to Gilroy. 'Give me the photograph, Jack, will you.'

Gilroy extracted the photograph of Harley and the blonde taken at the golf club cocktail party and handed it to Fox. 'Have a look at that, Ozzie,' said Fox. 'See if you recognise anyone there.'

Bryce studied the photograph for a second or two and then glanced up at Fox. 'I don't know the bloke,' he said. 'But the bird is the one who was at the funeral. Susan something she was called. Got it. Harley. Susan Harley.'

'What else can you tell me about her?'

'She didn't seem too upset,' said Bryce. 'She done the right thing at the burying, like. Crying and mopping her mascara with a handkerchief. All that. But once it was over we drove for a bit and then stopped at a boozer for a few drinks. Well, I tell you, you'd never have thought she'd just planted her old man. Life and soul of the party, she was. It was almost as if she was celebrating, not mourning.'

'Did she travel in the hearse, then?'

'No, she had her own motor, but she met up with us later ... at the boozer.'

'And how much did you get for this little enterprise, Ozzie?'

'Five hundred notes. But that included the use of the hearse.'

'Naturally,' said Fox. 'Business is business. One other question. Where did you pick this coffin up from?'

'Kingston,' said Bryce without hesitation. 'A big drum just off Kingston Hill.'

'I presume you know the precise address.'

'Yeah, course I do. I drove the bloody hearse there, didn't I?'

Chapter Eleven

'It seems to me, Jack,' said Fox, carefully placing a copy of *The Times* on his coffee table, and then putting his feet on top of it, 'that we are getting nowhere fast with this damned enquiry.'

'Oh, I don't know. All we've got to do is find Thomas Harley and Jane Meadows and I reckon we've cracked it, sir,' said Gilroy.

Fox gave his detective inspector a withering glance. 'Have you ever thought of applying to go to the Police College, Jack? If you'll forgive me for saying so they're very impressed by such blinding flashes of the bloody obvious down there.'

Gilroy looked hurt. 'Well, guv. What else can we do? All we've got so far are two bodies. One dead and one alive. Messrs Dixon and Murchison respectively. Apart, that is, from a brace of slag in the shape of Bryce and Meek.'

'Yes,' said Fox reflectively. 'And Harley is presumed dead ... if only by himself. So wherever he is he'll be using another name.'

'I reckon he would be anyway, guv'nor. Particularly as it's a racing certainty he's getting his leg over the gorgeous Jane Meadows somewhere. Probably in the South of France.'

'Can't blame him for that, Jack. Not when he's got a wife with all the sex appeal of a London cab. But why the South of France?'

'Well that's where some of the jewellery turned up.'

'Indeed it did, Jack, but don't forget that we found most of the tomfoolery down a hole in Cray Magna. Now they weren't planting it there in the hope that it might grow. They will return ... sooner rather than later.'

'Might have abandoned it altogether, guv,' said Gilroy. 'Once they'd got stuck with Dixon's topping, they might have decided it was too hot to knock out.'

Fox pondered that. 'Maybe,' he said slowly, 'but they did knock some of it out, didn't they? In France.'

'Could put an obo on the churchyard then, sir,' said Gilroy and immediately regretted it.

'Well if you feel like doing that, Jack ...' Fox grinned. 'No,' he said, 'That could be weeks, even months. My reckoning is that they'll be working on another job back here.' Fox leaned forward and picked up his cigarette case from the table. 'They can't resist it, you see, Jack,' he continued loftily. 'It's in the blood.' He thumbed his lighter. 'Just as it's in my blood to have the bastards off.'

'Well I reckon we can risk circulating him in *Police Gazette* now, sir,' said Gilroy.

'A leopard does not change its spots, Jack,' said Fox profoundly.

'Yes, guv, I had heard that.'

'Then we'll apply it, Jack. If our friend Harley's good at screwing hotels he's going to do it again. Particularly as it's his trade ... and has been for at least a couple of years. So, circulate details in *PG* together with a request that CID officers warn local hotels — worthwhile ones, not these bed and breakfast hovels that one finds in places like Blackpool — so that if our friend turns up anywhere we might just have a chance of laying hands on his collar. And don't forget to put it on the computer, either. I'd hate for this clown to get stopped for speeding then drive off again because our uniformed colleagues hadn't read *Police Gazette*.'

'And what about Jane Meadows, sir? Include her in the circulation?'

'Yes, why not? Give it a run, Jack.'

*

It was a long shot and even Fox did not expect immediate results. Which was just as well, because he didn't get them. What he did get was a surprise call at the Yard.

'There's a Mr Jeremy Benson at Back Hall asking to see you, sir,' said DS Crozier.

'Is there now? Well, well,' said Fox. 'Fetch him up.'

Crozier descended to Back Hall, as the front entrance to New Scotland Yard is perversely called, and conducted Benson to Fox's office.

'Well, Mr Benson, grown tired of the delights of Nice, have you?' Fox stood up and shook hands.

'Not exactly,' said Benson hesitantly, looking round Fox's office with the curious gaze that newcomers to the headquarters of the world's greatest police force so often display before they realise that it is just another office block. 'I've been mulling things over and I thought I'd better come and tell you the full story about Jane.'

'Sit down.' Fox indicated one of the easy chairs in the corner of his office. 'Coffee?'

'That's very kind of you. Thank you.'

Fox picked up the phone and ordered coffee before sitting down opposite Benson. 'What have you to tell me, Mr Benson?'

'I don't really know where to begin, Mr Fox, but, to put it bluntly, I've been a fool. A damned old fool.'

'How so, may I ask?'

For a few moments, Benson stared at his feet as if hoping that he might find the answer to his problems there. 'She wasn't my wife,' he said eventually, looking up at Fox.

'I see. But she called herself Mrs Benson?'

'Yes. The fact of the matter is that I was convinced that she would consent to marry me. I suggested that to use my name was merely anticipating events and she was happy to go along with it.'

'How did you meet her?' Fox realised that Benson needed some help to formulate his thoughts.

'There's a weekly column in *The Times*,' said Benson. 'I think it's called Saturday Rendezvous, or something like that.' Fox nodded. 'I put an advert in there some seven or eight months ago.'

'What sort of advert?'

'It was a damned silly thing to do. I realise that now. Asking for trouble really. But I was lonely. My wife died a couple of years ago, you see.'

'What did you say … in the advert?'

'I've got it here.' Benson took out his wallet and produced a cutting. 'I wanted a holiday companion.'

Fox skimmed through it and tutted. 'Oh dear,' he said, and handed it back. 'Bit silly, that. You should never tell them that you've got money. I take it that your Jane answered this advert?'

Benson stared miserably at Fox. 'Yes.'

'And she gave her name as Jane Meadows, did she?'

'Yes.'

'And did she send the photograph you asked for?'

'Oh yes. I was amazed at my good fortune when I got it. She seemed to be the answer to a prayer. Thirty years old, really good looking. And when I met her she said that she preferred the company of older men. She was a marvellous girl.'

'And did she move in with you?'

Benson was clearly embarrassed by the question. 'Not straight away. We went on holiday together ... Well, of course that's what I'd advertised for.'

'But she moved in with you when you got back?'

Benson hesitated for a moment. 'Yes,' he said softly. 'It was only a tentative suggestion on my part, but she agreed eventually. I must say she appeared a little reluctant.'

'I can imagine,' said Fox drily. He knew from previous experience that play-acting formed a part of this sort of scam. 'And presumably she was willing to go to bed with you?'

Benson nodded without looking up. 'Yes,' he said. 'It was too good to be true.'

'Yes, I think that goes without saying. Incidentally, where did you go for this holiday? South of France?'

'Yes. She adored Nice. That's why I went back there, but it was no good.'

'What was no good?'

'I couldn't find her, you see.'

'I'm sorry,' said Fox, silently directing Swann to put the coffee on the table between them, 'but I'm afraid you've lost me there.'

'After she left me, I mean.'

'And when did that happen?'

Benson, surprisingly for a man who seemed to have been so emotionally attached to this wonderful woman, pulled out his diary. 'The nineteenth of July,' he said.

'Did she tell you she was going?'

'No.'

'Leave a letter? Anything like that?'

'Nothing!' Benson spoke the word savagely.

'So you had no idea that she was going to leave you.'

'Not an inkling. Everything between us had been idyllic. Just like a dream. Then suddenly she'd gone.'

Fox stirred his coffee and took a sip. 'How much of your property did she take with her, Mr Benson?' he asked resignedly.

'How did you know that?' Benson looked up sharply.

'I'm afraid it's a familiar pattern. Especially when one knows as much as I do about this particular young lady.'

'I've been a damned fool,' said Benson, shaking his head wearily.

'Yes,' said Fox, 'but you haven't answered my question.'

'She took all my late wife's jewellery.' Benson had a sad expression on his face. 'I was going to give it to her anyway, when we were married.'

'I think the French police may have recovered that for you.'

'Really?' For the first time, Benson looked a little more cheerful.

'Did she take anything else?'

'She took money as well.'

'How much?'

'About twenty thousand pounds.'

'As you say, Mr Benson,' Fox said, 'you've been a damned fool, but how did she get her hands on it? Surely you didn't keep that much cash in the flat.'

'I'm afraid I was foolish enough to allow her access to my bank account.'

'You mean that you changed it into a joint account?'

'Yes.' Benson looked directly at Fox, pleading to be understood. 'I was convinced that we were going to be married, you see.'

'And presumably the arrangement was that either of you could draw on that account?'

Benson nodded miserably. 'Yes,' he said. 'I thought I could trust her.' He put his cup and saucer down on the table and looked up. 'But I was wrong,' he added.

'Why didn't you go to the police about it ... or tell me when I saw you in Nice?'

'Because I didn't really want anyone else to know what an idiot I'd been.'

'That's how people like her get away with it, Mr Benson ... time after time,' said Fox.

'I realise that now,' said Benson, 'but I suppose I didn't want to face up to what had happened.'

'So you packed up here and went to stay in Nice?'

'Yes, but there was a method in my madness. I was still hoping to get her back, you see.'

'You went there to look for her, then?'

'Yes.'

'Why there?'

'Well, as I said, she loved the South of France. We went to Nice three times in the short time we were together. She absolutely adored it. I went hoping that I could find her and persuade her to come back to me.'

'She worked, I think you said, when we spoke before.'

'Yes. I wanted her to give it up, but she said it was an interest for her. I didn't argue.'

'You say you went on holiday on three occasions?'

Benson paused only briefly. 'Yes.'

'How did she get that much time off from work?'

'Oh, that was no problem. As I said, she was a partner in this business and could take time off whenever she wanted it. As a matter of fact, she said that sometimes she was combining business with pleasure. She had people to see on the Côte d'Azur. Sometimes she would be away all day. A couple of times she was away overnight.'

'And she described this business to you as something to do with the hotel trade, yes?'

'Well, I was never quite sure. I didn't really go into it with her, but yes, something to do with the hotel business.' Benson bowed his head so that his chin touched his chest.

'And the man Dixon was her partner. That's what you said before.'

'Yes.'

'You don't happen to know what their business was called, I suppose?'

Benson thought about that. Then he looked up. 'Yes,' he said suddenly. 'Marloes. I remember now because she said to me once that if I answered the phone and it was for Marloes, it was for her.'

'Yes, I can imagine,' murmured Fox. 'However, you didn't find her when you went looking?'

'Not to speak to.'

'You mean you saw her?'

'Oh yes. I was walking along the Promenade des Anglais one day. That's that marvellous road along the seafront.'

Fox nodded. 'Yes, I know it.'

'And I was just about to cross the road when I saw her go past in a car. I waved, but she didn't see me.'

'Was she with anyone?'

'A man,' said Benson in a downcast voice. 'A younger man. Younger than me, I mean.'

'And you're sure that it was her? There are a lot of pretty girls in Nice, Mr Benson.'

'I'm absolutely certain. When you've been living with a girl you don't forget what she looks like.'

'And what about the man? Did you recognise him?'

'No. Never seen him before.'

'D'you think you might recognise him again?'

Benson shrugged. 'Maybe,' he said. 'I don't know.'

Fox stood up and walked across to his desk. 'Have a look at this,' he said, handing Benson a copy of the golf club photograph of Harley. 'I showed it to you when I came to see you in Nice and you said you didn't recognise him.'

'But that was before I saw her ... and him.' Benson looked at the photograph and shook his head. 'No,' he said, handing it back. 'It could be, I suppose, but I'm not certain. You see, Jane was sitting in the passenger seat, and I was on that side of the road. I didn't get a very good view of the driver.'

'But enough to tell you that he was younger than you?'

For the first time since coming into Fox's office, Benson smiled. 'I think that's what I expected,' he said. 'So that's what I saw.'

'And I suppose you didn't get the number of the car?'

Benson shook his head. 'No, I'm sorry.'

Fox leaned back in his chair and tossed the photograph on to his desk. 'Mr Benson,' he said, turning back, 'would you have any objection to police examining your bank account?'

'Whatever for?'

'It is possible, in view of the fact that it was a joint account with Jane Meadows, that it might give us some indication as to her movements. We know that she told a neighbour that she was going to Morocco —'

'Morocco?'

'That's what she said, but of course she may not have done.'

'I didn't know anything about that. When was this?'

'I don't know exactly. But the chauffeur was taking her luggage out one morning when this neighbour met her. Jane told her she was going on holiday to Morocco ... alone. Perhaps it was the day she left you.'

'Chauffeur? I didn't have a chauffeur. I wonder what made this neighbour think it was a chauffeur. Perhaps it was a hire-car. A mini-cab, maybe.' Benson paused. 'Was it Lady Morton, by any chance?'

'Yes, as a matter of fact it was.'

'Yes, it would be.' Benson smiled. 'Well, yes, you can have access to my account if you think it will help. D'you think that Jane's mixed up in something else, then?'

'I'm afraid we think that she may have been concerned in a murder, Mr Benson.'

'Oh my God!' Benson ran a hand through his thinning hair and then looked up. 'The murder of the man Dixon, d'you mean?'

'Quite possibly,' said Fox. 'Incidentally, Mr Benson, when was this that you saw Jane Meadows in Nice?'

Benson did not hesitate. 'Last week,' he said. 'After you'd been to see me.'

*

'That circulation in *Police Gazette*, Jack. The one on Jane Meadows,' said Fox. 'You might throw in that she could have made a habit of fleecing lonely old gentlemen who've got lots of money. Somehow, I don't think that our friend Benson was the first.'

'Might not be necessary now, sir.' Gilroy looked quite excited. 'Just had a phone call from Pierre Ronsard, sir.'

'Who?'

'Ronsard, the French policeman we did business with in Nice.'

'Oh, him. What about it?'

'He's got a lead on Jane Meadows, sir. The jeweller she unloaded that gear on spotted her in the town apparently.'

'Is that a fact?' Fox folded his newspaper untidily and dropped it in the waste-paper basket.

'Went racing down to the nick, and Ronsard put a couple of his blokes on it. They've got an address for her, but he hasn't nicked her. Reckons it might spoil our murder enquiry.'

'How very civil of him,' said Fox. 'Have to buy him a plate of frogs' legs when I see him again.' For a moment he looked thoughtful. 'Crozier speaks French, doesn't he, Jack?'

'I think so, sir.'

'Good,' said Fox. 'Get hold of him. I've got a job for him.'

Chapter Twelve

'Ron, they tell me you speak French.'

Detective Sergeant Crozier returned Fox's gaze with a bland expression. 'Not exactly, sir. I can find my way through a French menu ... and perhaps order a couple of beers.'

'Good enough,' said Fox. For a moment or two, he gazed thoughtfully at Crozier. 'You know all about extradition treaties, don't you, Ron?'

Crozier looked doubtful. 'Well, a bit, sir.' It was always the same with Fox's enigmatic questions. Before you knew where you were you'd been lumbered with something complicated. And usually a bit dodgy.

'Enough to know that it's a long and complicated business to get someone extradited to this country?' continued Fox. 'Particularly when the bloody French are involved,' he added darkly. 'And particularly when you haven't got a shred of evidence.'

'Yes, sir.' Crozier did not feel any happier. He could sense what was coming next.

'Right. How d'you fancy a little holiday? All expenses paid by the Commissioner?'

'Where, sir?'

'South of France, dear boy. Place called Nice, as a matter of fact. The weather's superb at this time of year they tell me.'

Crozier held his hands up. Metaphorically. 'What's this all about, guv?' he asked warily.

'Sit down, Ron.' Fox smiled. 'Fancy a Scotch?' he asked, moving towards his drinks cabinet.

*

'Pierre? It's Tommy Fox. In London.' Fox shouted into the telephone.

'Sacrebleu!' said Inspecteur Principal Ronsard.

'What?'

'I said it is a bad line, M'sieur Fox. How are you?' Ronsard was beginning to realise that Scotland Yard's senior officers were no different from his own and that when Fox telephoned it was not to enquire after Ronsard's health.

'Look, Pierre, I'm sending one of my lads over to hijack this Jane Meadows —'

'Hijack?'

Fox thought better of it. 'To talk to her, Pierre. Assist with our enquiries. Bit of a holiday for him, really.'

'Oh, I see.' Ronsard was not happy. Suddenly he knew why Jack Gilroy so often had a downtrodden look about him.

*

The holiday season was still in full swing and Nice Airport was crowded with people wandering in that aimless and lost way that so often marks out the inexperienced international traveller. Detective Sergeant Ron Crozier walked on to the concourse, pushing his way between little groups of passengers, and looked around. With an instinct possessed by detectives the world over, he identified the well-dressed man standing near the bookstall as being in the same trade as himself.

'M'sieur Ronsard?'

'Ah! M'sieur Crozier, yes?'

Crozier dropped his bag on the floor and shook hands. 'Ron Crozier, from Scotland Yard.'

'Of course. I am called Pierre. Your Mr Fox telephoned to say that you would be coming. He said he was sending you on holiday. That is not right, surely? It would not happen here in France.'

'It doesn't bloody well happen in London either,' said Crozier.

'What is it, then?'

'Can we get a drink somewhere?' asked Crozier.

'Of course.' Ronsard picked up Crozier's bag and led him into a bar just off the concourse.

Crozier gazed reflectively at his beer and offered Ronsard a cigarette. 'It's like this,' he began. 'My guv'nor, Fox, wants me to have a chat with this Jane Meadows. See if she knows anything.' He took a sip of beer. Fox's briefing had tasked Crozier with more than a chat. 'We know she unloaded some of the proceeds over here in Nice, but quite frankly, Pierre, we haven't got any real evidence to tie her in with this heist —'

'Heist?' said the French detective. 'What is that?'

'Sorry,' said Crozier. 'It means robbery. A theft. The one Fox was talking about when he was here. At the hotel in London.'

'Ah, the one he talked to the man Benson about. But a murder also, yes?'

'Yes, quite possibly.'

'OK,' said Ronsard. 'Just tell me what I can do.' He took a sip of pastis. 'If you want her arrested, just say the word. It is no problem, but I thought it better if we waited, yes?'

'I'd rather we did.' Crozier stubbed out his cigarette. 'As I said, there's hardly any evidence at this stage.'

'Ah well, I suppose you know what you are doing, Ron, but it seems a little strange to me.' Ronsard picked up his glass again and then paused. 'I hope there's nothing illegal about all this,' he said, 'but your Mr Tommy Fox is a little, what … unorthodox?'

'You're dead right there,' said Crozier with a grin, 'but believe me, this is dead straight. I've got my pension to worry about.'

Ronsard laughed. 'Me too,' he said.

*

'Have we heard from Ron Crozier yet, Jack?' asked Fox.

'Bloody hell, guv'nor,' said Gilroy. 'He's only been there an hour.'

'Yes.' Fox gazed at the clock over the doorway of his office. 'Time enough to have made a start.'

'You did tell him it was a holiday, guv.'

'Yes,' said Fox, 'but I was only joking.'

*

Ronsard's information was that Jane Meadows, now calling herself Jane Spencer, was living in a small villa on the outskirts of Nice. The rental agreement was in the name of a Mr Spencer, but no one had seen him.

Whether Ronsard had located the girl in the way he had described didn't matter. Crozier thought that it was probably one of the French detective's string of informants who had tracked her down. Ronsard did not say. And he certainly would not have been prepared to reveal such an informant so that Crozier could talk to him … or her. But that was understood. No detective in the world will reveal his sources of information. Even to other detectives. Particularly to other detectives.

Where Ronsard had been helpful was in fixing Crozier up with a reasonably priced hotel. Not an easy thing to do in Nice at any time, but particularly in the height of the season. And Crozier knew, with an instinct of more than twenty-two years' service, that when he got back to London Fox would query his expenses. Detective chief superintendents always queried expenses. That was what detective chief superintendents were there for. Or so it seemed to junior officers.

Crozier's first full day in Nice was a Wednesday. Dressed in a Breton cotton shirt and white trousers, he had driven, in a small Renault provided by the Police Urbaine of Nice, to the wide, tree-lined boulevard where Jane Meadows was staying. So it was said. But Crozier knew that Sod's Law of Detection might come into play, and that she could have moved. He was lucky. Skilled in the art of covert surveillance, he had been parked up for Jess than half an hour when she emerged.

Crozier watched as she threw a beach-bag into the back of a small white Fiat and drove slowly out of the road.

Some twenty minutes later she drew into a parking place on the Promenade des Anglais opposite one of the less populated beaches facing the Baie des Anges. Fortunately there was a parking place behind her car and Crozier edged his way into it. Quite deliberately, and just as she opened the door of her car, he nudged the rear bumper of her Fiat, enough to give her the slight jolt that would tell her that she had been hit.

Crozier leaped from his car, a carefully contrived expression of anguish on his face. '*Ah, ma'moiselle, pardon* —' he began and then intentionally faltered, holding out his hands.

'I'm sorry,' said Jane Meadows. 'I'm English.'

'Oh,' said Crozier with a smile, 'thank God for that. So am I. I'm most awfully sorry. Not looking where I was going.'

The girl walked round and looked at the back of her car. 'It's all right,' she said. 'There's no damage done.'

'I always have this horror of having an accident when I'm abroad,' said Crozier. 'Apart from the language problems, I always get the feeling that it'll all become terribly complicated.'

'Me too.' The girl smiled. 'Well, if you'll excuse me,' she said. 'I'm going for a swim.'

Crozier waved a hand. 'Enjoy yourself,' he said. 'And, once again, I'm sorry.'

Jane Meadows smiled. 'No harm done,' she said and walked briskly towards the beach.

*

'Had a call from Ron Crozier, sir,' said Gilroy.

'And?' Fox looked up from a file he was studying.

'He's made contact, sir. Literally. Ran into the back of her car.'

'Oh, bloody brilliant.' Fox threw down his pen. 'And had to show out, I suppose? Exchanged names and addresses? All that? Now we'll have reports from the French police and the commander'll be asking what the hell's —'

'No, sir,' said Gilroy firmly. 'He did it on purpose, just to make her acquaintance. There was no damage.'

'Thank God for that.' Fox looked slightly relieved.

'Well, softly softly catchee monkey,' said Gilroy.

'What's that supposed to mean?' asked Fox suspiciously.

'It was one of Baden-Powell's favourite expressions, sir.'

'Oh yeah! In the job, was he, this Baden-Powell?'

*

Crozier left it for a day, during which he wandered through the narrow alleyways of tall buildings in old Nice, climbed the town's highest point to watch the castle waterfall, strolled through the flower market and finished up gazing at the Palais de la Méditerranée, a casino he knew he could never afford to enter. Not on a detective sergeant's pay anyway.

On Friday, Crozier parked his car near Jane Meadows' villa again. She came out at the same time as on Wednesday, apparently intent on another visit to the beach. Once more Crozier followed, and once more parked on the Promenade des Anglais, but this time some way from where she had left her car. From a distance, he watched her as she walked along the beach until she found a reasonably uncrowded stretch.

Crozier leaned on the railing alongside the road and watched Jane Meadows as she undressed. When she was wearing nothing more than the bottom half of her bikini, she stretched herself out on her towel and started to cover herself with sun-tan oil.

Crozier waited until she appeared settled and then made his move. By the time he reached her, she was lying back and facing the sun through large sunglasses. 'Good morning,' he said. 'It is you, isn't it?'

The girl raised her head slightly and tipped her sunglasses forward. 'Oh, hallo.'

Crozier grinned. 'For one awful moment,' he said, 'I thought I'd made a mistake. It was you I bumped into the day before yesterday, wasn't it?'

The girl smiled. 'Certainly was,' she said.

Crozier squatted on the shingle beside her. 'Been in yet?' He nodded towards the sea.

Jane Meadows shook her head. 'Not yet. I might in a minute. How about you?'

'No. But I was thinking about it.' Crozier looked round. 'Mind if I settle here?'

The girl put her sunglasses back on. 'Not at all,' she said. 'It's a free country, so they tell me.'

'Oh? You don't sound too impressed with France.'

'I love it. This part, anyway. But it can get a bit boring in the evenings.'

'You must be joking,' said Crozier. 'All these cafés … and the casinos.'

'Not when you're on your own,' she said.

'So am I,' said Crozier.

'It's all right for you. You're a man.'

'How about I take you out for a drink this evening, then?' he asked.

Jane Meadows opened her eyes and carefully appraised Crozier. 'Thank you,' she said. 'I'll think about it.'

'Name's Ron Crozier.' He reached across and held his hand out in the girl's direction.

Slowly she put up her hand and took his. 'Jane.' There was a momentary pause. 'Jane Spencer. You're on holiday, I take it?'

'Sort of. Business and pleasure, really. I've come over to buy a villa.'

'What, here in Nice?' Jane Spencer suddenly became interested.

'Yes. Seems a decent place.' Crozier grinned.

'They're fearfully expensive, you know.'

Crozier shrugged. 'No sense in having money if you don't spend it,' he said casually. 'Can't take it with you.' He pulled his shirt over his head and slipped out of his trousers. 'Right, Jane,' he said. 'Race you into the water.'

*

'Ron Crozier went swimming with her yesterday, sir,' said Gilroy.

'I don't want a blow-by-blow account, Jack,' said Fox. 'I just want to know when there's a result.'

'He did say she'd made a clean breast of it, sir.'

'You mean she's confessed?'

Gilroy grinned. 'No, sir, just that she went swimming topless. But I think he's making progress. He took her out to dinner last night as well.'

Fox looked up and frowned. 'Next time you speak to him, Jack, just tell him to watch the bloody expenses.'

*

They were sitting outside a café in the Rue Messena watching the world go by. It was five days since Crozier had engineered their meeting on the beach and since then he and Jane Meadows had spent most of their waking hours together, swimming, drinking in the cafés and eating out. And during that time, with careless throwaway comments, Crozier had convinced her that he was a rich and unattached playboy. It was useful that dress was no longer an indication of wealth in the South of France ... but cars were. In order to further his image, he had returned the Renault to the local police and was now using taxis, despite knowing that Fox would have a seizure when he saw Crozier's expenses.

But he had insisted on the relationship between him and Jane Meadows remaining strictly platonic. He knew what could happen to CID officers who crossed the boundary between duty and pleasure. He had seen colleagues wriggling in the witness box at the Old Bailey and had no intention of risking either his career or his reputation.

'What made you come on holiday on your own?' Crozier slipped off his jacket and put it on the back of his chair.

'I was supposed to be meeting a friend. Last week, as a matter of fact.'

'And she didn't show up?'

'He,' said Jane holding Crozier's glance with her clear grey eyes.

Crozier shrugged. 'Sorry,' he said. 'None of my business.'

'I tried ringing him, but I haven't been able to get hold of him.'

'Here in France?'

'No, in England. I don't know what can have happened.'

'Are you worried?' asked Crozier, adding, 'Tell me to mind my own business, if ...'

'It's all right. No, he's a friend. A close friend.' She shot a sideways glance at Crozier. 'I'm sorry if that —'

'If what?'

'I hope you don't think that I've been deceiving you.' This was the first time that she had mentioned having a boyfriend.

'Not at all.' Crozier grinned. After all, he hadn't mentioned his wife and two teenaged children in Orpington. 'What are you going to do?'

'I don't know. I can't hang on here much longer or my money will run out.'

'Why not go home, then?'

'I can't afford to do that either.' She turned to him, concerned. 'Quite frankly, I don't know what to do. You see, he paid for the rent of the villa up to the end of this week. Said he'd be here by now. Long before, actually. But now ...' She held her hands out. 'What the hell am I going to do, Ron?' There was an appealing look on her face.

Crozier studied her and wondered if she had been looking for someone like him to pay her fare home. Lying on the beach every day, wearing next-to-nothing, just waiting for the first punter who came along. Not that it mattered. He had, after all, been hoping that something like this might happen. Been working at it, in fact. 'No problem,' he said. 'I'm going home tomorrow myself. Come with me —'

'But, I told you —'

'I'll put it on my credit card. Give me your address in England, and I'll come and collect. Any time. There's no rush.'

Suddenly she leaned across and threw her arms round Crozier's neck. 'Ron, you're an angel,' she said, and kissed him. She took out pen and paper. 'I'll write my address down for you.'

'It's no big deal,' said Crozier. And if Harley was found at that address it would have been worth every penny.

*

'I'm taking her back to England tomorrow, Pierre.'

Ronsard looked slightly alarmed. 'You mean —'

Crozier laughed. 'Don't look so worried, mon inspecteur, I'm not kidnapping her. She's returning voluntarily.'

'But what about the little matter of trying to sell the stolen diamonds here in Nice?'

Crozier grinned. 'Reckon you can prove it?'

'No!' Ronsard laughed. 'So she's going back with you, eh?'

'She ran out of money, so I offered to pay her fare back to London.'

'Ah,' said Ronsard with an exaggerated Gallic gesture, 'you English policemen are so generous.'

'It's my Commissioner who's being generous, Pierre, but if you want another drink, just bloody well say so.'

Inspecteur Principal Ronsard of the Police Urbaine of Nice — a detective just like Crozier — pushed his glass across the table. 'Pastis, you old bastard,' he said and grinned.

*

British Airways Flight 342 from Nice arrived at Heathrow at just after half past three in the afternoon. More as an insurance than a courtesy, Crozier carried Jane Meadows' travel bag for her, and escorted her through immigration and customs.

Once on the concourse, she turned to face Crozier. 'I'm ever so grateful, Ron,' she said. 'And as soon as I get the money I'll pay you back. I gave you my address, didn't I?'

'Sure.' Crozier glanced over the girl's shoulder and was pleased to see Gilroy and WDC Rosie Webster approaching, accompanied by another police officer, probably a Special Branch man stationed at the airport.

'There is just one thing though, Jane …'

She looked surprised. 'What's that?'

'You didn't give me your right name. You're Jane Meadows, not Jane Spencer.'

Crozier's confrontation took her completely by surprise. 'I — what d'you …?' she faltered. 'How did you know?'

'I'm a police officer and I'm arresting you in connection with the theft of a quantity of jewellery.' It was a pity really; Crozier had quite got to like the girl. She was attractive and good company. But he had a job to do.

Jane Meadows looked round and realised that she was surrounded by police. Not ostentatiously. More like a group of relatives who had come to greet her. Her first thought, that she might escape, was stillborn. Her shoulders drooped and she let out a sigh. 'Fine friend you turned out to be,' she said to Crozier.

'The address you gave us last night, Ron,' said Gilroy. 'The one this young lady gave you …'

'What about it, guv?' Crozier had telephoned the Yard the previous evening to pass over details of where Jane Meadows said she lived. He had hoped that DI Gilroy was going to tell him that the Squad had arrested Thomas Harley.

'Duff,' said Gilroy.

Crozier smiled at Jane Meadows. 'And a fine friend you turned out to be, too,' he said.

Chapter Thirteen

Thomas Harley was going down for the jewellery heist at the hotel, of that Fox was certain, and with any luck he would be able to put him on the sheet for the murder of Donald Dixon too. Although there were a few other odds and ends, like forgery and concealment of death, they were evidence of intent to murder rather than separate counts on the indictment. But first, the Flying Squad had to find him.

Based on Crozier's account of his conversations with Jane Meadows in France, Fox thought that she was probably the weakest member of the conspiracy and he hoped that she would tell him where Thomas Harley was. Had she been found in England, Fox would have had her put under surveillance in the hope that she would have led the police to him. Nevertheless, Fox was convinced that she knew a lot about Harley's activities both before and after the jewellery heist.

She had maintained a cool demeanour since her arrival at Bow Street police station, but there was always a possibility that deep down the episode had unnerved her. She had no previous convictions, and interviews with the police were, doubtless, a novel experience for her.

'Well, Mrs Meadows, you seem to have got yourself into a spot of bother,' Fox began. He glanced at Rosie Webster. 'Turn on the tape recorder, Rosie,' he said, and then redirected his gaze to the short-haired blonde sitting on the other side of the table. 'I am recording this interview,' he continued, 'and anything you say may be given in evidence. Do you understand that?'

'Yes.' Jane Meadows nodded. 'But I don't know what this is all about.'

It was the sort of defensive opening that Fox had come to expect from suspects. 'Nor do I,' he said cheerfully, 'but I intend to find out. Firstly, you were living in a villa in Nice that had been rented by a man called Spencer.'

'Yes. Is that a crime?'

Fox ignored the sarcasm. 'That man's real name is Thomas Harley.' He was guessing now.

'Yes, I know.' Her response was listless.

Fox's expression remained impassive. 'On the twelfth of July last a quantity of jewellery was stolen from a hotel in the West End of London. Jewellery to the value of some one hundred thousand pounds.'

'I don't know anything about that.' Again an automatic response.

'Thomas Harley, whom we know was concerned in this theft, left his employment at that hotel on the day of the theft. You also disappeared from London on that day. More than a coincidence, surely?'

Jane Meadows surveyed Fox with cool reserve, and it looked as though his hope that she might confess to everything was misplaced. She was certainly showing no signs of cracking. 'It's a free country,' she said. It was the same phrase she had used to Crozier on the beach at Nice.

'And why did he decide to leave … on that particular day?'

Jane Meadows remained silent for a moment or two. 'Have you thought of asking him?' she enquired.

'Yes,' said Fox, 'but right now I'm asking you.'

'I don't know.'

'I think you do.'

'It's difficult,' she said. 'You see, I don't want to get him into trouble.'

Fox smiled. 'He's in so much trouble now, Mrs Meadows, that a bit more won't make a great deal of difference.'

The girl began hesitantly. 'He told me that when he was working at another hotel — a year or two back — some money had gone missing.' Fox nodded. 'And that he had been suspected because he had been the night duty manager. But he hadn't taken it,' she added hurriedly. 'Anyway, on the day of the jewel robbery —'

'The one you know nothing about, you mean?'

Jane shrugged. 'Only what he told me. But neither of us had anything to do with it. Anyway, Tom said that he was bound to be suspected, because of the other business with the money, and that it would be best if he left there and then.'

Fox decided against telling the girl that Harley had not waited to find out whether he was suspected of the previous theft but had disappeared rather promptly. And had changed his name to Wilkins. 'But why did you leave?' he asked again and pushed his cigarette case across the table.

The girl shook her head. 'I don't smoke, thank you,' she said.

'Well?' Fox allowed a small cloud of cigarette smoke to drift upwards.

Jane Meadows stared at him, her grey eyes unwavering. 'We're going to get married,' she said.

'Oh, that's nice.' Fox toyed briefly with his cigarette case. 'And presumably his wife is willing to give him a divorce in order to facilitate this arrangement?'

If the girl was surprised to learn that Harley was married she did not show it. 'So he says,' she replied coolly.

'And it was Thomas Harley who paid for your villa in Nice ... and who you were expecting to join you?' Fox wanted to make absolutely sure that his guesswork had been on the right lines.

'Yes,' she said in a tired voice, as though the whole thing had become too much trouble.

'How long have you and Harley been acquainted?'

'About two years, I suppose.'

'How did that come about?'

'I'm sorry ...?'

'How did you meet?'

'Oh, I see. At the golf club we both belonged to. It was a Saturday, I think. He hadn't got a partner and neither had I. So we went round together. Then we had a few drinks in the bar. After that it became quite a regular thing.'

'But he's not been seen at that golf club since the day of the jewel theft. And neither have you.'

'No.'

'Go on, Mrs Meadows.' If Fox believed that she was yet another girl who had fallen for the blandishments of a smooth-talking villain he might have felt sorry for her. But he was convinced that Jane Meadows was a very shrewd criminal.

'He invited me out for dinner and we got to be very good friends. It sort of went on from there.' She looked down at the table, a sad expression on her face. 'We became lovers.'

'How very romantic,' said Fox. 'Did he ever tell you what he did for a living?'

'Not immediately, no. He said afterwards that he was something to do with insurance. He never said exactly what, but I think he was a broker. Something like that.' She toyed briefly with a dress ring on the little finger of her left hand. 'But later on, he said he had moved into the hotel business. Said he was fed up with insurance and wanted a complete change.'

'Really?' said Fox. 'Well, there's a thing.' He changed direction. 'Let's leave Mr Harley for a moment and talk about another of your romantic exploits, shall we?'

For the first time, Jane Meadows appeared to be disconcerted and looked sharply at Fox. 'I beg your pardon?'

'Let's talk about Jeremy Benson.'

'I'm sorry, am I supposed to know someone of that name?'

'Mrs Meadows,' said Fox quietly, 'we know all about your relationship with Mr Benson. And most of the information came direct from Mr Benson himself.'

'Well, the truth is that our relationship — Tom's and mine — had cooled off and I'd gone to live with Jeremy at Marble Arch. But it didn't work out.'

'So you upped and left him.'

Jane Meadows looked reproachfully at Fox. 'That's one way of putting it, yes.'

'Taking twenty thousand pounds of his money when you went.'

'He could afford it.' She tossed the statement defiantly into the conversation. 'Anyway,' she added, 'I didn't steal it. We had a joint account, and he said I could draw what I wanted.'

'And when you left you also took some of his jewellery with you.'

'Is that what he told you?' The girl looked genuinely surprised.

'I suppose your version is different.'

'Jeremy gave me that jewellery. He told me that it had belonged to his wife. Actually,' she went on, 'things had started out very well. He was generous to a fault and he took me out to restaurants and the theatre. But then he started to get moody and demanding. In fact, he turned out to be an absolute pig. Well, there's a limit to what you can put up with, so we had one tremendous row and I told him I was leaving. That's when he threatened that he would make trouble for me. That's why he told you that I had stolen the damned stuff, I suppose.'

'Yes,' said Fox amiably, 'there might just be something in that.' And, he thought, a jury would probably take the same view. Despite the appeal for information in the *Police Gazette*, nothing had come in about Jane Meadows, although Fox was convinced that she made a living out of milking rich, lonely widowers. Unfortunately, rich, lonely widowers were rarely prepared to admit that they had been taken for a ride; it had certainly demanded a deal of courage on Jeremy Benson's part to tell Fox about his experience with Jane Meadows. 'You left Benson in about the fourth week in July, I believe?'

'Possibly. I can't remember.'

'How very convenient,' said Fox. He took out a cigarette and tapped it thoughtfully on the outside of the case. It was a deliberate act to separate what he had been saying from what he was about to say. 'Why did you pretend to be Mrs Susan Harley and arrange the burial of Thomas Harley well knowing him to be alive?'

The voice was harsh and the question came so suddenly and out of context that it clearly stunned Jane Meadows. For a second or two she stared at Fox. Then she took a deep breath. 'I — er ...' she began, but faltered almost immediately as her mouth went dry.

Rosie Webster poured a glass of water and placed it on the table in front of the girl.

'What makes you think that I did?' asked Jane, having recovered her composure sufficiently to collect her thoughts and say something.

'The telephone number that was given to the vicar of Cray Magna was Jeremy Benson's, in whose flat you were living at the time.' Fox was beginning to tire of this barren exchange. 'Benson denies all knowledge of the matter, and I believe him.'

'It was all his idea.'

'Whose idea, Mrs Meadows? Harley's?'

'Yes. He was certain that because of the trouble with the money at the last hotel he would be suspected of stealing the jewellery this time. He said that the only way out was to fake his own death so that he could lose his identity completely.'

'Why should he do that?' asked Fox.

'I told you, because of the business at —'

'Mrs Meadows,' asked Fox, a certain edge to his voice, 'are you telling me that Harley was prepared to commit several crimes of forgery and falsification to prevent himself being arrested for two other crimes that he claimed he hadn't committed?'

'Well, I —'

'And you allowed yourself to be dragged into this, for no reason at all? What was in it for you?'

'I told you, we were going to get married.' She paused. 'And I loved him. But I had nothing to do with any funeral.'

'But you knew about it?'

'Only what Tom told me.'

'I see.' Fox switched his line of questioning again. 'And did he tell you what this coffin contained?'

'He said that there were bags of sand in it to give it the right weight.'

'How fascinating,' said Fox. 'And you believed that?'

'Yes, I did.'

'Well don't expect me to believe it, Mrs Meadows. Why should he go to all that trouble? Why didn't he just disappear and change his name? Which he did anyway ...'

'I don't know.' The girl shrugged her shoulders.

'I'll tell you, Mrs Meadows. The reason is that it was a convenient place to hide the proceeds of the jewel theft —'

'Eh?' That revelation appeared to surprise her.

'Come, come, Mrs Meadows. Don't pretend you didn't know that,' said Fox. 'Jewellery which you and he were going to share once you had established a new identity for yourselves. That's what he told you, but in fact he had no intention of sharing it with anyone. He's left you high and dry, Mrs Meadows.' Fox paused to allow that to sink in. 'We arrested one of your co-conspirators, a man called James Murchison, who obligingly told us all about it.' Fox wished Murchison *had* told him all about it, but he was fairly convinced that he would be persuaded to do so if that became necessary. 'There is, however, something far more serious than either of those things. The coffin did not contain sand. Apart from the jewellery, it contained the body of another of your associates, one Donald Dixon. And, Mrs Meadows, he had been murdered.'

For a second or two, Jane Meadows stared at Fox, then her eyes rolled and she slipped off the chair in a dead faint.

'Interview terminated on account of prisoner fainting.' Rosie Webster directed the statement at the microphone in matter-of-fact tones and with a sigh got up and turned off the tape recorder. 'D'you reckon that amounts to a statement of admission, guv?' she asked as she bent to attend to the prostrate girl.

Fox screwed out his cigarette in the ashtray. 'Unfortunately, Rosie,' he said, 'I don't think it even amounts to guilty knowledge. I think that Dixon's murder has come as a very nasty shock to her. But it's a damned nuisance. I'd hoped to wrap this up tonight.' He glanced down at Jane Meadows, now showing signs of recovering consciousness. 'Better get the divisional surgeon to have a look at her. Don't want any nasty allegations.'

Chapter Fourteen

There is a method, a certain style, followed by the police in the apprehension of criminals who are known to them. It differs from the way in which, for example, a hitherto distinguished City banker will be arrested for fraud. He will usually surrender himself at a police station, by arrangement, in the company of his legal adviser. It is all very civilised.

Nathaniel Barber was not, however, in the distinguished City banker bracket. Mr Barber, inevitably known to several generations of detectives as Ali, was a low-life, all-time-losing, petty villain. He knew more about the admission procedure at Her Majesty's prisons than most of the officers who dealt with it. But that was because he had started his prison career before most serving screws had been born.

But the arrest of Ali Barber was no less civilised for all that.

Detective Sergeant Fletcher and Detective Constable Bellenger had drawn the short straws in Fox's lottery and therefore found themselves on a doorstep in Catford at six o'clock in the morning. They were not accompanied by a team of the specially trained firearms officers who occasionally grace television screens, doing set-piece poses, and aiming at nothing in particular.

Nor was there what viewers call back-up. No white Transit vans blocked off the street. No tapes crossed the ends of roads. No traffic police put in expensive diversions resulting in announcements on the wireless.

It was just Fletcher and Bellenger.

Fletcher banged on the front door.

And waited.

He banged again.

And waited again.

The woman who came to the door knew who they were. Even though she had never seen them before. She took in Fletcher's kindly face and Bellenger's stocky figure. 'You want Ali, I s'pose,' she said in resigned tones.

'Yes, love,' said Fletcher.

'He's in bed. Come in and I'll give him a shout.' She stopped, one foot on the bottom stair. 'D'you want a cuppa?' she asked.

'Wouldn't say no, love,' said Fletcher.

'Hang on, then. But I'll give Ali a shout first.'

Some ten minutes or so later, the forlorn figure of Nathaniel Barber appeared in the doorway of the kitchen. 'Hallo, Mr Fletcher.' He wore a dull tartan dressing gown and looked as though he hadn't shaved for a week. But then he always looked as though he hadn't shaved for a week.

'Hallo, Ali. How y'keeping?'

'Oh, not bad. Back's playing up a bit.'

'It's the weather, Ali.' Fletcher took a sip of Mrs Barber's tea. 'I'm afraid you're going to have to come down the nick, old pal.'

Barber shrugged. 'What is it this time, Mr Fletcher?'

'Seems you helped Ozzie Bryce and Sid Meek out with a funeral, Ali.'

'Yeah, s'right. What about it?'

'Turns out the bloke you took down to Devon had been topped.'

'Oh, my oath,' said Barber. 'I'd better get me duds on, then.' He stopped at the door. 'Time for a couple of kippers, have I, Mr Fletcher?'

*

'Are you fully recovered now?' asked Fox. He had decided to suspend the interview with Jane Meadows after she had fainted the previous evening. It had been close to ten o'clock anyway, and although he preferred to interrogate prisoners fully as soon as possible after their arrest he had had little alternative but to break off. But in the event it probably did not matter. He was starting to think that Jane Meadows knew less than he had originally thought.

'Yes, thank you.' Despite her reply, the girl looked pale and drawn. Her arrest — and the discomfort of a police cell — had prevented her from getting much sleep.

'Last night, I was talking to you about the body of a man that we found in a coffin at Cray Magna. The unusual aspect of which, you may recall, was that he had been murdered. I put it to you again, Mrs Meadows, that you arranged that funeral and were present at the interment. What d'you have to say to that?' Before Jane Meadows could reply, Fox added, 'I must remind you that you are still under caution.'

'I didn't know anything about there being a body in that coffin,' said the girl and paused. Then, 'Oh, God, I've been a fool.'

'D'you want to tell me about it?'

'Where shall I start?' The girl looked imploringly at Fox.

For a moment or two, Fox studied the girl's face. It was evident that she was no longer acting. 'At the beginning, I suppose. Wherever that is.'

'I was divorced about four years ago. There were no children and my ex-husband disappeared straight after the decree absolute, so there was no chance of getting any money from him. Not that I would have wanted it anyway. Then I met Tom, as I said, at the golf club.'

'And he took you out to dinner —' Fox interrupted himself. 'How many times did that happen, incidentally?'

Jane shrugged. 'I don't know. Four or five, maybe.'

'And where did you go to make love?'

The girl's colour rose sharply. 'I don't see how that —'

'Just answer the question, Mrs Meadows.'

'At a hotel usually.' She stared down at the table.

'The one where the theft occurred?'

'Once he'd started working there, yes. It was quite easy to arrange. He was the deputy manager.'

'That's what he told you, was it?' Fox sighed. 'He never took you to his house?'

'No. I didn't know where he lived.'

'You knew him for four years, but you didn't know where he lived?' Fox didn't believe that. He realised, too late, that it would have been better to have had the girl followed from the airport instead of arresting her the moment she landed on British soil. In that way she might have led them to Harley. But there again, he'd not had much option. Someone as strongly suspected as Jane Meadows could not be allowed to roam free. 'Right,' said Fox, leaving that enigma for a moment, 'let's get back to Jeremy Benson. Tell me about that.'

'I answered an ad in the paper. It said that a recently widowed man was seeking a companion to go on holiday with him. All expenses paid. I wrote and sent a photograph. That's how we met.'

'But it didn't work out?'

'No. He told me originally that he was in his early fifties, but he was nearer sixty-five. And it was obvious after a while that there was only one thing he wanted.' She added the last comment bitterly.

'Which you gave him, of course.'

Jane Meadows looked scathingly at Fox, a blush rising on her face. 'Everything has to be paid for,' she said profoundly. 'Particularly expensive holidays in the South of France.'

'You told Benson that you were a partner in a business. A business vaguely connected with the hotel trade?' The girl nodded. 'Why? Benson was prepared to keep you in luxury, wasn't he?'

'Well, I —'

'All very plausible, Mrs Meadows, but it won't wash. You were in league with Harley, and your so-called romance with Benson was at Harley's instigation. Furthermore, you were a willing accomplice. You had known Harley for some time — you've admitted that — but it was you who suggested he got a job at the hotel because of the rich pickings. Benson's advert in the paper was a bonus and you both shared the proceeds of what you stole.' Fox paused to light a cigarette. It was largely speculation, but Fox was an experienced detective and he knew that she would probably confess to a conspiracy to steal as soon as he put his next proposition to her. 'You, Murchison and Harley conspired to murder Donald Dixon so that you could share the proceeds of the theft from the hotel. Then the three of you disposed of the body in a way that you thought was foolproof.'

'No, it's not true.' Jane Meadows' voice almost reached hysteria, and a red flush started to creep up her neck. 'I don't know anything about a murder, honestly. You've got to believe me.' Her eyes opened wide and stared straight at Fox.

'Then you'd better tell me how much you do know,' said Fox quietly.

'All right. Tom did organise the stealing of the jewellery. He told me that himself. There were some others in it, too —'

'Names?'

She gave a brief shake of the head. 'I only know the one. Murchison. But there were others. Another man, and a woman. A blonde, I think. That's what Jim said.'

Fox produced the post-mortem photograph of Dixon. 'Was he one of them?' he asked.

The girl looked at the dead face and turned away quickly, her face going pale. 'I, er —'

'I see you know him.'

She nodded miserably. 'Yes,' she said. 'That's Don Dixon.'

'I think you'd better stop pussy-footing about, Mrs Meadows. We are talking about serious charges here.'

'Tom said that after the job he and I would go to the South of France for a holiday. He said we might even stay there to live if his plan came off.'

'What plan was this?'

'He said that as he'd done the dangerous bit it was only right that he should take all the proceeds and leave everyone else out.'

'And it was at that point that you and Harley decided to get rid of Dixon.'

'No!' There was still anguish in the girl's voice. 'I keep telling you, I knew nothing about Don's death. Tom told me his plan about faking his own death and asked me to help. Well, it didn't seem very risky at all —' The girl broke off and felt in the pockets of her skirt.

'Here.' Rosie Webster handed her a tissue from a box on the window-sill.

'And Murchison helped in this, of course?' asked Fox.

'Yes.'

'And you pretended to be the widow.'

'Yes.'

'Who else was involved in this funeral?'

'A couple of men I'd never seen before.' Jane glanced at Fox, anticipating the next question. 'I only knew them as Ozzie and Sid,' she said. 'They acted as pall-bearers.'

'That's all very interesting,' said Fox, 'but tell me, where did you go after the heist? When Murchison dropped you and Dixon at Marble Arch?'

Jane Meadows stared at Fox. 'I don't know what you're talking about,' she said. 'I didn't have anything to do with the actual robbery.'

'Then who was the blonde woman, about your build and age, who took part in the theft?'

'I've no idea. I'm sorry.'

'Harley didn't tell you?'

'No. I'd already been in Nice for a week when the robbery happened. That's where I was living when your policeman found me.' She looked at Fox reproachfully. 'Tom rang me to say that it had all gone off all right, and that he was coming over to join me.'

'So you are saying that when this theft occurred you were miles away. In a villa in Nice. Yes?'

'Yes, I was.'

'Is there anyone who can vouch for that? Anyone you met or saw on that day?'

She appeared to think carefully about that. 'Not that I can recall,' she said. 'It's a long time ago now.'

'A pity, that,' said Fox. 'And afterwards Tom flew over and joined you?'

'Yes. But then we came back and fixed up the fake funeral. We used Jeremy's phone number and I was to pretend to be the undertaker's secretary if there was a call.'

'And what would have happened if Jeremy had answered the phone ... to someone asking for Marloes?'

She didn't seem at all put out by the question. 'I told him that was the name of my firm.'

'And once this bogus funeral was over, you both went back to Nice and assumed the identities of Mr and Mrs Spencer? Is that right?'

For some reason Jane Meadows seemed surprised that the police should know that. 'Yes, but Tom only stayed a day or so, and then he went back to London again.'

'Why did he do that, Mrs Meadows? Why did Harley return to this country so soon after arriving in Nice?'

There was a lengthy pause before Jane Meadows answered. Then, 'He said he wanted to collect the rest of the jewellery from Cray Magna.'

'And why didn't he?' asked Fox.

'I don't know really. He rang me from England to say that it was going to take a bit longer.'

'Was it because he'd heard that Murchison had been arrested?'

'I don't think he knew. I certainly didn't, and he never mentioned it.'

'And you waited ... and waited, but he didn't turn up.'

'No, he didn't.' The girl looked momentarily sad at having been let down by a man who, she now realised, probably had no intention of marrying her after all.

'No,' said Fox. 'I think he's abandoned you, Mrs Meadows. But while you were there, you sold the jewellery you had stolen from Jeremy Benson.'

'I certainly sold it, but I hadn't stolen it. I told you before, Jeremy gave it to me.'

'And you also sold some of the jewellery that had been stolen from the hotel,' said Fox.

'Yes.' The girl spoke softly and looked despairingly at Fox. 'What's going to happen to me?'

'That's a matter for the Crown Prosecution Service,' said Fox. 'But for a start you'll be charged with handling stolen property, if not with stealing it.' He paused. 'Then there's the murder of Donald Dixon. You were certainly instrumental in helping to dispose of Dixon's body —'

'But I didn't know that that was what had happened.' She sounded desperate.

Fox smiled. 'So you say, Mrs Meadows. So you say.'

Chapter Fifteen

'What do we do next, sir? Trip to Brixton to talk to Murchison?' asked Gilroy.

'Certainly not,' said Fox. 'I've had enough of being ponced about by that little toe-rag.'

'But he's got to find some answers, guv. Like why his dabs were all over the house at Kingston Hill when he reckons he never went anywhere near the place. But more to the point, how he came to be burying Dixon when he reckoned he'd never heard of him.'

'We didn't mention Kingston to him, Jack.' Fox sighed. 'But even if we had, he'd have denied being there. He said that he drove a man and the blonde, whoever she turns out to be, and dropped them off at Marble Arch after the heist. Then he said that he was supposed to meet this Harry bloke in a boozer in Dulwich to pick up his wages. He reluctantly admitted to having heard of Harley under the name of Wilkins, but denied ever having met him. As for having buried Dixon, he could put up the same defence as Madam Meadows, namely, he didn't know what was in the box.'

'So what's the plan, sir?'

'The plan, Jack, is to wait until I've got enough to screw that little bastard good and proper. Jane Meadows has told us some of the story, admittedly, but I don't think she knows it all. I want some more before we have another go at Murchison. I think it's a waste of time talking to him again ... yet, anyway. You see, Jack ...' Fox paused to light a cigarette. 'The trouble with small time tea-leaves like Murchison is that it's second nature for them to tell lies. It's the way they're brought up. Anyway, he's not going anywhere.' He stood up. 'In the meantime, we'll have a look at Benson's bank account, and while we're about it we'll have a look at Harley's as well ... both the Harleys.'

'Do we know where the Harleys' account is?'

'Oh yes. Mrs Harley obligingly left the address of her bank with the furniture depository in Wimbledon. So get Crozier to get a warrant.'

'Under the Police and Criminal Evidence Act, sir?'

'Of course, Jack.'

'Application has to be made to a judge, sir ... by an inspector.'

'So it does, Jack,' said Fox. 'Well, just got yourself a job, haven't you?'

*

The manager of Jeremy Benson's bank looked unhappily at the letter of authority that Fox had obtained from Jeremy Benson and shook his head. 'We have a problem here, Chief Superintendent,' he said.

'Do we really?' said Fox. 'Oh dear. And what might that be?'

'Well, it's a joint account. Mr Benson's letter of authority needs to be signed by Mrs Benson as well. Otherwise, I can't grant you access.'

'Unfortunately, Mrs Benson is in custody,' said Fox. 'And I'm afraid the law is so protective that we cannot ask her to provide evidence against herself. Apart from which, she isn't Mrs Benson at all. She is Mrs Meadows.'

The bank manager pushed his glasses back up his nose. 'Oh!' he said, and blinked. 'Unfortunately, that does not alter my position.'

'Can't win 'em all,' said Fox with a shrug. 'Still, I'm sure that a warrant issued by a Crown Court judge will set your mind at rest.'

The bank manager smiled. 'If you can get one,' he said.

'Oh, we shall,' said Fox. 'Don't go away.'

It took an hour and a half, and Fox and Gilroy returned to the bank just before closing time. 'There we are,' said Fox, producing the warrant. 'Now we can get down to business.'

'Ah, yes, quite so,' said the manager, who did not seem any happier than on their last visit.

Fox and Gilroy settled themselves in an ante-room and started on the tedious task of going through the Bensons' account. Apart from regular drawings, cheques for moderate amounts had been cashed at intervals in Nice, confirming what Benson had said about the couple's frequent travels to the South of France. Some were signed by him, others by Jane Benson. The interesting one was for twenty thousand pounds, and that was dated the nineteenth of July. And had been drawn by Jane Benson.

Fox tossed the cheque across to Gilroy. 'Well, he was certainly right about her having twenty grand out of his account, Jack,' he said and turned to the manager. 'This cheque,' he continued. 'Would you have queried it? Being so big?'

The manager pushed his glasses up his nose once again and studied the cheque. Then he turned it over. 'We did, as a matter of fact,' he said. 'I remember it quite clearly. It was a much larger sum than was usual for that account and the cashier referred it to me. Because it was a joint account, I considered it prudent to speak to Mr Benson.'

'And what did he say?'

The bank manager looked surprised by Fox's question. 'He approved it. Said it was all right to go ahead and honour it.'

'How interesting,' said Fox with a satisfied grin. 'It's got bugger all to do with anything but we shall have another little chat with our Mr Benson, Jack.' He glanced again at the documents in front of him and a minute or two later jabbed a finger at an entry. 'Can you tell me which of the account holders made that drawing?' he asked the manager.

The manager glanced at the item that had attracted Fox's interest. 'Yes,' he said and referred to one of the other printouts in front of him. 'It was Mrs Benson.'

'Oh dear,' said Fox. 'Have a look at that, Jack. That requires some answers. And there's another thing, Jack ...'

'Yes, sir?'

'There have been several payments to a credit card company. Have a word with them. I seem to recall that we've had a bit of luck with them in the past.'

*

'Call for you on line seven, guv,' said the DC on duty in the main office of the Flying Squad as Gilroy walked in.

'Who is it?'

'Duty officer at Kingston, sir. Something to do with that drum on Kingston Hill you turned over last week.'

Gilroy picked up the phone and pressed down the switch. 'DI Gilroy.'

'Inspector Pebble, duty officer at Kingston.'

'Inspector who?'

'Pebble ... as on beach.'

'Oh, right. What can I do for you, Mr Pebble.'

'That house on Kingston Hill that was searched ...'

'What about it?' asked Gilroy.

'Well, I looked it up in the Premises Searched Register and found your name against it.'

'Yeah,' said Gilroy. 'You would have done. I put it there.' He looked up at the ceiling, then glanced at the DC who had taken the call. 'Tell Mr Fox something's come up about the Harley's house at Kingston, lad, quickly.'

'Well,' continued Inspector Pebble, 'I've got a man in the nick now. Reckons he's the owner of the house and that it's been broken into.'

'It was,' said Gilroy. 'Police broke in.'

Fox appeared in the office. 'What have you got, Jack?' he asked.

Gilroy put his hand over the receiver and quickly repeated the story before speaking to Inspector Pebble again. 'What name did he give?' he asked.

'Davidson,' said Pebble.

Gilroy turned to Fox. 'Says his name's Davidson, sir.'

'Are you still there?' asked Pebble.

'Yeah, hold on a minute,' said Gilroy. 'I'm just repeating this to my guv'nor.'

'Saucy bastard,' said Fox. 'So Harley's now calling himself Davidson. Like the motorbike, see. Harley Davidson. Tell them to hang on to him … on my authority, Jack.'

Gilroy repeated the instructions to the Kingston duty officer. 'We'll be down there before you can say Sweeney Todd,' he added.

Fox's driver, the mournful Swann, sat stoically behind the steering wheel of the Ford Granada and pushed it to unbelievable speeds on the way to Kingston. The siren and the circulating blue light, attached to the car's roof by magnets, ensured that other traffic kept well out of its way. Fox sat hunched in the front seat, occasionally rocking forward as if to urge the vehicle on to even greater speeds.

Twenty-three minutes after leaving Scotland Yard, Swann steered the car into the yard at Kingston police station. Fox and Gilroy hurried inside, leaving Swann to follow them at his usual slow amble. 'Here, mate,' he said to a PC. 'Where's the canteen?'

'Well?' demanded Fox as he strode into the front office of the police station. 'Where's this Davidson, or whatever he calls himself?'

'This way, sir,' said Inspector Pebble, and led them through the custody suite to an interview room. 'I'll have him brought up.'

The man who appeared a few minutes later was about sixty years of age and was clearly of Indian origin, albeit light skinned. 'What is the meaning of this?' he demanded. 'I come in here to inform the police that my house has been broken into and the next thing is I'm arrested.'

'You're Mr Davidson?' asked Fox, an element of doubt in his voice.

'Of course.'

'Oh!'

'If you're wondering why I have an English name,' said Davidson. 'It came from my grandfather on my father's side. He was a regimental sergeant major in the Indian Army.'

'Fascinating,' said Fox. 'Now about this house that you say you own —'

'But I do own it. And I want to know why I am arrested because of it. It was broken into, you know.'

'Yes, I do know, Mr Davidson. It was the police who broke in. The house was properly secured, but if any damage was done our Accident Claims branch will —'

'But why? Why did you break in?'

'The fact is, Mr Davidson, we are investigating a murder.'

'A murder? Whose murder? In my house?'

'I must apologise for the over-reaction of the officers at this station,' said Fox, ignoring Davidson's question, 'but I'm sure that as a responsible citizen you would wish to assist the police. Particularly when I say that you are probably the one man who can help us solve this dastardly crime.' Fox smiled disarmingly.

'Well, of course,' said Davidson, somewhat mollified. 'Naturally.'

'Good, good,' said Fox. 'I knew the moment I set eyes on you that I could rely on your every assistance. Now then, have you ever heard of a man called Harley, Thomas Harley?'

'Of course. He is the man who rented my house.'

'When would that have been, Mr Davidson?'

'The twenty-fifth of March,' said Davidson promptly. 'He agreed to take it for six months.'

'I see. Where did he come from, this Thomas Harley?'

'He told me that he had been living abroad. In the South of France, actually.'

'Yes, I'll bet he did,' said Fox.

'Please?'

'Did he produce references?'

'Of course. I would not have let him have the house otherwise.'

'Can you remember details of any of these references, Mr Davidson?'

'Certainly.' Davidson opened his Filofax and thumbed through the pages. 'Ah yes, here we are. There were two from persons who had previously let their houses to him in France, and one other in London.'

'And did you follow them up?'

'Most certainly. One has to be very careful to whom one lets one's house, you know.'

Fox grinned. 'Of course. Do you have the telephone numbers or the addresses there, by any chance?' He pointed at Davidson's open Filofax.

'Yes, indeed. I'll write them down for you.' Davidson scribbled the addresses and telephone numbers on a separate sheet and tore it from the book. 'There you are,' he said.

Fox read through them and then handed the piece of paper to Gilroy. 'Funny how that Marble Arch telephone number keeps cropping up, isn't it, Jack? Get on to our friend Inspector Ronsard in Nice and ask him to take a look at the other two.' He turned back to Davidson. 'This Marble Arch address, did you go there or did you telephone?'

'I telephoned.'

'Who did you speak to?'

Davidson referred once more to his Filofax, and Fox offered up grateful thanks to whoever ordained that Harley's erstwhile landlord was such a meticulous man. 'I spoke to a lady. A Mrs Jane Benson. She knew Mr Harley socially, she said, and could vouch for him absolutely. She said he was a jolly good chap. She even offered to give me a banker's guarantee if there was likely to be any problem.'

'And did you take her up on that?'

'No, I did not think it was necessary. Anyway, Mr Harley paid in advance for the whole six months and, of course, I required a substantial deposit against possible damage.'

'And what about the French references?'

'I don't speak French, but I got a friend of mine to telephone them. The same. All very satisfactory.'

'Yeah,' said Fox, standing up, 'they would be. Well, thank you very much indeed, Mr Davidson. I can't begin to express my gratitude for all the assistance you have given me,' he continued blandly. 'It is very refreshing these days to find someone prepared to spare a little time to help the police. In fact, I shall get my Commissioner to write you a letter of thanks. And I do apologise, once again, for the mistake that caused you to be detained by the officers at this station. I merely told them that I wanted to talk to you. Believe me, I shall speak to them most severely about the need to understand instructions correctly.'

Davidson waved a deprecating hand. 'My dear sir,' he said. 'Please do no such thing. It is comforting to know that the police are so keen to apprehend wrongdoers. I just hope you catch this one.'

'Everything all right, sir?' asked Inspector Pebble as Fox and Gilroy watched Davidson leave the station.

'Yes,' said Fox gravely. 'It is now. By dint of some fast talking I managed to persuade Mr Davidson not to make an official complaint that you had wrongly arrested and falsely imprisoned him.' But he winked at Gilroy as he said it.

Inspector Pebble's mouth was still silently open as Fox swept out of the police station.

*

'I think that Mrs Harley knows more about all this than she told us, sir,' said Gilroy.

'You do catch on quickly, Jack. What in particular prompted you to say that?'

'She didn't say anything about the house being rented. And this reference — Jane Benson — she must have known about that, surely?'

'As you say, Jack, as you say. I look forward to talking to her again. When we can find her. So send a message to all forces and all ports. And while you're about it, a blue-corner circular to Interpol.'

'That's a bit heavy, guv,' said Gilroy.

Fox smiled. 'Yes, it is, isn't it?'

*

Detective Sergeant Percy Fletcher was very familiar with the West End of London, and when Fox told him to find Sandra Nelson he knew exactly where to look. But he had dealt with prostitutes before, so he took WDC Rosie Webster with him.

In fact, Sandra Nelson all but gave herself up. Fletcher, who had had the foresight to tell Rosie Webster to stay some distance from him, was moving casually through Shepherd Market when Sandra stepped out from a darkened doorway. 'How d'you fancy a little bit of fun together, darling?'

'What a good idea,' said Fletcher. 'You're nicked.'

'You rotten bastard,' said Sandra in a shrill voice. 'Can't a girl earn an honest living any more?'

Fletcher laughed. 'Not tonight, Josephine,' he said.

Sandra looked as though she was going to make a run for it, but as she turned she came face to face with Rosie Webster. 'Oh God,' she said, 'it's you.'

Rosie smiled. 'Yes, it's me, Sandra. We want to have a word with you. Or rather my guv'nor does, down at Rochester Row.'

'What are we going there for? We usually go to Vine Street or Savile Row when we get nicked.'

'We are going there because that's where Mr Fox wants you to be. And he wants a chat with you, my girl,' said Fletcher.

'What for? What's this about?' There was panic now in Sandra Nelson's voice.

'Something to do with a large quantity of jewellery that's been nicked. And a murder,' said Fletcher.

'What?' Sandra Nelson now looked thoroughly alarmed. 'I'll own to tomming, but I don't know anything about a murder. Honest, I don't. And I've already said I don't know anything about any jewellery.'

When they got to Rochester Row police station, Sandra was placed in an interview room in the care of a uniformed WPC while Fletcher rang the Yard.

'I'm Thomas Fox ... of the Flying Squad.' Twenty minutes later Fox strode into the room and sat down in the chair opposite Sandra Nelson.

'I don't care who you are,' said Sandra. 'I don't know anything about any murder and I want a solicitor.'

'Do you know one professionally, then?' asked Fox. 'His profession, I mean, not yours,' he added.

'Very funny,' said Sandra.

'Now,' began Fox, 'you remember when you and Murchison were arrested —'

'Not likely to forget it,' said Sandra sulkily. 'Those horny bastards made me do a strip-tease in reverse.'

'They have my sympathy,' murmured Fox. 'But when you were arrested my officers found a blonde wig in the room.'

'Don't know anything about it,' said Sandra.

'Look,' said Fox, 'I want the truth about that wig. Was it yours?'

'I told you. I'd never seen it before. I wouldn't be seen dead in a wig, blonde or any other colour.' Sandra stared at Fox. 'Can you imagine what would happen if a punter was giving it all he'd got and right at the crucial moment my bleeding wig fell off.'

'Probably demand his money back,' said Fox. 'But if it's not your wig I'm sure you won't mind giving us one or two sample hairs from that ample crop of yours.'

'What the hell is this? Are you kinky or something?'

Fox smiled. 'If it's not yours you've nothing to worry about. I just want to satisfy myself that the hair found inside that wig doesn't match yours, and we do that by scientific comparison.'

Sandra plucked a few strands of hair from her head and laid them carefully on the table. 'There you are,' she said. 'My pleasure.'

'Good.' Fox stood up. 'Record those as an exhibit,' he said to Fletcher, 'and release Miss Nelson on police bail.'

Sandra looked up in surprise. 'You mean you're not doing me for soliciting him?' She nodded at Fletcher.

'No,' said Fox. 'He'd never live it down.'

*

'Interesting, isn't it, Jack,' said Fox, as Swann swung the Granada on to the A3, 'that the Harleys should have their bank account in Guildford? He lived in Kingston, robbed in London, frequented the South of France, played golf somewhere near Richmond and claimed a connection with Cray Magna.'

'Yes, sir,' said Gilroy.

'So why does he have his bank account in Guildford?'

'I don't know, sir.'

Fox grunted and then lapsed into silence for the remainder of the journey.

The bank manager had never seen a warrant issued under the Police and Criminal Evidence Act before and read it suspiciously. Then he laid it on his desk and looked up. 'I think I shall have to consult my head office,' he said.

'There are quite severe penalties for contempt of court,' said Fox, a certain menace in his voice, 'and the warrant is addressed to you personally, not to your head office.'

'Well,' said the manager reluctantly, 'it appears to be in order. What exactly is it that you want to see?'

'Don't know, really,' said Fox cheerfully. 'Better go through the lot, I suppose.'

'Oh!' The manager pressed a switch on his intercom. 'Beverley, ask Clive to bring in all the papers on the Harley account, Thomas and Susan, will you.'

Ten minutes later, during which time the manager had talked about little else but the weather, a young man appeared, laden down with computer printouts and a ledger or two, and hovered expectantly in the doorway of the manager's office. 'The Harleys' account, sir,' he said.

After twenty minutes or so, Fox let out a sigh and leaned back in his chair. 'This is all too bloody straightforward, Jack,' he said. 'There are all the usual things, like household bills, weekly drawings, cheques for credit card payments, standing order for the rent of the Kingston Hill house, TV licence renewal, car tax … all that sort of stuff. It's too damned honest. This bloke Harley doesn't put himself on offer for anything.'

'Well, he's not going to get caught out for not buying a TV licence any more than he's going to get stopped for having no car tax, is he?'

'No, he's not.' Fox pushed the printout away. 'To be frank, Jack, I don't think this is the only account Harley's got.'

'Oh,' said the bank manager, 'did you want to see the other one? I thought it was just the joint account you were interested in.'

Fox bit back a retort and waited another ten minutes while the manager's assistant, Clive, found another set of papers. After some fifteen minutes of close examination, Fox looked up with a satisfied expression. 'That's better,' he said. 'And there's an address in Godalming, Jack. Make a few enquiries, will you.' He paused. 'Better go mob-handed.'

Chapter Sixteen

'The house in Godalming, sir. It's a non-starter.'

Fox gave Gilroy a pessimistic stare. 'I thought for one minute you were going to surprise me there, Jack.'

Gilroy grinned. 'A Mr and Mrs Makins own the house now, guv. Bought it a year ago. They only met Mrs Harley a couple of times. And never saw our Thomas. The first time was when they looked at the house, obviously. And the second time to make sure that they hadn't gone away with a false picture.'

'And had they gone away with a false picture?'

'I don't know, guv. But Mrs Makins said that Mrs Harley was probably in her late twenties, blonde and good looking.'

*

The shop in Regent Street was expensive. The moment that Gilroy stepped through the door he detected that it was an establishment whose customers did not concern themselves about cost so much as quality.

'May I help you, sir?' The girl, a petite Chinese, smiled.

'I'm a police officer,' said Gilroy. 'I'd like to speak to the manageress, if I may.'

'That's me.'

'Good. I'm interested to know what this credit card transaction was for.' Gilroy produced the details.

The Chinese girl laughed. 'Well, there's only one thing it can be,' she said. 'That's all we sell.'

Gilroy laughed too. 'Yes, I know,' he said. 'But can you tell me exactly what it was?'

'No problem. Won't keep you a moment.' And the girl disappeared into a back room.

*

'I've been doing a bit of digging, sir,' said DS Percy Fletcher, sidling round Fox's office door.

'Not found another body, I hope.'

'In a manner of speaking, guv.'

'Oh!' Fox put down his pen and leaned back in his chair. 'Let's have it then, Perce.'

'You know that Jane Meadows said she was divorced about four years ago, guv?'

'Yes.' Fox leaned forward again, a sudden look of interest on his face.

'She wasn't. I thought I'd spend a few hours up at St Catherine's House, having a bit of a poke about.'

'Yes ...' said Fox again.

'She's still married, guv. And her old man's in the nick. Doing seven for blackmail,' Fletcher grinned triumphantly. 'Copped it about four years back.'

'Well, well,' said Fox. 'Now there's an interesting thing. D'you have paper to support this proposition of yours?'

Fletcher placed a pile of files on Fox's desk. 'His CRO microfiche, and the General Registry docket, sir.'

'Why wasn't she done? She was part of this scam, whatever it was, surely?' Fox couldn't believe for one moment that Jane Meadows was not involved in her husband's chicanery.

'DPP's office wouldn't have it, guv. Reckoned she was young, pure and innocent. But mainly innocent.'

'Bloody tossers,' said Fox.

*

Gilroy laid the sheet of paper on Fox's desk. 'That's a printout of her credit card account, sir.'

'So it is, Jack, so it is. And?'

'That item makes interesting reading, sir.' Gilroy pointed at an entry that was highlighted on the printout.

'Oh yes, doesn't it just? Have you confirmed it?'

'Yes, sir, and it's what you think it is.'

'Interesting,' said Fox. 'However, that transaction was made after the jewellery heist.'

'Yes, I know. Thought it might interest you though, sir.'

'Oh, it does, Jack, though I've got this nagging feeling that it's just a coincidence. But we'll keep it in mind. The other thing about both the bank account and the credit card is that they interest me for what's missing rather than for what is there.'

'Yes, sir,' said Gilroy, not for a moment understanding Fox's enigmatic comment.

*

'Got a minute, sir?' asked DS Fletcher.

'What is it, Perce?'

'Got the results of the hair comparison, sir.'

'The what?' asked Fox.

'The hair comparison, sir. You know, the hair in the blonde wig that we found when we nicked Murchison and Sandra Nelson, the tom.'

'Oh yes. What about it?'

'No go, sir,' said Fletcher. 'The hair inside the wig was definitely not Sandra Nelson's.'

'Terrific,' said Fox. 'Got any more good news for me?'

Fletcher grinned. 'Yes, sir. None of the prints found at the Kingston Hill house matched Sandra Nelson's. Nor any of those found in the Bensons' flat at Marble Arch.'

Fox stared despairingly at Fletcher. 'No, they wouldn't, would they?'

*

'Oh, Mr Fox. Good morning. Have you come to see me?' Lady Morton emerged from the lift just as Gilroy was about to press the button.

'Good morning, Lady Morton. No, as a matter of fact I've come to see Mr Benson.'

She lowered her voice to a conspiratorial whisper. 'He's back, you know.'

Fox beamed. 'How very fortunate, Lady Morton,' he said. 'Well, mustn't hold you up,' he added and stood to one side.

Jeremy Benson did not appear pleased to find the two detectives at his front door. 'I rather thought that I'd be seeing you again,' he said. 'Come in.'

The sitting room was identical in shape and size to the one in the flat opposite, but whereas Lady Morton favoured antiques Benson had opted for a curious mixture of art deco and art nouveau. In Fox's view they fitted uneasily together.

'Well, what can I do for you? Have you come to tell me that you've found Jane?'

'Not specifically,' said Fox, 'but she is in custody.'

'I see. And is she implicated in this murder?'

'She's certainly involved, but to what extent is not yet clear. However, that is not why I'm here.'

'Oh, there's something else, then.'

'Yes, Mr Benson. We took advantage of your authority to inspect your bank account —'

'You did?' Benson sat up.

'You sound surprised.'

'Well it was a joint account and I didn't imagine that they'd let you see it without Jane's authority.' Benson paused. 'But she wouldn't have given permission, surely?'

'No, we didn't ask her,' said Fox. 'Not cricket, you know, asking suspects to convict themselves. Her Majesty's Lords of Appeal in Ordinary take a rather dim view of that sort of thing.'

'Well then how —?'

'We got a warrant from a circuit judge.'

'Oh!' Benson eased himself into a more comfortable position, as though it had all become too much for him.

'One of the things that fascinated me, Mr Benson,' said Fox, 'was that the last time I spoke to you, you said that Jane Benson had stolen twenty thousand pounds from you. She had drawn it from your account, you said. And yet when I spoke to the manager of your bank he said that he'd queried it with you, and you'd given authority for that cheque to be honoured.'

Benson sighed and let his arms hang loose over the sides of his chair. 'It was blackmail,' he said.

'Was it really?'

Fox waited for some time before speaking again. 'Well, are you going to tell me about it?'

'I think I've got myself into trouble here,' said Benson.

'Well, I shan't know unless you explain.'

'What I told you about advertising for a holiday companion was true. Well, I showed you the cutting …' Fox nodded. 'It wasn't until later that I realised that I'd become the victim of an elaborate trap. We were in bed one night — it must have been about eleven, I suppose — when the bedroom door opened and this man walked in.'

'And who was he?' Fox thought he knew.

'It was Jane's husband. At least that's what he said, and she agreed with him.'

'Oh dear,' said Fox. It demanded a great deal of will-power on his part not to smile at Benson falling for one of the oldest tricks in the book.

'And how did he get in?'

'He said he'd found the key in her bag and followed her.'

'How did that happen? I thought she was living there with you.'

Benson shrugged. 'How it happened didn't really matter. The fact is, it had happened. After you came to see me I thought about it and realised that it must have been planned. She probably gave him the key and told him where and when to come.' He had a resigned look on his face. 'Well, you can imagine the scandal that it would've caused if it had got out.'

'Scandal?' Fox couldn't quite see where any scandal would arise.

'Of course. I am a respected businessman, Mr Fox. What d'you think my partners would have said if they'd heard that I'd been sleeping with a girl many years my junior? Particularly as it happened to be someone else's wife. I'd never have been able to look my neighbours in the face again.'

Fox certainly understood Benson's concern about that and tried to imagine the devastatingly censorious glance that Lady Morton, for example, would be able to summon up. 'It was then that they made their demands, was it?'

'Not they ... him,' said Benson miserably. 'But there was more to it than that.'

'Oh?'

'He said that he was expecting a phone call for a firm called Marloes —'

'You mentioned that before,' said Fox.

'Yes, but he said that if I didn't play along, he'd make sure that my fellow directors got to hear about me sleeping with his wife, and that he'd probably make up some story about me interfering with children as well. I couldn't afford that sort of story to circulate, could I?'

So that was what Benson meant about scandal. Fox's eyes narrowed. 'And have you interfered with children?'

'No, of course not.' Benson's answer was spirited.

'So what happened next?'

'Nothing, as a matter of fact, but I suspected that something illegal was going on ...'

'What made you think that?'

'For one thing, I didn't like this man's menacing attitude, and then there was the man Dixon. He seemed to know the other man, and they both came and went more or less as they pleased. It was as if they'd taken over my flat.'

'But what about Jane?' asked Fox. 'Why did you go after her to the South of France, if she'd been blackmailing you?'

'I didn't think she had at first. I thought that she was just as much an innocent party as me. Once or twice, when I got her on her own, she said that she was terrified of the other two, but begged me not to do anything about it, or they would kill her.'

'Why did you agree to the payment of the cheque, then?'

'I did it for her. I thought that she was in trouble and I didn't want anything to happen to her.'

Fox stretched out his legs. 'Well, I've got news for you, Mr Benson. Mrs Meadows' real husband is serving seven years' imprisonment ... for blackmail. Same MO as yours.'

'I'm sorry? Same what?'

'MO, Mr Benson. It's short for the Latin, *modus operandi*. They've been at it for some time, apparently. Attractive young girl, rich elderly man, and suddenly in through the door comes the husband. Pay up or else.'

'Good God!' said Benson. 'But then why isn't she in prison?'

'Very simply, because she always played the innocent party. The Director of Public Prosecutions, in his infinite wisdom, decided that there was no case against her.'

Benson shook his head unbelievingly. Then he looked up and smiled. A crooked smile. 'No fool like an old fool, eh?' he said.

'This so-called husband. Was it the man in the photograph I showed you, Mr Benson?'

'Yes, it was.' Benson frowned. 'D'you mean you knew all along?' he asked.

Fox smoothed his hand across his knee. 'We had a pretty good idea,' he said, and stood up.

'Will I be in any sort of trouble over this?' asked Benson as he escorted his visitors to the front door.

'That I can't say, Mr Benson. The matter will of course be the subject of a report to the Crown Prosecution Service, but I shouldn't worry too much if I were you.'

*

Detective Constable Ransome of the Sussex Police snatched up the phone. 'CID Brighton,' he said tersely, and for the next few minutes listened intently. He asked one or two questions and advised the caller to keep the information to himself. Then he dipped the receiver rest and dialled the direct-line number for the Flying Squad at New Scotland Yard. 'DI Gilroy, please,' he said when the Squad operator replied.

*

'I am Inspecteur Principal Ronsard, m'sieur. You are Anton Desfarges?'

'That is so, m'sieur.' The café owner wiped the copper top of the bar and dropped the cloth out of sight. 'You would like a drink, perhaps, m'sieur?'

'Beer.'

Desfarges turned away and paused. '*Pression*?' He was about fifty and heavily built. There were a few strands of black hair across his otherwise bald head and he had a large moustache. He had the look of a man who perspired a lot. He was perspiring now.

'Yes.'

Desfarges began the laborious task of filling a glass with frothy beer. When he had finished he put it on the bar, pointedly placing the till receipt next to it. 'How can I help you, m'sieur?'

'You know an Englishman called Thomas Harley?' Ronsard took a sip of beer.

'Perhaps.' Desfarges shrugged.

'I suggest that you think carefully,' said Ronsard. 'It is a serious matter.'

'It is difficult,' said Desfarges. 'So many customers come here in the season. So many English.'

'Perhaps this will help.' Ronsard laid a copy of the golf club photograph on the bar. Knowing Harley's predilection for Nice and

Cannes, Fox had left several copies with Ronsard when he had been over to see Jeremy Benson.

Desfarges looked closely at the photograph. 'Ah yes, of course. Now I remember ... and that is his wife, Jane, isn't it?'

'She was here with him?'

'Sometimes.'

'You knew him well, this Harley?'

Desfarges shrugged again and held out his hands, palms uppermost. 'A little.'

'Well enough to give him a reference when he wanted to rent a house ... in England.'

Avoiding Ronsard's gaze, Desfarges screwed up the till receipt and tossed it on the floor behind him. 'It was business,' he said.

'What sort of business?'

'May I be perfectly frank, M'sieur l'Inspecteur?'

'I hope that you would not be anything else,' said Ronsard.

'I was doing him a favour. He has been in here many times over the years. Spends a lot of money. One day he asked me if I would vouch for him if I got a telephone call. It was of no importance. As you say, he wanted to rent a house. He asked that if anyone was to telephone to enquire if he was a reliable person ...' Desfarges waggled his head from side to side. He seemed to be sweating more now. 'There was no harm. It happens all the time. It is business.' Desfarges looked nervously at Ronsard. 'I hope there is no trouble, m'sieur. Has M'sieur Harley done something wrong?'

'The English police think that he may have committed a murder, m'sieur,' said Ronsard and laid a ten-franc piece on the bar before walking out into the sunshine.

*

'Just had a call from the CID at Brighton, sir,' said Gilroy.

'Oh yeah, and what did they want?'

'They think that our man's surfaced at one of the bigger hotels down there, sir.'

'Really?' Fox sounded less than enthusiastic. 'How many's that we've had, Jack?'

Gilroy thought for a second or two. 'About twenty-five, I suppose, sir.'

'Damned right,' said Fox. 'Cornwall, Sheffield, Edinburgh and Manchester, to name but a few. What's so special about this one?'

'This bloke claims to have worked in the South of France until the end of the season and has produced references to back it up. They've taken him on as a floor waiter.'

'Ah!' said Fox, 'that's a bit better. Whereabouts in the South of France?'

'Nice, sir.'

'And have they checked the references?'

'No, sir.'

'Bloody marvellous,' said Fox. 'And these people wonder why they get ripped off. Send Fletcher down there and tell him to take a discreet look at this finger and see what he thinks. And tell him to get photostats of those references. We'll get Ronsard in Nice to make a few enquiries. What name's this character using, incidentally?'

'Spencer, sir.'

Fox sighed. 'You could have said that in the first place, Jack.'

Gilroy grinned. 'I thought I'd keep the best bit till last, guv,' he said.

*

The clerk placed a form on Fox's desk. There was a sheaf of receipts attached to it.

'What's that lot?' asked Fox.

'DS Crozier's expenses for his trip across to France, Mr Fox.'

'He didn't waste any time,' said Fox. Slowly he stood up and jabbed a finger at the total. 'Is this a bloody joke?' he yelled.

But the clerk had already gone.

*

Gilroy tapped on Fox's office door and went straight in. 'Fletcher's just back from Brighton, sir,' he said. 'He had a good look at this Spencer, the floor waiter, and he reckons it's definitely Harley ... at least, as far as he can tell from the photograph. And that's the best we can do until we nick him. There's no way that we can get Hawkins to ID him, of course. Not until Harley's in custody. Apart from which it might bugger up the case ... when eventually we get it all to court.'

'Hawkins? Who's Hawkins? I'm losing track of this job, Jack.'

'Hawkins is the manager of the hotel that was ripped off, guv.'

'What about the references, Jack?'

'Already in hand, sir. They were faxed across to Ronsard yesterday.'

'I'd better give him a bell,' said Fox. 'Just to gee him up a bit.'

*

'There are times when I think that I'm doing more work for this M'sieur Fox of Scotland Yard than I'm doing for France,' said Ronsard, sighing heavily as he put down the phone after yet another conversation with the head of the Flying Squad.

The first call he had to make on Fox's behalf was to finish off the enquiry about the references that Harley had given when he rented the house on Kingston Hill. But at least this call was almost a pleasure.

It was a large and elegant villa, discreetly hidden by palm trees, in the Carabacel district, not far to the west of the Quai Gallieni. The maid who opened the door bobbed briefly before leading Ronsard into a richly furnished room and inviting him to take a seat. A few moments later she returned with a glass of pastis and a jug of water.

Ronsard was just taking his first sip when the door opened again. Madam Calmet was at least sixty but in extremely good shape for a woman of her age. Her short dark hair was immaculately arranged and she wore a flowing, floor-length gown. When she saw Ronsard she held out both hands, each heavy with costly rings, and advanced on him. 'My dear inspector,' she said. 'What a pleasant surprise.' She took his right hand in one of hers and gently patted the back of it with the other as she spoke.

'Madame.' Ronsard inclined his head.

'But, you are looking well.' Madame Calmet beamed at him. Then she relinquished her hold on his hand. 'Wait,' she said, 'I have something to show you.' She walked towards the door and spoke briefly to someone in the hall. Seconds later, she ushered in an attractive girl of about nineteen dressed in a diaphanous chiffon creation that dipped daringly at the neckline. 'This is Lisa, my latest girl. Do you not think that she is beautiful?'

'Very,' said Ronsard. 'But, madame, I am here on business. Police business.' He smiled at the older woman.

Madame Calmet shrugged and spread her hands. 'It is a dull day when you cannot take a little time for pleasure, m'sieur,' she said, shepherding the young woman out again and closing the door behind her.

Ronsard laughed. 'You are always trying to tempt me, madame,' he said.

Madame Calmet laughed too. 'And one day I shall succeed, m'sieur,' she said. 'Now what is this important police business you wish to discuss with me? There are no irregularities here. You must know that. Everything is conducted properly —'

Ronsard held up his hand. 'Madame,' he said, 'this concerns a man you may know. An Englishman called Thomas Harley.'

Madame Calmet clapped her hands together. 'Of course,' she said. 'A real English gentleman.'

'How did you come to meet him?'

The woman shook her head gravely. 'You are making jokes, m'sieur?' she asked. 'How do you think I met him? He is a client here. As I said, he was the perfect gentleman. He treated my girls so well. Always courteous. And he always gave them little gifts, you know. A very generous man.' She looked dreamily at the large ormolu clock on the mantelshelf behind Ronsard. 'If I had been a little younger, who knows …'

'You knew him well enough to give him a reference when he was renting a house in England, then?'

'Of course. What are these questions about?' Madame Calmet suddenly became incisive again.

'It is an enquiry from Scotland Yard.'

'From Scotland Yard? Now you are definitely making jokes. You are telling me that Scotland Yard are making enquiries about a man renting a house in England? Pah! I do not believe it.'

'It is true, madame.'

'But why? What is wrong with that?'

'There is nothing wrong about renting the house, madame, but murdering people is against the law in England … as it is in France, and it seems that —'

'Murder!' Madame Calmet put both hands to her cheeks. 'I do not believe it,' she said. 'There must be a mistake.'

'It is not known for certain, of course.'

'And to think that he would come here regularly and would be with my girls … alone. It is terrible.'

'Do not distress yourself, madame. It was not that sort of murder. I do not think that your girls were in any sort of danger, and even if he comes here again —'

Madame Calmet let out a hoot of derision. 'Come here again, m'sieur? I tell you, he will not set foot in my house again. A murderer indeed.'

'That is not known for certain, madame,' said Ronsard again. Wearily this time. 'The police in London want to talk to him about a murder. It does not mean he did it.'

Madame Calmet shook her head slowly. 'There was always something about that one,' she said. 'Something that I did not like. He had a beautiful wife, you know.'

'So I have heard, madame.'

'I saw him with her at a restaurant one evening. At least, I imagine it was his wife. They weren't talking to each other very much …' Madame Calmet gave an elegant shrug of the shoulders. 'She had good hips, that girl. So why, I asked myself, should he have to come here? I don't understand why he wanted my young ladies.'

'There is an English saying,' said Ronsard, 'that a change is as good as a rest.'

'Huh!' said Madame Calmet scornfully. 'He would never have got a rest here. Not with my girls.'

*

'Ronsard's been on the phone, sir,' said Gilroy. 'Reckons his *commissaire* wants to know if we're going to put him on our payroll.'

'Bloody frogs,' said Fox darkly. 'Any joy?'

'Not a lot, guv,' said Gilroy. 'The two hotels where Spencer claims to have worked have never heard of him, and certainly never gave references to a person of that name. According to Ronsard they expressed some surprise that anyone should think that they'd employ an Englishman as a waiter in the first place.'

'Chauvinist bastards.'

'As for the two references that Harley gave Davidson when he took the house at Kingston Hill, guv'nor, well they both exist, for what that's worth. One's a bar-keeper who saw Harley from time to time … as a customer only. The other keeps a brothel. Harley was quite a regular visitor there, it seems.'

'Hope he caught something nasty,' said Fox.

*

'We'll play this low-key, Jack,' said Fox. 'It doesn't matter how few people we tell, some bastard'll let the cat out of the bag, that's for sure.'

'What d'you want me to lay on, then, sir?'

'You and Percy Fletcher can hover. And I want Henry Findlater and his team standing by, ready to house this character if I can persuade him to take it on the toes. And you can tell Henry from me that if he loses him I'll have his guts for garters.' Fox smoothed his hand across the top of his desk and smiled. It was a disconcerting sort of smile. 'Rosie Webster and I will do the business. Simple.'

Gilroy sighed inaudibly. 'Yes, sir,' he said. He had been involved in some of Fox's simple jobs before. And some of them had gone horribly wrong.

Chapter Seventeen

The following afternoon, the Flying Squad went to Brighton. Not all of them, of course, but enough. Swann drove Fox's Ford Granada with Fox and Rosie in the back, and Gilroy and Fletcher were in a second car, which, Fox had said, should make its own way there. Discreetly, he added. Whatever that meant. He did not, he emphasised, want a convoy turning up at the hotel. DI Henry Findlater had made his own arrangements. His task was to make sure that the man the Squad had gone to Brighton to see was not lost.

At about four o'clock the Granada swept on to the forecourt of the hotel and stopped. Immediately, a top-hatted linkman stepped forward and opened the door. Despite his attempt at restraint, he found his gaze transfixed by Rosie Webster's nylon-clad knees as she swung her long legs gracefully out of the car. It was only when she stood up that the linkman discovered that she was taller than he was. He hurriedly redirected his attention to Fox and touched his hat. 'Will your chauffeur be staying at the hotel, sir?' he asked.

'Certainly not,' said Fox, and taking Rosie's arm led her into the entrance hall.

'Do you have a booking, sir?' asked the receptionist.

'Yes,' said Fox airily. 'Mr and Mrs Newman.'

Rosie Webster turned away to examine a show-case full of china animals, unable to restrain a smile.

The receptionist fiddled briefly with her computer terminal and then returned. 'Room two-one-seven, sir,' she said, and touched a bell on the desk.

A bell-boy appeared in traditional livery complete with pill-box hat. 'D'you have any luggage, sir?' he asked.

'Only this,' said Fox handing over his briefcase.

'This way, sir. It's on the second floor,' said the boy and led the way across the lobby.

Despite his earlier intention not to inform anyone of the Squad's operation, Fox had realised that he would have to take the hotel manager into his confidence. Otherwise, he might have finished up on a floor that was not served by the man under surveillance.

It was an elegant room, looking out on to the front of the hotel, dominated by a large double bed and comfortably furnished with armchairs and a coffee table.

'With any luck we'll only be here half an hour,' said Fox as the door closed behind the bell-boy, 'so you needn't make yourself at home.'

'Nothing was further from my thoughts, sir,' said Rosie with an impish grin and a glance at the bed.

'Good.' Fox opened his briefcase and taking out his personal radio made a call to satisfy himself that DI Findlater and his men were in position. Then he rang room service and ordered a bottle of Bollinger. 'The Commissioner can pay for that,' he added as he put the phone down.

It was a good seven or eight minutes before the knock came at the door, by which time Fox and Rosie were seated in the two armchairs. The waiter entered, placed the ice bucket containing the champagne on a side-table, and put the two flutes beside it.

'Shall I open the bottle, sir?'

'Yes, please,' said Fox.

As the waiter went about the business of stripping off the foil and easing the wire cage from the top of the bottle, Fox studied him. He was of medium height, and had the smooth, refined features so often to be found in thieves who specialised in hotel crime. His hair was combed flat to his head, conveying an indefinable air of servility, and although the style was different from that in the photograph taken at the golf club there was no mistaking the facial similarity. Fox was quite satisfied that the man now gently twisting the cork from the champagne bottle with an assiduous panache was Thomas Harley.

'Isn't your name Harley?' asked Fox, managing to inject an inflection of doubt into his voice.

There was not a flicker of reaction, save for a slight tightening of the waiter's grasp on the neck of the bottle as he poured the champagne. 'I think you must be confusing me with someone else, sir,' he said calmly, shooting a quick sideways glance at Fox. 'My name's Spencer, sir.' With a deferential smile, he handed one flute to Rosie and the other to Fox.

'Will that be all, sir?' he asked, in the manner of a servant confidently expecting a tip.

Fox took a sip of champagne. 'I must be mistaken, then,' he said, 'but you look very much like a man called Harley. I've got it. There was a picture of him in the papers. Something about him being missing from home.' He paused, a puzzled expression on his face. 'Or was it something to do with a jewel robbery …?' There had been nothing in the papers to connect Harley with a jewel robbery; Fox had made sure of that. But Harley could not be so certain. 'Perhaps you just look like him,' added Fox.

'I'm sorry, sir,' said Spencer. 'I've only recently returned from the South of France. Been there for some years, as a matter of fact.' He carefully replaced the bottle in the ice bucket and walked slowly towards the door. Then he paused with his hand on the knob. 'If there's anything else, sir, just ring. I'm the waiter for this floor.'

As the door closed, Fox leaned over and took his personal radio from his briefcase once again. 'He's a cool customer, I'll say that for him, Rosie,' he said, and then addressed himself to the radio. 'Henry, this is Fox. Our man's up and running. Or I'm a Dutchman,' he added. Then he took another sip of champagne. 'Good health, Rosie,' he said. 'Be a shame to waste this.'

'As a matter of interest, sir, why have you decided not to nick him straightaway?'

'Because, Rosie, I am hoping that he'll make for his bolt-hole, wherever that is. And that if we wait long enough his blonde accomplice will turn up.'

DI Henry Findlater's team of surveillance officers were fanned out around the hotel, covering the service entrances as well as the main door. Findlater was in his element with this type of operation and had spent several years as the officer in charge of one of the Criminal Intelligence Branch's surveillance units before transferring to the Flying Squad. Fresh-faced and youthful-looking, he had barely met the minimum height limit prevailing at the time he had joined the police. That, added to his portly appearance and the owl-like glasses he wore, made him seem an unlikely policeman. All of which was an advantage to a surveillance officer.

Nevertheless, the speed at which the bogus waiter departed nearly took them by surprise. It was obvious that he had only paused to strip off his white waiter's jacket and put on a blazer before running out of the back door of the hotel into the car park. He made his way quickly to a red Ford Escort XR3i and drove off at high speed.

Swann, eating a sandwich and sitting behind the wheel of Fox's Granada, saw Spencer's racing start and smirked. 'That's it, my son,' he said to himself. 'Give it all you've got.'

But Findlater's team were a match for the fleeing waiter, and by the time Spencer had cleared Brighton on the A23, the surveillance officers were well placed to maintain observation. One vehicle was ahead of Spencer and two behind. All three changed places from time to time — a system the police called leap-frogging — but just to be on the safe side Findlater had deployed two motorcyclists as well. Each was a former traffic patrol officer and had passed out of the Hendon Driving School with an advanced classification.

It had obviously not crossed Spencer's mind that he could have been followed, particularly as Fox had been careful not to reveal that he was a police officer. Nevertheless, he studiously observed the speed limits, and even on the motorway resisted the temptation to drive faster than seventy miles an hour. He certainly had no desire to be stopped by the traffic police.

At Junction 7, Spencer joined the M25, going clockwise, and merged with the heavy traffic. But Findlater's men were still with him.

When Spencer reached Junction 10, still driving impeccably, he turned off the motorway, north towards London. All the time the surveillance officers maintained a running commentary and succeeded in keeping their target in sight.

Fox and Rosie, meanwhile, had finished their champagne and were being driven by Swann over the same route as that taken by the suspect. From time to time Fox told Swann to slow down; wherever Spencer was going, he would be surrounded by surveillance officers and would not be allowed to escape until Fox arrived.

After following the A3 for a short distance, Spencer turned off at Pain's Hill and eventually came to a standstill in the driveway of a secluded house in the countryside around the pretty Surrey village of Stoke d'Abernon.

*

It was nearing seven o'clock when Swann drove slowly into the road leading to Spencer's final destination.

Fox got out and walked up to Findlater's car. 'Well done, Henry,' he said. 'Anything to report?'

'He arrived about forty minutes ago, sir. Let himself in with a key. Then we sighted him through the downstairs front-room window. He switched on the lights and just before he pulled the curtains he turned on the television and poured himself a Scotch. Well, I think it was Scotch, sir.'

Fox grinned, 'I'll forgive you if it was cold tea,' he said. 'How many of you on this stunt, Henry?'

'I used eight altogether, sir. I hope that was all right.'

'Perfect,' said Fox. 'Hang on.' He walked back to his car and opened the boot. Returning to Findlater, he handed him a bottle of Scotch. 'That's for your lads,' he said. 'But not before you've put the cars to bed. You can send them home now. And thanks.'

Gilroy and Fletcher joined Fox and Rosie Webster. 'What's the score, guv'nor?' asked Gilroy.

'Get the cars out of sight, Jack, then we'll go and have a chat with our Mr Spencer ... or in my case, another chat. I've got some scores to settle with him personally.'

Fletcher was deputed to knock at the front door while the other three remained out of sight.

After a few moments Spencer opened the door. Since arriving, he had changed into a pair of casual trousers, a shirt, and a sweater with a motif on it.

'Tom Harley?' asked Fletcher.

'Yes.'

'Jim Murchison sent me,' said Fletcher and offered to shake hands. With an involuntary reaction, Harley held out his hand. In one fast flowing movement, Fletcher seized the other's wrist, jerked it and turned his man so that Harley suddenly found himself with his face against the wall, his arm secured in a painful hammer lock and bar.

'What the bloody hell —?'

Fox appeared from outside. 'Well done, Perce. Not bad for an old man.'

Harley turned his head. 'Look, I can explain,' he spluttered, still believing that Murchison's friends had come to sort him out.

'Oh, you're going to, my son, believe me,' said Fox. 'In fact, you and I are going to do quite a lot of talking.'

Recognition dawned. 'Here,' said Harley, 'I know you. What's the problem?'

'The champagne was not chilled to the correct temperature,' said Fox and beckoned Rosie and Gilroy to come into the house.

For a moment Harley believed him. 'You surely haven't followed me all this way just to —' He stopped suddenly as the absurdity of his own words became apparent to him. 'What the hell's going on here?' he asked.

'Release him, Perce,' said Fox, 'and make sure he's not carrying.'

Fletcher let go of his prisoner and quickly searched him. Then he stepped back. 'Clean, guv,' he said.

'I am Thomas Fox … of the Flying Squad,' said Fox, 'and you and I have got some serious talking to do. Oh, as a matter of interest, where is your blonde girlfriend?'

'I'm saying nothing,' said Harley.

'Interesting,' said Fox. 'That means she's expected. Perce, go and loiter in the bushes, there's a good chap, so that when her ladyship arrives she won't be tempted to do a runner when she finds that we're holding a party in her house. She's got form for doing a runner.'

Fox led the way into the sitting room, turned off the television and looked round. 'Do yourself quite well, don't you, Thomas?' he said.

'Now look here.' Harley spoke with an upper-class drawl which Fox presumed was his natural accent. 'I don't know what this is all about, but if you haven't got a search warrant you'd better get off my premises now.'

'We don't need a warrant,' said Fox, still appraising the richly furnished room. 'You invited us in.' He met Harley's gaze. 'Now sit down and make yourself comfortable. This could take some time.'

Harley sat down and crossed his legs, looking perfectly composed. 'What exactly do you want?' he asked. He had lost none of the coolness that he had displayed when Fox had confronted him in the hotel.

'We have quite a few questions to put to you about certain matters,' said Fox. 'But I think it would be a good idea if we waited until your accomplice arrives. When is that likely to be?'

'As you're so damned clever,' said Harley, 'I suggest that you find out. If I remember correctly, I'm not obliged to say anything unless I wish to do so.'

'My word,' said Fox. 'You sound as though you've been in trouble with the police before.' But Fox knew that Harley had no criminal record ... so far. 'Or is it that you just watch a lot of television?' He glanced at the ceiling, apparently in thought. 'No,' he continued, 'it can't be that, otherwise you'd have muttered some American jargon about reading your rights.' He looked at Harley and smiled. 'Well,' he said, 'you needn't think that I'm going to sit here all night waiting.' He turned to Gilroy. 'We'll take Mr Harley to Bow Street and lock him up, Jack. Leave a team here and wait for the woman. When you've arrested her you can take her to ...' Fox looked thoughtful. 'Better make it Paddington, I think. Then we can talk to them another day. Next week, even ... if it takes that long.'

'I don't know what you're talking about.' Harley clearly did not like the sound of the arrangements; he was showing his first signs of panic. Until now he had thought that he might be able to talk his way out of whatever the police suspected him of. But then he didn't know Tommy Fox, and he didn't know just how much Fox knew. Furthermore, he had never fallen foul of the Flying Squad before. And that, he was about to discover, was a whole new experience.

'They all say that,' said Fox.

'I tell you, I don't know this blonde woman you're talking about,' said Harley regaining his composure. 'But I warn you, when I get hold of my solicitor you're going to have a lot of explaining to do.'

'Yes.' Fox appeared unconcerned by the threat.

'Yes, really. Forcing your way into my house, assaulting me, holding me prisoner and making threats.'

'Sounds quite serious,' said Fox conversationally, allowing his glance to travel round the room once more. 'I must say, Thomas, old fruit, you seem to have done awfully well for a waiter. They obviously pay you handsomely in the South of France. I'm surprised you came back.'

'I'm beginning to wish I hadn't,' said Harley with feeling.

'Rosie,' said Fox suddenly. 'Have a gander round upstairs. See if you can see any trace of a female resident.' For the next few minutes Fox ambled about the room humming an unrecognisable tune.

'Nothing, sir,' said Rosie, returning from her examination of the bedrooms. 'There's no clothing, no perfume, and nothing in the bathroom that would indicate a woman's presence.'

'Oh, well.' Fox shrugged. 'There's no future in that, then.'

Fletcher was called back inside and instructed to send for reinforcements. Within forty minutes of his putting the phone down, six Flying Squad officers in the shapes of Detective Inspector Denzil Evans, Detective Sergeant Crozier and four DCs arrived at the front door of Thomas Harley's house at Stoke d'Abernon.

'Right,' said Fox. 'Got a job for you, Denzil.' He took a form from his briefcase, filled in a few details and scrawled his signature at the bottom. 'Just to be on the safe side,' he said, 'as we're in alien territory, there's a superintendent's written order to search. So get searching. You know what we're looking for.' He held on to the form for long enough to make Evans hesitate. 'And don't bugger up any fingerprints, Denzil. They could be crucial in this case.'

'Right, sir,' said Evans, piqued that Fox should think he needed telling.

'And now,' continued Fox, turning to Rosie, Gilroy and Fletcher, 'we shall remove our Mr Harley to Bow Street police station.'

*

'What d'you make of him, then, guv'nor?' asked Gilroy in the car on the way back to London.

'Bogus,' said Fox. 'Very bogus. Probably the sort of chap who carries a comb.'

Chapter Eighteen

Detective Inspector Denzil Evans was not greatly taken with being dragged away from a promising observation in order to search some damned house that was not even in the Metropolitan Police District. Particularly as the observation might, just might, have led to the arrest of a villain he had been seeking for some time. But a summons from the head of the Flying Squad was not a thing to be ignored.

The simple solution, as far as Evans was concerned, was to search the house as quickly as possible. And the only way to do that, without incurring Fox's wrath for missing something that might be important, was to do it methodically.

He split his team up and directed them to start with the loft, the garage, the outhouse and the dustbins because in his experience, the lofts, garages, outhouses and dustbins were nearly always the places where searching policemen found what they were looking for. Good, hard, incontrovertible evidence.

Evans himself, working on the principle that the leader of the team should not add to the confusion by taking part in the search, wandered around the ground floor of the house, looking at various books and ornaments. In the large sitting room he came across Thomas Harley's grand piano, a huge white instrument. Evans sat down and opened the lid of the keyboard. He rubbed his hands together and with a brief smile of pleasure, started to play a Rifkinesque version of 'The Entertainer'. To him it seemed eminently suited to the occasion.

To the accompaniment of Evans' ragtime, DS Crozier and DC Bellenger climbed reluctantly into the loft and started poking about. And got dirty. But they also got lucky.

'Guv!' Crozier shouted down through the loft trap. There was no reply. He shouted again and the music stopped.

'What?' Somewhat irritably, Evans closed the lid of the piano and stood up.

'There's something in the cold water tank. Up here in the loft.'

'It's not a ball, about five inches in diameter, attached to the side of the tank by a metal rod, is it?' asked Evans sarcastically as he mounted the stairs.

Crozier groaned. 'No, guv. It looks like a plastic box.'

'Bloody hell,' said Evans, and climbed the loft ladder.

'Mind you don't put your foot through the ceiling,' said Crozier helpfully as Evans joined him.

'I have been in a bloody loft before,' said Evans. 'Now, what are we looking at?'

'It's in the tank, guv.'

'I know it's in the tank. Give us some bloody light.' Evans took the proffered torch and directed the beam into the water. Lying on the bottom of the tank was a plastic box about nine inches long by six inches wide. 'What's that, then?'

'Dunno, guv.'

'Well fetch it out.' Evans stood upright and banged his head on a beam. 'Sod it!' he added.

Crozier, remembering that Fox had made a point about not ruining any fingerprints, said, 'Bit risky, guv'nor. We might cock it up. I think it'd be a good idea if we got the fingerprint blokes down here straightaway and let them do it. They've got all the gear. If there's any dabs on the outside of that thing, we might smudge them.'

For a moment or two, Evans gazed intently at his sergeant. 'Yes,' he said slowly, 'I think you're right, Ron. Get on the dog-and-bone and give 'em a bell, there's a good chap.' Crozier sighed and started to descend the loft ladder. 'And once you've done that, you can give the other lads a hand with the garage,' added Evans, looking down through the trap.

*

The fingerprint team arrived two hours later and made a big thing of examining what they described as 'the problem.' They drained the cold water tank and carefully removed the plastic box with a pair of giant callipers.

'Ever tried your hand at one of those machines in an amusement arcade where you try to pick up a bar of chocolate?' asked Evans, leaning against an upright with his hands in his pockets.

The fingerprint experts placed the box in a large container and put it in the back of their van.

'Can't you tell me what's in it?' asked Evans, who was now thoroughly irritated by the whole procedure.

'Yeah,' said the fingerprint officer, 'when we get back to the Yard. It's all taped up, you see.' He paused on the doorstep. 'You coming then, guv?'

'Don't seem to have much option,' said Evans moodily. 'Bloody prima donnas,' he added as he followed them out of the door.

*

'We've just had a message from Denzil Evans, sir,' said Gilroy.

Fox yawned and stretched. 'What did he have to say?'

'He's found a package in the cold water tank of Harley's house at Stoke d'Abernon.'

'Well, what's in it, Jack? Or is Denzil keeping that a secret?'

Gilroy shrugged. 'No idea, sir. Denzil said he didn't want to bugger up the fingerprints, so he got the experts to go down there and take it back to the Yard.'

'Bloody terrific,' said Fox.

*

Woman Detective Constable Marilyn Lester glanced at the monitor in the Special Branch office at Heathrow Airport and saw that the Air France Boeing 727 from Nice had touched down right on schedule at twenty minutes to one. For a brief moment she considered skipping it and going to lunch. Then she changed her mind, picked up her suspect book, and strolled out to the controls.

The flight was packed, mainly with the sort of well-heeled passengers who could afford not only to go to the South of France, but could do so mid-week, to avoid the package holiday crowds.

The blonde caught WDC Lester's eye immediately, mainly because she was wearing a shoulder-length wig, albeit an expensive one. Tall — she must have been five feet nine even without her three-inch heels — and with an enviable figure, she was dressed in a cool ice-blue dress and wore dark glasses of the same discreet good quality as the soft leather overnight bag she carried. She placed her passport firmly in front of the immigration officer and glanced away with a bored expression.

'Would you mind removing your sunglasses, madam?' said the IO.

The woman did so, slowly and with a slightly disdainful look of appraisal as though the IO had recently crept out from under something unsavoury.

'Thank you,' said the IO, adding with a smile, 'but the photograph is not a very good likeness.'

'Are they ever?' said the woman.

The IO was in the act of returning the passport when Marilyn Lester leaned across and took it from him. The photograph was of a woman with short brown hair and horn-rimmed glasses. The detective compared it with the face of the woman in front of her and could see that, in addition to the wig, she was now wearing contact lenses. 'Mrs Susan Harley, I am a police officer,' said Marilyn. 'Would you come over here, please.'

Still keeping hold of the passport, WDC Lester stepped away from the immigration desk. The two or three passengers who had been waiting immediately behind Susan Harley stared with that conceited expression of innocent curiosity that international travellers reserve for other people they think have just been caught by the customs or some other branch of authority.

'What is this about?' asked Susan Harley haughtily.

'There is a warrant in existence for your arrest,' said WDC Lester, 'in connection with a jewellery theft.'

'What on earth are you talking about?'

'The warrant has been taken out in the name of Detective Chief Superintendent Fox of the Flying Squad,' said WDC Lester. 'More than that I can't tell you, I'm afraid.'

'Good God, is this what you get for reporting your husband missing?' said Susan Harley bitterly. 'I answered all that man's questions. Anyway, I'm hardly running away, am I? I'm actually coming into the country ... and travelling on my own passport.'

'Is there any reason why you should not travel on your own passport, Mrs Harley?' asked WDC Lester drily, and taking the woman's arm by way of token apprehension, led her to the Special Branch office.

*

Fox put his head round the door of the Flying Squad office. 'Any messages?' he asked.

'Yes, sir,' said a DC. 'Two. One's from Special Branch at Heathrow. They've nicked Susan Harley.'

'Have they now?' said Fox. 'Well, well. And the other?'

'From DI Evans, sir. Came in just after you left for Bow Street this morning. The package they found in Harley's house at Stoke d'Abernon contained a firearm.'

'Really?' said Fox. 'What sort of firearm?'

The DC glanced down at the message form. 'A three-eight Smith and Wesson, guv. They're doing it for dabs and ballistics now.'

'Splendid,' said Fox, beaming round at the occupants of the office. 'Every day in every way, things are getting better,' he said to no one in particular.

The DC waited until Fox had left the office, slamming the door behind him, and turned to his colleague. 'What the hell did that mean?' he asked.

*

Fox looked at Susan Harley — at the blonde wig and the ice-blue dress that did little to disguise her shapely figure — and wondered if the dowdy and unbecoming clothes she had worn previously had been a deliberate deception. 'Well, Mrs Harley, quite a change in appearance, eh?'

'I told that woman who arrested me that I've answered all your questions. This is an outrage. All I did was to report Tom missing. I demand to see my solicitor.'

'I'm sure you do,' said Fox, drawing a chair up to the table and laying out his cigarette case and lighter. He knew that only one person could actually have fired the gun that killed Donald Dixon, and the most important thing right now was for that person to be charged with his murder. Fox had not ruled out Jane Meadows entirely, but he was fairly certain that she had been telling the truth when she claimed to know nothing of Dixon's death, even though she had helped to bury him. Added to which, it was fairly evident that she had been cruelly used by Harley, who had tossed her aside when she had served her purpose.

That left the Harleys, husband and wife, and he couldn't wait to see them start accusing each other.

'Incidentally,' began Fox, pointing, 'that is a tape recorder and everything you say will be recorded and may be used in evidence.' He nodded to Rosie Webster, who switched on the machine. 'Now then,' continued Fox, 'I have reason to believe that you and your husband were both involved in the theft of a quantity of jewellery from a London hotel on the twelfth of July last —'

'Is this some kind of a joke?' asked Susan Harley.

Fox raised his eyebrows and assumed a pained expression. 'Talking of jokes,' he said, 'why did you inform the police that your husband was missing from home when it now appears that you knew precisely where he was?'

Susan Harley half raised her hands and then allowed them to fall to her lap. 'I didn't know where he was,' she said in resigned tones. 'In fact, I still don't.' For a moment or two she looked thoughtfully around the predominantly green interview room. 'I can't say I'm surprised, though,' she said.

'Oh? Why is that?'

'Women,' she said simply. 'He spent all his money on other women.' She paused to allow herself a sly smile. 'I suppose he thought that by disappearing he could just start up again somewhere else with whoever's taken his fancy this time.'

'I see,' said Fox, giving the impression that he believed every word. 'Let's discuss this jewel theft, then.'

'I've no idea what you're talking about,' said Susan Harley and suddenly started to cry. It was a very convincing performance, but one to which Fox was quite accustomed. And it was one of the reasons why Rosie Webster was sitting only feet away from the woman, watching her impassively. Fox was unimpressed and waited for the act to finish.

Susan Harley dabbed at her eyes, being careful not to smudge her mascara, and looked up. 'I'm sorry,' she said. 'But I just can't understand why you're talking to me about a jewel robbery.'

Fox was quite ready to destroy what he saw as Susan Harley's implausible play-acting, but he knew that the more he could get her to say, the more likely it was that she would finish up contradicting herself … and everyone else for that matter. 'Mrs Harley,' he said, 'your husband is strongly suspected of stealing jewellery from a West End hotel, jewellery to the value of one hundred thousand pounds.'

Susan Harley took a deep breath. She had gone pale and for a moment Fox thought that she was going to faint as Jane Meadows had done. But this woman was made of sterner stuff. 'This is all too fantastic for words,' she said slowly. 'My husband is an insurance broker. He arranges cover against things being stolen. He doesn't steal them himself.' She gave a brief, bitter laugh. 'It ... well, I mean —'

Fox threw the post-mortem photograph of Donald Dixon on the table. 'Know this man, do you?' he asked.

Susan Harley leaned forward. 'Yes,' she said, and sat back sharply.

'Tell me about it.'

'But what is it? What's this man ...?' She lapsed into silence, apparently unable to take in the events of the day.

'That man is Donald Dixon,' said Fox, 'and I'm particularly interested to know how he finished up in a grave in the middle of Devon, in a coffin with your husband's name on it.'

'Devon? A coffin? Tom's name?' Susan Harley was clearly becoming genuinely distraught.

Fox, however, was not yet convinced that this woman opposite him was not a brilliant actress. 'How did you come to know that man?' Fox pointed at the photograph.

Susan Harley sighed. It was a sigh of resignation. 'He came to the house one day.'

'With another man?' Fox took a guess.

'Yes.' She spoke softly.

'Would you speak more loudly, Mrs Harley, please.'

'Yes,' she said again.

'What did they want?'

'They pushed their way in and started making threats. They said that if Tom didn't pay up they'd kill him. I was absolutely terrified. I had no idea what it was all about.'

'What did you do?'

'My first priority was to get them out of the house. To be quite honest, I thought they were going to rape me.'

'Where was your husband at this time?'

'Away on business, or so I thought. On reflection, he was probably with some woman somewhere.'

'And what did he have to say about the visit of these two men?'

'Oh, he just laughed it off. Said something about these people not understanding the way the system worked, and that they would get paid. He told me not to worry.'

Fox took a cigarette from the case on the table, tapped it thoughtfully and then lit it. 'As a matter of interest, Mrs Harley,' he said, 'why didn't you tell me of this visit when I saw you the first time ... at Kingston?'

Susan Harley appeared to give the question serious thought before answering. 'I suppose I half believed what my husband told me ... about it being all right. I wanted to believe it, but I was apprehensive. I honestly didn't think that it had anything to do with his disappearance. And anyway, I was scared that they might come back ... which they did. It's all very well to tell the police these things, but if they'd come back and threatened me ...' Her shoulders dropped resignedly. 'And they did.'

'I see. Another thing, Mrs Harley ...'

Susan Harley looked up. 'Yes?' She sounded drained of emotion.

'Why didn't you tell me that the house at Kingston was rented?'

'Why should I have done?' The question was hostile. 'I don't see what possible relevance that could have had to his being missing.'

Fox shrugged. 'No,' he said, 'but then you weren't investigating his disappearance.' Susan stared blankly at the detective. 'Your husband, Mrs Harley,' Fox went on, 'has been engaged in a life of crime — serious crime — for at least the past two years. He was dismissed from his job as an insurance broker because he had got into heavy debt. And it was debt of the worst possible kind. Bookmakers. Did these men say anything about gambling debts?'

Susan Harley shook her head miserably. 'No,' she said. 'But it's true about horses. Tom always liked racing, but I never thought that he was in trouble over it.'

'I think the short answer to that,' said Fox, 'is that he was forced to commit crime to appease the people to whom he owed these large sums of money. Fifteen thousand pounds is a figure that's been quoted.'

'Good God!'

'And you maintain that you knew nothing about your husband's criminal activities?'

'No, not a thing.' She sat in silence for some time and then looked up at Fox. 'D'you know where my husband is?' she asked.

'Your husband is in Cell Number Two at this police station,' said Fox.

'What?' Susan Harley was clearly astounded by Fox's revelation. 'Where did you find him?'

'In a house in Stoke d'Abernon, as a matter of fact.' Fox had decided that it was time to drive a wedge between husband and wife. 'He had been living there — on and off, as you might say — for the last year. We also arrested a very attractive blonde who was living with him.' That was not quite true, but it would do. 'They were going to get married, so she said. Prior to that, he lived in a house in Godalming, presumably with the same woman. I take it you knew nothing about that?'

'No.' Susan Harley gave an involuntary shudder and stared at Fox for some time. Then she pointed at his cigarette case. 'D'you think I could have one of those?' she asked.

Fox gave her a cigarette and then thumbed his lighter, holding it towards her.

She placed her hand on his and drew it towards the tip of her cigarette. 'I knew he was a womaniser,' she said resignedly, 'but I didn't know anything about this house in —' She broke off, a quizzical expression on her face.

'Stoke d'Abernon.'

'To think he's been cheating on me all that time.' She shook her head in disbelief. 'Well, I don't give a damn about the consequences. Not any more.'

'Why did you report your husband missing, Mrs Harley?'

'I honestly thought he'd been murdered by those two thugs, and I didn't see why they should get away with it.'

Fox leaned forward. 'You haven't told me everything, have you?'

For some time, Susan Harley sat unseeing, a glazed expression on her face. Then she sighed deeply. 'I knew there was something wrong,' she said at last. 'Men coming to the house, often late at night. Once they brought a van and put something in it out of the garage.'

'Could it have been a coffin?'

She looked at him, unbelieving, as though it was all a dream. 'I don't know,' she said and shrugged. 'I was in bed. To be honest, I didn't want to know.'

Fox rolled the ash carefully from his cigarette. 'Despite what you said previously, Mrs Harley, I would suggest that your husband was away from home more often than he was there.'

'Yes.'

'And that he returned after the time you said you saw him last?'

'Yes.'

Fox smiled at the thought that Dixon's body, in its coffin, was probably in the garage when DCI Barker from Kingston interviewed her. He would enjoy telling him that. 'Are you going to tell me why you suddenly disappeared after I saw you last, Mrs Harley?'

Susan Harley exhaled a long puff of smoke. 'I suppose that no matter what happens, a wife will always try to defend her husband,' she said.

'What happened?'

'One of the men who came to the house before came again. There was another man with him. Not that man …' She pointed at Dixon's picture. 'I'd not seen the other man before.'

'What did they want?'

'They said that they knew that I'd talked to the police about Tom and that if I knew what was good for me I wouldn't do so again. And just to make sure, they told me to go to France and stay there. Out of the way. They said that if I didn't, they would kill me.'

Fox held his hand out towards Rosie Webster. 'Give me that picture of the chap we've got banged up in Brixton,' he said being careful to avoid naming Murchison. 'Seen this man before?' he asked, handing the print to Susan Harley.

'Yes, that's him. That's …' She paused for a moment. 'That's Murchison,' she said.

'He told you his name, did he?'

'Yes. He said he was a business partner of Tom's.'

'So you went to France?'

'Yes. I was absolutely terrified. I didn't know where Tom was and I had no idea what was happening. The whole thing had become a nightmare.'

'Why then did you come back, Mrs Harley? What caused you to think that you would now be safe?'

'I saw it in the papers. That Murchison had been arrested, and that Dixon had been murdered. There was a photograph. That one.' She pointed at the photograph of Dixon that still lay on the table, the one that police had released in their first attempts to identify him.

'That wig you're wearing, Mrs Harley …'

'What about it?' She stroked at it self-consciously.

'How long have you owned it?'

'Oh, goodness, I don't know.' She thought for a moment. 'Must be about two years, I suppose.'

'And have you ever owned another?'

'No. Why d'you ask?'

Fox ignored the question. 'Would you be prepared to give a sample of your own hair. For scientific comparison.'

She looked puzzled, and then shrugged. 'Yes,' she said, 'but why?'

'Just to satisfy me that it does not match hair found in a wig used at the jewellery theft I was talking about earlier.'

'Yes, of course. I've nothing to worry about there. I told you, I know nothing about it.' She suddenly looked at Fox with a penetrating stare, and for the first time the hard lines around her mouth were quite marked. 'Who was this woman he was living with?' she asked.

'A very good-looking girl called Jane Meadows. Your husband told her that he was going to marry her and that they were going to live in the South of France. On the proceeds of the jewellery theft.'

Far from expressing signs of jealousy, Susan Harley just laughed. 'Silly little bitch,' she said. 'Didn't know what she was letting herself in for.'

Chapter Nineteen

Fox had decided to listen to the tape recording of his interview with Susan Harley before putting any questions to Thomas Harley. In fact he listened to it twice.

Then he sent for Denzil Evans. He wanted a first-hand account from him about what had been found in the house at Stoke d'Abernon.

'We took every bit of paper we could find, sir,' said DI Evans, 'although I suspect that most of it'll be bloody useless. But the most important thing of all was the gun.'

'Good bit of work that, Denzil. In the cold water tank in the loft, I believe?'

'Yes, sir.'

'Any particular reason for looking there?'

'Got to look everywhere, sir.' Evans sounded self-righteous. 'Start at the top and work your way down to the bottom. Found some interesting things in cold water tanks and lavatory cisterns in my time.'

'All right, Denzil, I know you're good. You keep telling me.'

'It was a three-eight Smith and Wesson, sir. The same calibre as the rounds they took out of Dixon. The shell cases were in there too.'

'Really? That's odd. When can we expect a result?'

'The lab boys are running tests now, sir. Shouldn't take long, sir. They'll let you know as soon as possible. The fingerprint lads have already given it the once over.'

'And?'

'Still waiting, guv.' Evans shrugged. 'Of course, there's not only the pistol, there's the box as well.'

'Box? What box?'

'The pistol was in a plastic box. One of those self-sealing things that you put your sandwiches in.'

'Put my sandwiches in? What the hell are you talking about, Denzil?'

'Well not you, perhaps, but some people, guv.' Evans backtracked rapidly.

'Really? How extraordinary.'

'It was sealed up with tape, sir, to stop the water getting in. So to be on the safe side I got the fingerprint lads to undo it. Like you said, didn't want to bugger up any impressions. Anyway, with any luck, there'll be some dabs on that too.'

'What about the house?'

'They've turned up several sets there, sir. They're checking those against main and scenes-of-crime collections now. The only thing they can be sure of to date is that Murchison's prints were not at Stoke d'Abernon.'

'I suppose that's useful,' said Fox. 'But for the moment I can't work out why.'

*

'It looks as though we're going to run out of custody time for Harley before Fingerprint Branch have finished, Jack,' said Fox as he and Gilroy drove from the Yard to Bow Street police station.

'Unless we charge him, sir,' said Gilroy.

'I'd rather not do that yet,' said Fox. 'We'd be safe enough putting him on the sheet for the theft, certainly, but I want him to think he's in the clear. Just for a while, anyway. And you can bet that he won't let us take his prints voluntarily. Not that a magistrate's order would be much good. Ever tried taking fingerprints by force, Jack?'

'Not lately, sir.'

'So we're just going to have to pretend.' And for the rest of the journey, Fox whistled variations on extracts from Bizet's *Carmen*. His own, unrecognisable variations.

The custody sergeant appeared with Thomas Harley, and went through the necessary paperwork before retiring to his office.

'Sit down and make yourself comfortable,' said Fox. 'This could take some time.'

'I am making a formal application to see my solicitor,' said Harley.

Fox glanced briefly over his shoulder as if expecting to see a High Court judge waiting there. 'What, now? But you haven't heard what I've got to say.'

'Unless you're about to say that you're releasing me with an apology, I'm not interested.'

Fox smiled. 'There's one thing that always impresses me, Jack,' he said to Gilroy. 'And that is a sense of humour in the face of adversity.'

'I'm quite serious about this,' said Harley. 'Apart from making a complaint to the appropriate authorities, I intend to start proceedings for wrongful arrest and false imprisonment.'

'Yes,' said Fox in an absent sort of way. 'I was about to say that it would be a waste of your money, Thomas, old dear, but then it's not your money, is it? You've nicked it all.'

'I'm warning you —'

'We have your wife in custody,' said Fox mildly.

Harley raised his eyebrows. 'You've what?'

'She was arrested yesterday, returning from Nice.'

Harley leaned back, a satisfied smile on his face. 'I'll bet she didn't like that.'

'No, she didn't. What she liked even less was to learn that you'd been screwing Jane Meadows.' Fox flicked a crumb off the table.

'How did she —? What d'you mean by —?'

'If you're wondering how she knew, I told her,' said Fox.

'You've no right —'

'And she also told us that you were responsible for the theft of the jewellery at the hotel on the twelfth of July, Thomas. The theft which has been occupying so much of my time.' Fox blithely reeled off the lie; it sounded convincing even to Gilroy. 'And a few strange tales about things that go bump in the night.'

'It's a pack of lies.'

'You had nothing to do with this jewellery theft, then?' Fox looked uninterested.

'It's the most ridiculous thing I've heard,' said Harley. 'I was in the South of France. It's obviously a case of mistaken identity.'

'Then you're prepared to give us the name of some person who can verify that. Madame Calmet at the brothel in Nice, perhaps?' Fox grinned insolently.

'I don't know what you're talking about. That stupid bitch of a wife of mine imagines these things,' said Harley.

'Yes,' said Fox casually, 'I should think that imagination plays quite a large part in your life. Anyway, time will tell. We've searched your house, by the way.'

'About the only jewellery you'll find there will be a couple of Susan's bead necklaces, I should think,' said Harley caustically. 'She's the one you ought to be talking to about jewellery theft.'

'But your wife claims that she knows nothing of the house at Stoke d'Abernon, much less been there,' said Fox. 'Anyway, we've recovered the jewellery.'

That clearly shook Harley. 'If you've recovered this jewellery you've been talking about, then,' he said, 'surely you've arrested someone?' But the statement was flat and unconvincing.

'Yes. A man called James Murchison. And he's not too impressed with you, Thomas, old love. Reckons you've tried to have him over.' Murchison hadn't actually said as much, attempting as he was to disengage himself from the heavy part of the proceedings, but Fox enjoyed mixing it for members of the villainry.

'I've never heard of him,' said Harley.

'Is that so? Then why, Thomas, were you so ready to shake hands with someone who knocked at your front door the other night and announced that he was Murchison's messenger?' Fox leaned across and took the pocket book that Gilroy was holding and turned a page. 'And to say, and I quote, "I can explain everything"?' Harley said nothing. Just sat and stared at Fox. 'And that brings me to my next point,' Fox continued. 'When we dug up the coffin — your coffin, Thomas — we found therein the body of Donald Dixon. You will also know that he had been murdered. I may say, purely as an aside, that the vicar of Cray Magna takes rather a poor view of people who con him into burying murder victims in his churchyard.'

'What has that to do with me?' Harley regarded Fox with a supercilious sneer. 'Thomas Harley is not exactly an uncommon name. I imagine there are quite a few graves with that name around the country. Are you going to produce someone who says that I had something to do with it? Someone in your debt, perhaps, who will perjure himself to say that I was there when in fact I was in the South of France.'

Fox leaned across the table until his face was within inches of Harley's. 'Cut the crap, mister,' he said. 'We've found the gun that killed Dixon, and we found it in the water tank in the loft of your drum at Stoke d'Abernon. And what's more, my friend, it's got your fingerprints all over it.' That wasn't true, of course. There were fingerprints on the box, certainly. But it had yet to be decided whose prints they were. Nor, indeed, had the gun yet been identified as the murder weapon.

Harley smiled disarmingly. 'I hate to say this,' he said, 'but your chaps must have made a mistake. Either that or it's one of these frame-ups that one hears so much about these days.'

'I thought you'd say something like that,' said Fox and waited patiently.

'It was my wife and Murchison,' said Harley after a while.

'Oh, is that a fact.'

'They were having an affair.'

Fox hooted with derisive laughter. 'Oh, do leave off,' he said. 'Whatever else you might say about your wife, she's a bit above having it off with a slag like Murchison. She's really quite a classy bird, isn't she?'

'You're trying to con me,' said Harley. 'I've heard about this sort of thing. You haven't got a shred of evidence that will prove I had anything to do with this ridiculous business.'

Fox leaned forward menacingly. 'Just listen, Thomas,' he said, 'and listen good. I'll repeat what I said just now. Point One. We found the weapon that killed Dixon in the water tank in the loft of your house. Point Two. Your fingerprints were on it. With me so far?' He leaned back and paused. 'That evidence will be put before a jury at the Old Bailey ... probably. I suppose it might be Guildford Crown Court, on the other hand. But I'm quite satisfied that there's enough there to put you away for life, so I don't really care what you've got to say about it. It's irrelevant, Thomas. All that remains for me to do now is to charge you with the murder of Donald Dixon and get you remanded in custody by the Bow Street magistrate tomorrow morning. None of that's a problem to me.'

Harley suddenly realised that this policeman opposite him, despite his bantering and almost light-hearted approach, was not playing games.

'All right,' he said, 'I admit that I helped them to hide the gun, but what else could I do? They killed the bloody man in my house —'

'Which house?'

Harley paused.

'The one at Stoke d'Abernon,' he said.

'Bad luck,' said Fox. 'Wrong one. You see, Thomas, old love, Murchison's fingerprints were found only at Kingston Hill. There was no trace of them at Stoke d'Abernon. Apart from on the box that contained the weapon. And I told you, your prints were on that too. However, I shall leave you to simmer gently while we have another chat with Jane Meadows,' he added. 'Get the gaoler to fetch her up, Jack, will you.'

That obviously had some impact on Harley. 'What the —?'

'Oh yes,' said Fox. 'Didn't I mention that? Yes, we've arrested Jane Meadows. Been telling us some enthralling stuff about funerals in darkest Devon, Thomas old love.'

*

Jane Meadows' confidence appeared to have increased rather than diminished in the time she had been at Bow Street police station. She was composed, and despite the spartan accommodation of a police cell, still managed to look very attractive. She had taken care over her make-up and her short blonde hair was immaculate. She sat now, one nylon-clad leg crossed over the other, cool and collected, and with a half smile on her face.

But Fox soon put a stop to that.

'When Harley rented a house on Kingston Hill,' he began, 'you undertook to provide a reference for him, and even offered to furnish a bank guarantee if necessary. The telephone number you used was that of Benson's flat. The same number, in fact, as the one you gave to the vicar of Cray Magna. Then, more than a year ago, you pretended to be Mrs Harley when you helped Harley to dispose of his house in Godalming. So from now on we'll work on the basis that your association with him was a little more than an innocent friendship arising out of a few rounds of golf. Far from being dragged into his criminal activities, Mrs Meadows, I am in little doubt that you were a willing participant.'

Jane Meadows uncrossed her legs and sat up, swinging herself round to face Fox. 'I don't know what you —'

Fox cut across her. 'But more importantly, you blackmailed Jeremy Benson to the tune of twenty thousand pounds. And you won't walk out of that as you did when your husband went down for seven years,' continued Fox relentlessly. 'But that's not all.' He turned to Gilroy. 'Have you got those papers, Jack?'

Gilroy opened his briefcase and gave Fox the notes and photostats that had been taken at the bank and the credit card company. 'These, sir?'

'Those are the ones, Jack. Now, Mrs Meadows,' he said. 'You say that you were in the South of France — at the villa Thomas Harley had rented for the pair of you — on the twelfth of July, and that you had been there for some time before that? What were the dates exactly?'

'I can't remember ... exactly.' She tossed her head imperiously. 'It was from about the second of July, I think.'

'You've already admitted coming back to arrange the so-called funeral on the nineteenth,' continued Fox. Jane Meadows gave a brief nod. 'But did you return to this country at any time between the second and the nineteenth?'

'Of course not.' She dismissed the proposition scornfully. 'You don't go on holiday and come back halfway through.'

'It was a holiday, then?'

'I've already said so.'

Fox had decided that the time had come to start knocking down Jane Meadows' little house of cards. 'Let's get back to the twelfth of July, shall we? If those dates are correct, that was the second Thursday after your arrival in Nice. Can you recall what you were doing that day?'

'Now look ...' The composure gave way to anger. 'I've tried to help you as much as I can, but I'm damned if I'm going to sit here answering irrelevant questions. Either you release me or charge me.'

'That's no problem,' snapped Fox. 'D'you imagine that falsifying records of deaths, forging death certificates, making false declarations, blackmail and the theft of one hundred thousand pounds' worth of jewellery is something that you're going to walk away from? Well, before you go, Mrs Meadows,' he continued sarcastically, 'perhaps you'd like to explain how it was that on the twelfth of July aforementioned, when you claim you were living in a villa in Nice, you managed to draw a hundred pounds from a cash machine in Regent Street in the heart of London's West End.'

Jane Meadows leaned forward and stared at the papers on the table in front of Fox. 'Where the hell did you get those from?' she asked angrily.

'From your bank.'

'And what gave you the right to inspect our bank account?' Irritated by Fox's Cockney accent, she allowed her restraint to slip once more.

'Under a warrant granted by a Crown Court judge,' said Fox with a helpful smile. 'And,' he added, 'I'm still waiting for your answer, Mrs Meadows.'

'That wasn't me. It must have been Jeremy.'

'Did he have your cash card, then?'

'Yes, of course he did.'

'I see. And when did he return it to you, Mrs Meadows?'

'He didn't. He's still got it.'

'Really?' Fox smiled at her. 'How come we found it in your handbag when you were arrested, then?' Jane Meadows said nothing, just confined herself to a shrug. 'Two days later, that is, on the fourteenth of July,' continued Fox, 'you purchased a blonde wig from a shop in Regent Street.'

Again there was a brief spasm of surprise as the thoroughness of the police enquiries became apparent to the girl. 'So what?' she demanded truculently.

'Why buy a blonde wig?'

'I like to be able to change my appearance from time to time,' she blurted out, but then chewed her lip in anguish as she realised the implications of what she had just said.

'Yes, I know,' said Fox. 'But what happened to the one you already had?'

'I lost it.'

'So you did have one previously?'

Too late, the girl realised that Fox had trapped her. 'Yes,' she said quietly.

'What happened there, then? Blow off in a gale, did it? Or did you just happen to leave it in a Jaguar XJ6 driven by one James Murchison?' Fox let that rhetorical question hang in the air for a moment or two. 'The linkman at the hotel can identify you, Mrs Meadows,' he continued. He didn't think that there was much chance of that, but he threw it in just for the hell of it. 'D'you know,' he added, 'it's a fatal mistake for a glamorous woman to commit a crime. Male witnesses tend to remember her. Furthermore,' he continued, 'it is my intention to take samples of your hair in order that a scientific comparison can be made between them and the hair found inside the blonde wig recovered from the possession of James Murchison when he was arrested. You can either give those samples voluntarily, or I shall seek — and undoubtedly obtain — a justice's order to take them.'

'I want a solicitor.' All the fight had gone.

'I think you're very wise, Mrs Meadows, because this time you're going down the steps.' Fox smiled at a sudden thought. 'D'you know,' he said, 'if your husband gets full remission for good conduct, he'll just be coming out when you're going in.'

Chapter Twenty

The prison officer returned to the gate lodge from the inner office. 'Sorry, guv,' he said, 'but Murchison is refusing to be interviewed by police any further.'

Fox nodded. That, of course, was the right of a prisoner on remand. It was one of many rules that had been designed to protect criminals from their just desserts. But it would take more than that to dissuade a detective of Fox's experience. 'Is that a fact?' he said. 'Well, perhaps you'd be so good as to pop back and tell our Mr Murchison that he can either talk to me, or I'll send an escort to take him back to Bow Street where I shall take great delight in charging him with several additional serious offences.' It was an empty threat. Once a prisoner was remanded into the custody of a prison governor it was very difficult to get him out again. But Murchison probably wouldn't know that. 'Mind you,' Fox added, 'I shall hotly deny ever having said such a thing.' Then he grinned.

So did the prison officer. 'It'll be a pleasure, guv,' he said. 'Hang on.'

A sullen Murchison was escorted into the interview room. 'What's all this crap about?' he asked, slumping into a chair.

Fox did not believe in going straight to the nub of an enquiry, not when he had plenty of other material to use. He much preferred to approach the apogee slowly, metaphorically zig-zagging, and allowing his suspect to lay his own land-mines ... and eventually step on them. 'When you drove hell-for-leather from the hotel, Jim —' he began.

'I never admitted that I —'

'Don't interrupt, Jim, it's rude,' said Fox. 'Apart from which, you did admit it. Would you like Mr Gilroy to read out the answers you made on a previous occasion?' Fox waited expectantly, but Murchison said nothing. 'When you left the hotel, you conveyed two persons, now known to be the lovely Jane Meadows and the late Donald Dixon, to Marble Arch.'

'So?'

'At what stage did Jane discard her blonde wig?'

'Eh?'

'Oh, stop poncing about, for Christ's sake, Jim. You know precisely what I'm talking about. Jane took off her wig and left it in the car, and you took it out before you dumped the wheels. And that's the wig we found in Sandra Nelson's pad the morning we nicked you, right?'

'Yeah. So what?'

'So what nothing. I just wanted to be sure, that's all.' Fox smiled. 'How many times did you go to the house on Kingston Hill?' he asked suddenly.

'I never —'

Fox held up his hand. 'Look closely at the tips of my fingers, Jim,' he said, 'and tell me what you see.'

'Fingerprints?'

'Exactly. And we found yours all over the place in the house at Kingston Hill. So I know you were there. And what actually happened after the heist was that you dropped Dixon and then drove Jane to the Marble Arch flat. Still in your chauffeuring costume, you collected her bags, took her straight to Heathrow Airport and put her on a flight for Nice.' Fox grinned at Murchison. 'How am I doing so far, Jim?'

'I never.' Murchison sounded angry. 'I dumped 'em at Marble Arch.'

'Have it your own way, Jim. Who hung on to the loot, incidentally?'

'Dixon did.'

'No, he didn't,' said Fox. 'You did, and you took it straight to Kingston.'

'What are you asking me for? You seem to know.'

'Yes, I probably do, Jim. What's more, you went to Kingston on more than one occasion. I just want to know how many times. There, that's not too difficult, is it?'

Murchison shrugged, defeated. 'I don't know. Three or four, I s'pose.'

'And the house at Stoke d'Abernon? How many times did you visit there?'

'Where?' Murchison's brow furrowed.

'Stoke d'Abernon, Jim. It's in Surrey.'

'Never heard of it, and that's straight.'

Fox thought that was the case, and Murchison's prints hadn't been found there, although he hoped that Fingerprint Branch would find them on the damaging piece of evidence that had been found in the cold water tank. 'Right.' Fox turned over a few pages in the file in front of him. 'Now, Thomas Harley, sometimes known as Wilkins, and Mrs Jane Meadows ...' He looked up. 'Bit of a quick-change artist, she is, Jim. Been known to abandon blonde wigs in other people's motorcars. However, both these persons have been arrested, and interviewed by police.'

'Oh, really?' Murchison folded his arms and leaned back in his chair, a sarcastic leer on his face.

'And,' continued Fox, 'they both put the murder of Donald Dixon firmly down to you.'

Murchison altered neither his position nor his expression. 'What d'you expect?' he asked insolently.

'Oh, I know, Jim.' Fox looked sympathetic. 'Happens all the time. Particularly when thieves fall out.'

'Well, it was nothing to do with me.'

'We found the gun, and we know that it was the gun that killed Dixon.' That, so far, was speculation.

'It had nothing to do with me.' Murchison was still desperately trying to convince Fox.

'That weapon was found in the cold water tank at the house at Stoke d'Abernon I mentioned earlier.'

'I told you, I never went near any house in Stoke whatever it was.'

'So you're saying that you know nothing about Dixon's murder and you had nothing to do with it. Is that right?'

'Dead right, mister,' said Murchison, but a tell-tale spasm of fear flitted across his face.

'The weapon was concealed in a plastic lunch box.'

'Oh yeah?'

'You know the sort of thing I mean, Jim. Housewives used to hold parties to sell them, before they decided that kinky underwear was a better bet. But that aside, your fingerprints were on the box too.' Fox hoped they were. 'Perhaps,' he continued, 'you would care to consider your position, as politicians are wont to say.' Fox waited patiently and lit a cigarette.

'Look,' said Murchison, an edge of desperation in his voice. 'Harley or Wilkins, or whatever his bloody name is, set the job up.'

'Yes

'I was just the wheelman.'

Fox shook his head. 'I think you were a bit more than that, Jim. You said at an earlier interview that you were approached by a man called Harry in a pub called the Oak and Apple in Dulwich, right?'

'Right.'

'Wrong,' said Fox. 'There isn't a pub by that name in Dulwich.'

'Well I must have got the name wrong, then.'

'That's not all you got wrong,' said Fox drily. 'Your friend Harry was Donald Dixon and he was the prime mover in this little enterprise. And you were his lieutenant. Let's face it, Jim, Harley hasn't got the intelligence to plan a job like that, but you …'

'All right, so I was a bit more into it than what I said.'

'But when the job was over, there was one hell of an argument about the split. And that's when things went pear-shaped, isn't it?' It was a wild guess on Fox's part, but he had dealt with enough robbers over the years to know that most crimes followed a familiar pattern.

Murchison was familiar with crime too, but from the other side, and he knew that interrogations like the one to which he was unwillingly being subjected now also followed a set routine. His chin sank on to his chest. 'Yeah,' he said eventually, 'but it was bloody Harley and that sodding fancy bird of his. They ain't at all professional, you know.'

Fox tutted. 'There you are then, Jim. That's what happens when you mix it with amateurs. So what happened?'

'It was Dixon. He reckoned that as he'd planned it all and put hisself on the line for nicking it into the bargain, he should have the biggest share. So he went down Kingston and put the arm on Harley and that blonde bitch of his.'

'How interesting,' said Fox. 'Tell me, if Dixon was the big wheel in all this, how come he gave you the proceeds of the heist to give to Harley? After all, it was Dixon who'd had it away. Harley didn't catch up until later. So why didn't he hang on to it until the split had been decided?'

'Bloody hell!' said Murchison, 'You don't think Dixon'd want to walk round London with a bleeding briefcase full of sparklers, do you? Daft, that'd be. S'posing he'd got a pull from the Old Bill? Anyhow, he reckoned it'd be safer to steer clear of Harley's place for a bit.'

'Very wise,' said Fox. 'But you still haven't told me about the split, dear boy.'

'Dixon was going to get half,' said Murchison sullenly, 'and Harley and his bird and me was going to get a third each —'

'That doesn't add up,' said Fox. 'Like the rest of your fairy story.'

'Don't follow you, Mr Fox.' True to form, Murchison, realising that he was in dire trouble, had slowly become more respectful.

'The sum of the parts is greater than the whole.'

'I still don't —'

'What I mean, Jim, is —' Fox broke off, exasperated. 'Never mind. What you meant was that Dixon was to take half and you, Harley and Meadows were to split the remainder equally.'

'That's what I said.'

Fox sighed. 'Go on, then.'

'But then Harley, who was going to knock out the gear on the continent somewhere, starts arguing the toss. He reckoned that as he was taking the risks in getting it across there, he ought to have a bigger share.'

'And what did you think about all that, Jim?'

Murchison ran a ruminative hand round his chin. 'Well, I reckoned we should've stuck to what was agreed.'

'Very noble. But that wasn't how it panned out, I take it.'

'Nah! There was a right dust-up down Kingston, and Harley pulls out a shooter and does for Don.'

'Oh dear. You were witness to all this, I take it?'

'Not likely. I never knew nothing about it till after. Harley gives me a bell and says as how we're all in it together and that if he gets caught he's going to grass, so I'd better get down there and give him a hand out.'

'And what form did this assistance take, Jim?'

'Well, when I got down there, they'd got it all planned, see. They'd done the shooter up in the plastic box and hidden it. That's what they said.'

'I see. Are you telling me that you neither saw nor handled this plastic box, then?' Fox studied Murchison with a rapier-like stare.

Just in time, Murchison recalled that Fox had told him that his fingerprints had been found on the box. 'It was lying about, see, so I said they'd better hide it, pronto. I picked it up and bunged it in a cupboard. Last I ever saw of it.'

'But you arranged the funeral.'

'Yeah, well, least I could do. I mean I knew a geezer what'd got a contact in the trade, like. He owed me one, so him and a mate come across with a coffin and a hearse.'

'Ozzie Bryce and Sid Meek, you mean?'

'Oh! You know about them, then?'

'Of course, James. I've nicked 'em.' Fox beamed at the prisoner.

'Oh!' said Murchison again, and gulped. 'Well anyhow, Harley was a dab hand at a bit of forgery — so he reckoned — and he'd nicked some forms from somewhere and done it all up kosher. Then this bird Jane. She done the phoning to some vicar —'

'In Cray Magna.'

'Yeah, well, down Devon some place. Yeah, that was it.'

'I thought you'd remember, Jim. After all, you drove the hearse, didn't you?'

'Yeah.'

'Why Cray Magna, incidentally?'

'Well, smart-arse Harley reckoned that if he picked some place miles away in the country we'd get away with it. We nearly did an' all.' Murchison looked momentarily regretful.

Fox laughed. 'You might have done if it hadn't been for Susan Harley. It was she who did for you, my son, reporting her husband missing to the police.' Fox suddenly flicked his fingers. 'That reminds me, Jim,' he said. 'I knew there was something else I wanted to talk to you about.'

Murchison gave Fox an apprehensive glance. 'Oh, yeah?'

'Yes. A little question of threatening to murder Mrs Susan Harley. I've told you before about going round threatening people, Jim.'

'Yeah, but that was before you told me the first time —' Murchison suddenly stopped.

'Yes,' said Fox with a grin. 'I know. But thank you for the admission, James. That can go on the indictment too. You should never put the arm on a woman. It has a nasty habit of bouncing back and hitting you behind the ear.' He paused for a moment as if a sudden thought had occurred to him. 'Of course, once the dear departed Dixon was out of the way it meant that you were going to get a bigger share, didn't it?'

'Yeah, I s'pose so, but I never thought of that.'

'Not much, you didn't,' said Fox. 'It's what's called motive, James. By the way, d'you know what happened to the bulk of the jewellery?'

'Harley said he'd taken it over to France and left it there in a safety deposit, and that he was fixing for a buyer.'

Fox threw back his head and laughed. 'Oh dear, Jack,' he said to Gilroy. 'Did you hear that?'

Gilroy grinned. 'Nice, that, guv'nor.'

'I don't see what's so bleeding funny about it,' said Murchison.

'What's so funny about it, Jim, is that the jewellery was in the coffin containing the late lamented Donald Dixon, and you helped to bury it.'

'What?' Murchison's face started working in anger at being had over. 'The double-dealing bastard,' he said.

'Like I said, Jim, that's what comes of mixing it with amateurs.' In fact Harley had admitted to abandoning the spoils altogether because, following the murder of Dixon, he had decided that the proceeds had become too hot to handle. But Fox didn't bother to tell Murchison that. It would have ruined the effect.

'Did you say you've got Harley banged up, Mr Fox?'

'Indeed I have. Why?'

'Nothing. But I've got a few friends on the inside, and thirty years'll be long enough to put matters right.'

'I hope that's not another threat to murder, Jim. How many more times d'you need telling? Anyway, I don't see why you should think that Harley will get thirty years.'

'That's about the going rate for a topping, ain't it?'

*

The ballistics experts and the Fingerprint Branch had both worked flat out. It was either that or have Fox constantly nagging them. Three days after Harley's arrest, Hugh Donovan, the firearms man, and Sam Marland, the senior fingerprint officer, appeared in Fox's office.

'Good news?' Fox rubbed his hands together in anticipation.

'I think you'll be pleased,' said Donovan. 'The weapon was definitely the one used to kill Dixon. No doubt about it. And the shell cases found with it were definitely those used in the weapon.'

'Splendid,' said Fox. 'And what about you, Sam? Any luck?'

'Yes,' said Marland. 'We got two sets of prints off the plastic box.'

'But you got nothing off the weapon itself, Denzil Evans tells me.'

Marland held up his hands and sighed. 'Did we ever? But it doesn't matter, as it happens.'

'So whose prints did you ID?'

Marland laid his report on Fox's desk and pointed to a paragraph. 'That's the bit that puts the finger on your murderer, Tommy,' he said. 'So to speak.'

Fox skimmed through the paragraph that Marland had pointed out. Then he looked up with a grin on his face. 'Now that's what I call evidence, Sam. There's no doubt, I suppose.'

'None whatsoever. I'm happy to go into the box with that.'

'Nice one,' said Fox.

*

'Well, James, I didn't think I'd be seeing you again so soon.' Fox beamed at Murchison and sat down.

'Now look here —'

'I've got some bad news for you, old son. And I'll tell you why. Before he moved into the hotel business and took to crime, Thomas Harley really was an insurance broker. He believes in insurance, passionately. And he made doubly sure on this occasion. Despite what you said about not seeing the gun until it was all neatly packed up in its plastic box, there's a flaw in that argument —'

'I never —'

'Just listen. When that box was found, it was examined by fingerprint experts. Examined very carefully. And d'you know what they found, Jim? They found your fingerprints —'

'Well, I said I'd handled it, didn't I?'

'But they found them underneath the tape with which the box was sealed. And they found them on the lid. Inside! And that, Jim, was because you sealed it up after you'd killed Dixon. It was the other way round, you see. You forced Harley into helping you out. Another threat to murder, I suppose.' Fox sighed. 'And he, in turn, conned Jane Meadows into assisting. That was why they cut and ran, and why Thomas Harley decided to fake his own death. He panics, you know,' he added as an aside. 'Unfortunately, Mrs Harley — Susan to you — went bent on the lot of you, and loosed her mouth off to the police. But being an amateur, Harley hung on to the gun, simply because he didn't know how to get rid of it. Bingo! You got nicked.'

'All right, so I packed up the shooter, but that don't mean I topped Dixon.'

'I mentioned insurance just now, Jim. And Harley's best bit of insurance was the cases.'

'The cases?'

'Yes, dear boy.' Fox smiled. 'The little brass things that the bullets are in when you put them in the chamber.'

'What about them?' asked Murchison nervously.

'Know what happened to them?'

'Well, Harley said he'd —' Murchison broke off, sudden fear strangling his vocal chords.

Fox laughed again. He was really quite enjoying himself. 'Harley, very carefully — with plastic gloves, I shouldn't wonder — picked them up, all three of them, and put them in another little plastic box inside the one containing the pistol.'

'What did he do that for, the berk?' Murchison was starting to sweat now.

'So that if the body was ever discovered, the identity of the murderer wouldn't be too difficult to work out. Harley knew you'd got form ... Well, he'd only got to look at you, hadn't he? Your mistake was to load the pistol with your bare hands.' Fox shrugged. 'But then most people do. Consequently, your dabs are on all three cartridge cases. How's that for being bang to rights, Jim?' Fox stood up and smiled at the unfortunate Murchison. 'In a way,' he added, 'I suppose it serves Dixon right for introducing you to a berk like Harley.' But the illogicality of that comment was lost on Murchison.

*

Lady Morton heard the milkman and opened the door.

'Good morning, young man,' she said.

'Good morning, m'lady.' The milkman paused. 'Excuse me for asking, m'lady,' he said, 'but you haven't seen Mr Benson lately, have you?'

Lady Morton stood up, clutching her pint of milk. 'No, not lately,' she said. 'Why d'you ask?'

'Well his milk's still there from yesterday.' The milkman pointed to a lonely bottle standing in front of Jeremy Benson's door.

'How very strange,' said Lady Morton thoughtfully. 'But I think you can leave that to me, young man.' She walked back into her flat and telephoned her friend Detective Chief Superintendent Fox of the Flying Squad.

Fox had other things to deal with and told Crozier to see to it.

Crozier did what Lady Morton should have done in the first place and telephoned Marylebone Lane police station.

Delta One answered the call and effected an entry, as policemen are wont to say, causing serious damage to the door frame in the process.

Jeremy Benson was in bed. Dead. On a side table was a note briefly explaining that he was convinced that he was to be prosecuted for his part in the affair of Harley, Meadows and company, and just could not face the scandal that would result.

It was the following day that Fox got a note from the Crown Prosecution Service saying that they agreed with his view that Benson had not been guilty of any crime.

*

Commander Alec Myers looked up from his paperwork. 'Ah, Tommy,' he said. 'Just the bloke I wanted to see. How did it go?'

'Harley got fourteen years, sir, and Murchison went down for life, of course. Recommended twenty-five years minimum. Bryce and Meek got a league each.' Fox grinned. 'But then they had got a bit of form, guv'nor.'

'And the woman?'

'Jane Meadows got two years with twelve months of it suspended.' Fox sounded quite depressed about that. 'The judge reckoned that she'd acted under the evil influence of Harley. He mentioned a couple of fingers called Svengali and Trilby. I suppose they'll come eventually.'

'What about Ali Barber?'

'Who, sir?'

'Ali Barber. The bloke who helped Bryce and Meek to bury Dixon.'

Fox grinned. 'Oh, him. Threw him back. Don't want tiddlers.'

'Good result, all the same, Tommy,' said Myers.

'Thank you, sir.' Fox turned to go.

'Oh, Tommy.'

'Yes, sir.'

'I've got DS Crozier's expenses here. A trip to the South of France. He seems to have been living it up over there, wining and dining. He said you authorised it …'

Printed in Great Britain
by Amazon